W9-DCJ-459

A Fine
GENTLEMAN

OTHER BOOKS AND AUDIO BOOKS
BY SARAH M. EDEN

THE LANCASTER FAMILY
Seeking Persephone
Courting Miss Lancaster

THE JONQUIL FAMILY
The Kiss of a Stranger
Friends and Foes
Drops of Gold
As You Are

STAND-ALONE NOVELS
Glimmer of Hope
An Unlikely Match
For Elise

A Fine
GENTLEMAN

✦ A REGENCY ROMANCE ✦

SARAH M. EDEN

Covenant Communications, Inc.

Cover image: *Couple* © Lee Avison / Trevillion Images; *Butterfly* © thawats, courtesy istockphoto.com

Cover design copyright © 2017 by Covenant Communications, Inc.

Author photo: copyright © Annalisa Photography

Published by Covenant Communications, Inc.
American Fork, Utah

Copyright © 2017 by Sarah M. Eden
All rights reserved. No part of this book may be reproduced in any format or in any medium without the written permission of the publisher, Covenant Communications, Inc., P.O. Box 416, American Fork, UT 84003. The views expressed within this work are the sole responsibility of the author and do not necessarily reflect the position of Covenant Communications, Inc., or any other entity.

This is a work of fiction. The characters, names, incidents, places, and dialogue are either products of the author's imagination, and are not to be construed as real, or are used fictitiously.

Printed in the United States of America
First Printing: March 2017

23 22 21 20 19 18 17   10 9 8 7 6 5 4 3 2 1

ISBN 978-1-52440-210-5

To Ranee`,
who offered a desperately needed ray of hope in a
difficult time and has stood as my friend again and again,
for giving me reason to hold on to this story and
believe it had a future

Acknowledgments

A HEARTFELT THANK YOU TO . . .

The British Postal Museum & Archive for invaluable insights and incredibly specific information, without which I could not have hoped to make this story anywhere near accurate.

Graham Bradley for coming to the rescue on the unexpectedly complicated matter of a very crucial Castilian expression, a seemingly small endeavor but one I greatly appreciate.

James Blevins for a thorough and expert check of my admittedly inexpert Spanish. Your insights and willingness to help made all the difference in the world. This story would have been a mess without your generosity.

Christina Parks for double-checking the French phrases used in this story and making certain I didn't make an utter fool of myself. Thank you.

The incomparable Pam Howell, who has been a cheerleader, an advocate, a listening ear, and a source of indispensable wisdom.

Bob Diforio, whose knowledge, professionalism, patience, and determination never cease to amaze me.

Sam Millburn, who takes these stories I craft and mold and makes them far better than I ever could on my own.

My family, for supporting me in this often ridiculous under-taking, for encouraging me, cheering for me, putting an arm of consolation around my shoulders when need be, and loving me through all the chaos and stress. You make life beautiful.

Chapter One

London, April 1815

THE COMMOTION OUTSIDE HIS OFFICE ought to have served as something of a warning, but Jason Jonquil, barrister and proud perfectionist, had done nothing more than glance up from his ruler-straight stack of papers when the first noises had drifted through his closed door. Thus, he was entirely unprepared when Hansen, his long-suffering clerk, hurried inside, a bit short of breath, to announce the arrival of a client.

"Miss Mariposa Thornton." The name rushed from Hansen's lips at precisely the instant a young lady Jason had never before seen glided into his office.

He stood automatically.

"And Mrs. Aritza," Hansen added as a second lady stepped inside. *Hobbled* inside was a more precise description, and Jason was nothing if not precise.

"You are Mr. Jonquil?" Miss Thornton asked, a hint of an accent in her words. She raised an ebony eyebrow in inquiry.

Though far shorter than he was, she somehow managed to look down her nose at him. Being the son of an earl had its advantages—Jason found he could quite easily squelch such pretensions. He might be a barrister and obligated to work for a living, but he was born to the aristocracy. "I am Mr. Jonquil," he replied repressively. "And I shall inform you now that I do not take on new clients without a recommendation."

"*Sí*." She seemed to sigh. "You are definitely Señor Jason." She made the realization sound oddly like an insult. The woman beside her shook her head of white hair as if in disapproval. "*Siéntese, Abuela*," Miss Thornton said to her companion, who shuffled to a nearby chair and sat, her wrinkled eyes narrowed on Jason.

"As I said, Miss Thornton," Jason repeated himself calmly. "I have a very full clientele and do not accept new clients without—"

"A recommendation, *sí*." She waved off his words and sat as well. "You have come very highly recommended, so we need not worry on such a thing."

That was not at all what he had meant. Jason straightened a stack of papers that had shifted askew when his office door had burst open so unceremoniously. The task allowed him a moment to push down his frustration. He was something of an expert at maintaining his calm.

"Miss Thornton," he said, "*you* are the one requiring a recommendation."

"What need have I for a recommendation? I am not a barrister."

"You misunderstand me—"

"Not a very reassuring example of your skills of communication." Miss Thornton looked rather unimpressed with him as she cut him off. Again. "I would think it *importante* for a barrister to be able to bring others around to an understanding of his position on any given issue."

"This conversation is in no way, I assure you, Miss Thornton, an example of my professional abilities. It is more a display of your own inability to understand what is said to you."

"Oh, I understand what is said in more than one language, Mr. Jonquil." He would wager one of those languages was Spanish. The other was clearly English, spoken nearly perfectly, with only the slightest of accents. How was it, then, that she struggled so much to understand him? "I find myself much concerned over you, sir."

"Over me?" Jason raised an eyebrow.

"Yes," she answered, seeming to study him. "You are something of a disappointment, if you must know."

"A disappointment?"

"I was told you were a very skilled barrister. *Quite talented*, I was told. And yet I find you cannot even hold up your end of a simple conversation." Miss Thornton shook her head in much the way a nursemaid would at a small child struggling with the smallest of tasks. "Perhaps, Mr. Jonquil, you are a bit *simple*." She whispered the last word as if it were a well-kept secret she was reluctant to disclose.

"A bit simple?" he asked, his exasperation growing by the moment.

"And you have a most disconcerting habit of repeating everything that is said to you," she added. "I am not at all certain that is what I wish for in a man of the law."

"I do not accept clients without a recommendation."

"Yes, you said that already," she answered extremely patiently. "A most unprofessional habit of yours. It is no wonder you have to be recommended in order to acquire clients."

"*I* am not the one who is recommended—"

"But you *were* recommended, which is particularly confusing, for I cannot imagine why. I had assumed I would, at the very least, find you competent. Perhaps advice given by one who is biased is not to be trusted." She said the last as if more to herself than to him. "Strange. I thought he was quite dependable."

"You thought who was dependable?" Jason asked, feeling a headache coming on.

"The gentleman who recommended you," she answered as if he ought to have known as much.

"And this was a close acquaintance of mine?" Jason hoped to get around to the identity of the ingrate who'd sent this babbling package of confusion to his office. He had every intention of locating the mischief maker and "thanking" him.

"Of course," Miss Thornton replied in that same tone of condescending exasperation.

"And who is he?"

"Mr. Jonquil"—she shook her head once more—"if you do not even know who your 'close acquaintances' are, I cannot see how you can possibly handle the many intricacies of the law."

"Again, you misunderstand me." A soft pounding began in his temples.

"Not a promising sign." Miss Thornton drew her eyebrows together, concentrating. "I am sorry, Mr. Jonquil, but I am afraid I am going to be forced to fire you."

"Fire me?" Jason was on his feet again. How utterly ridiculous.

"It is nothing personal, I assure you." She rose calmly. "I am certain you are a fine individual. You are simply a horrible barrister."

"I will have you know I am a fine barrister, and you cannot fire me—"

"But I must." She pressed a hand to her heart in a continental display of regret. "I am needing someone with experience, intelligence, and ability. So I absolutely must fire you, as much as it pains me."

"Experience? Intelligence? Ability?" Jason felt his patience slip further.

"You are repeating things again." She spoke gently, as if assuming he was unaware of it.

"I realize that," he snapped back.

"Then perhaps you can in time overcome that difficulty." A ponderous look crossed her face. "Maybe that is what you need, Mr. Jonquil. A chance to conquer your shortcomings. If I allow you to be my barrister again, could you accomplish what I am in need of?"

It was a rhetorical question, Jason felt certain. Yet he valued honesty above all character traits, save, perhaps, dependability. He would answer her question and without hesitation. "Of course I could, and I would do a far better job than any other barrister you could find in all of London."

She looked ever more doubtful. "I suppose I could give you a chance to prove yourself, though I am not entirely certain it would be a wise thing for me to do."

"On the contrary, it would be an extremely wise decision."

She shrugged, obviously still unconvinced, then resumed her seat and fished through her overlarge drawstring bag. "So long as you understand that I may, *qué lástima*, be forced to fire you at any time."

Of all the ridiculous notions. He'd never been fired in all his life. "I sincerely doubt you will find it at all necessary, Miss Thornton."

She smiled at him then, but it was not a companionable smile, nor necessarily a cheery smile. Once again, she put him in mind of a nursery maid indulgently watching over a particularly bumbling charge. "You did not even repeat anything that time, Mr. Jonquil," Miss Thornton said as if he ought to look on such a feat as a significant accomplishment. "That is promising."

Jason caught himself very nearly rolling his eyes, something his eldest brother, Philip, did quite regularly and, therefore, something Jason was quite careful *never* to do.

Miss Thornton produced several sheets of heavy paper. "These are papers," she said to him, her words enunciated quite carefully, her eyes focused on him with a hint of a pitying smile tugging at the corners of her unfashionably wide mouth.

Mrs. Aritza, who had remained silent and almost entirely still during the exchange, shifted quite abruptly in her chair, her foot striking Miss Thornton's shin in the process. A tiny, muffled yelp escaped Miss Thornton's throat, indicating the strike had carried more force than it had seemed to.

Miss Thornton patted the older lady's hand soothingly. "*Está bien*," she said gently to her companion. Then, turning to look at Jason, Miss Thornton said under her breath, "Old age, I fear, has taken its toll. She twitches now and again. It is, at times, most inconvenient, but she is such a dear old lady that one must overlook such things."

Another twitch sent the older lady's foot into Miss Thornton's shin once more. Jason could do little but nod his understanding and, for the briefest of moments, feel a twinge of sympathy for the exasperating young lady.

"What is the significance of these papers?" Jason asked, steering the conversation back to the topic at hand. "I am assuming these relate to the legal matter with which you require my assistance."

"Oh, yes. This is my father's will."

"Will?" Jason very nearly dropped his head into his hands. Barristers did not, in general practice, handle such trivial matters of civil law.

"Oh dear." Her black, arching eyebrows shot together in discouragement. "The repeating has begun again."

"Allow me to explain, Miss Thornton. Matters of estate and inheritance are the domain of solicitors. I, as I know you are aware, am a barrister."

"Oh. Then solicitors are far superior to barristers." She nodded decisively as if a great mystery had been solved.

"On the contrary, Miss Thornton," Jason interrupted, unable to let such an untruth go unchecked. "The distinction is quite the reverse. In fact, solicitors often are employed *by barristers*. To consult a solicitor rather than a barrister would be something of a step down."

"But if I understood you correctly," Miss Thornton said, "you suggested I take my pressing problem to a solicitor because you are unable to address this issue. Such an action does seem to indicate you feel your abilities lacking."

"I—"

"Just as I had originally suspected they were." Miss Thornton did not even pause for breath. "I truly must fire you, Mr. Jonquil. If you do not have confidence in yourself, how can I possibly have confidence in you?" She rose, placing her father's will inside her reticule once more.

"Allow me to be frank, Miss Thornton."

She nodded, but the wariness did not leave her expression.

"I can perform any legal service a solicitor can," Jason said. "And, I might add, would be far better at it."

She looked excessively doubtful.

Jason found it absolutely imperative that he count—slowly— before answering. He was very close to losing his calm, something he would never have believed right up until the moment Miss Thornton had entered his office.

"Have you ever even seen a will, Mr. Jonquil?" Miss Thornton seemed to expect him to deny it.

Of all the absurd! "Certainly, I have."

"Professionally, I mean."

That, at least, was slightly less insulting. Jason nodded, mentally working the tension out of his jaw.

"And you did not bungle the assignment too monumentally, I hope?" she pressed. A tiny *oof* followed when Mrs. Aritza's twitch resurfaced. Miss Thornton offered a tight smile to her companion.

"I did not bungle the assignment at all," Jason said.

"But if you had, you likely wouldn't tell me as much."

She doubted his honesty? Anyone who knew anything about him would never question his integrity. Though he had his failings, being a liar was not one of them.

"If you wish to consult Lord and Lady Cavratt on the matter, I am certain they would give you a full account of their satisfaction with my abilities."

"Ah yes." Miss Thornton nodded. "You require recommendations."

"That is not what I meant."

Miss Thornton placed her pile of papers on Jason's desk, very nearly upsetting a tidy stack. Jason carefully moved his other work to one side and took her papers in hand.

"My father's will is on top," Miss Thornton said. "Below it is my birth certificate and my parents' marriage lines. Below that is a signed statement from a priest, witnessing that my father has died."

"Not a death certificate?" Jason asked, surprised that she did not have anything more official than a letter. "What is it, Miss Thornton, you wish me to ascertain on your behalf?"

"Whether or not I have received any inheritance from my father."

"A simple reading should reveal that," Jason said.

"Wonderful." Miss Thornton rose once more, and Jason did as well, civility as ingrained as breathing. "Then I should not have to fire you after all." She pulled a calling card from her reticule and held it out to him. "If you would kindly send word when you have finished and inform me of whatever you discover, I would be most obliged."

Hardly believing he was to be so easily freed from the exhausting lady's presence, Jason eagerly accepted the card, placing it on her stack of papers. "I will, Miss Thornton."

She said something in Spanish to her companion, who rose a little shakily. Jason came around his desk to offer the older lady his arm, keeping enough of a distance to hopefully stay out of range of her twitch.

The look Mrs. Aritza gave him was very nearly commiserating. Jason chuckled silently to think that perhaps she realized Miss Thornton was exasperating.

He walked them to the door of his office before giving them over to Hansen, who was waiting quite properly to do his duty by his employer and accompany his clients to the front door.

Jason shook his head as he closed his office door. At least the problem she had presented was an easy one—a solicitor could easily have seen to the matter. It was not the area of law he generally worked in but would be simple enough.

As he added her papers to his stack of work to be completed, he couldn't help wondering with a disconcerting amount of confusion precisely how he had come to take Miss Thornton on as a client. He absolutely had *not* intended to.

Chapter Two

"THESE ARE PAPERS." ABUELA REPEATED Mariposa's earlier words, though she repeated them in her native Spanish. "Was it necessary to be quite so condescending?"

"Was it necessary to kick me quite so hard?" Mariposa countered.

"Which brings me to another grievance." The conversation continued in Spanish, Abuela not being nearly as comfortable with English as Mariposa was. "I have a twitch?"

"I thought it a splendidly brilliant means of explaining the situation. You very nearly brought the entire scheme crashing down around our heads. If Mr. Jonquil had realized for even one moment that I was not an empty-headed prattle box, he would have dismissed us without a second thought."

"Could you not have left off the part about me being such a very *old* lady?" Abuela eyed Mariposa with barely disguised amusement.

Mariposa's heart lightened at the sight of her grandmother's cheerful countenance. There had been too much of sorrow in both their lives.

"You repaid my mischief with a good number of kicks, so I feel we are quite reconciled to one another." After a moment's silence,

Mariposa voiced the thought running through her mind. "I believe we were right to go to Mr. Jonquil. So much depends upon our success, I could not possibly have trusted such a thing to someone unknown."

"And yet you do not know Mr. Jonquil," Abuela said.

"I feel as though I do. I feel as though I know all of the Jonquil brothers. The earl who acts the part of a fribble. The widower who has distanced himself from the world. The shy, gentle one. The brother destined to be a painfully respectable vicar. The mischievous youngest brother."

"And the high and mighty barrister," Abuela added.

Mariposa nodded. "We could not possibly have had a more vivid picture painted of Jason Jonquil, could we?" They both chuckled. "His professional dignity was every bit as palpable as I anticipated."

"Why did you not simply tell him who had praised his abilities so highly?" Abuela asked. "Surely he would have taken your case had you explained as much."

"All I learned of him, including the praise of his capabilities, was imparted during moments of extreme physical distress, at times all but forced out by fever." Mariposa's memories of a handsome golden-haired young man suffering so horrifically flooded her anew. Even amongst the myriad remembrances of pain and death that constantly lingered at the back of her thoughts, that young soldier's agony always pierced her. "I am not entirely certain I have leave to reference such personal confidences."

Abuela made a small noise of understanding. "Did you, I wonder, lose a little of your heart to that young man?"

"I did," she confessed, "but not in the way you are imagining." A sad sort of smile sighed out of her. All of her smiles were sad now, all that weren't entirely feigned.

The hack came to a stop at the narrow house Mariposa had let for the Season in a respectable but not quite fashionable section of Town. Though she had found work while they had been on the Continent and had saved every bit possible of that unforeseen windfall, the amount was not sufficient for anything truly fashionable. Respectability was their aim for the nonce. Having left behind a life in which survival had proven difficult in the extreme, respectability felt absolutely frivolous.

Mariposa tipped their driver and linked arms with her abuela as they took the steps to the door. Their efficient and not-at-all-commonplace butler anticipated them, opening the door as they stepped inside without so much as a pause.

"Señora Aritza. Señorita Thornton."

"Your *acento* is improving," Abuela told him with a nod of approval. "You will never *pasar* for a Spaniard, but you would not give us reason to be ashamed."

"Thank you, Señora," he answered, his fair English skin showing an immediate blush.

Mariposa particularly liked the fact that a hardened soldier—he must have been hardened to have survived as many battles as his myriad injuries indicated he had—could still do something as eminently uncorrupted as blushing.

"Been workin' on sayin' all them Spanish words more proper like," Black said, his color dropping to normal by degrees.

"Now you ought to put your mind to sayin' all them *English* words more proper like," Mariposa suggested.

Black's barking laughter filled the small entryway, as Mariposa had known it would. He liked straight talk and found her sometimes scathing wit amusing. She might have held her tongue if he'd been the more sensitive type. "Right ye are, Señorita Thornton," he said. "A proper butler don't say things like a deuced street sweep do."

"Perhaps you could begin by wiping the word *deuced* from your vocabulary."

Black looked alarmed at the suggestion. "But *deuced* is already less of a word than I'd been saying. I'll start soundin' like a little girl soon enough."

Mariposa clarified. "Remove it from your *butler* vocabulary. Below stairs or away from the house on your days off, you, of course, may speak as crassly and vulgarly as you choose."

"Wouldn't do nothin' to embarrass you," Black reassured her.

"I know that." Mariposa gently touched the stump of his right arm. "And I wouldn't be embarrassed. I would, in fact, be relieved to hear you had thoroughly scandalized the local servants' tavern with your constant muttering of every lower-class curse known to London."

His eye opened wide, his mouth dropping open a bit. Abuela, on the other hand, knew Mariposa too well to be shocked by anything she said.

"If you curse to your heart's content while you are away," Mariposa said, "I would know your tongue will not be tempted to say such things at less appropriate times simply because it missed doing so."

Another barking laugh echoed around her as Mariposa followed in her grandmother's wake. Black had improved by leaps and bounds since first coming to be in her employ. Getting that man to smile and laugh and generally enjoy life again had proven one of her most difficult undertakings.

She had seen far too much sorrow and felt too much of it herself to bear seeing such sadness in others. She had, over the years, teased and jested and reassured a good number of heavy hearts to lightness once more. Her own happiness, however, felt far more elusive.

She had not the slightest doubt that with very little effort, Mr. Jonquil would be able to answer the question she'd posed to him. Truth be told, she knew perfectly well she was entitled to an inheritance from her father's estate. Furthermore, she knew the exact amount of the bequest. She had read the will herself. A far bigger question lay at the heart of her inquiry, a question she could not risk anyone else discovering.

Somewhere in this vast, unfamiliar country, she had family, and she needed to find them. They did not know it, but their lives depended on her discovering their whereabouts.

She did not like playing the empty-headed fool, but she simply could not risk Mr. Jonquil's guessing that there was more than met the eye to her simple legal question. Giving the impression of stupidity and ridiculousness was the only way she knew to keep others, especially those as clever as Mr. Jonquil appeared to be, from looking too closely.

He would realize she had an inheritance awaiting her and could, she sincerely hoped, discover the name of the Thornton family's solicitor, an important piece of information she had been unable to discover on her own. Through their solicitor, she could locate her family without drawing undue attention to her search.

Secrecy was of paramount importance. She was not the only person looking for them.

❦

Jason never could manage to summon a great deal of patience when faced with the frivolous dandy his oldest brother, Philip, had become.

"The staff is already here. Save them from the boredom, Jason." Philip flicked a speck of invisible lint off his cuffs. "Sorrel's operation requires us to travel all the way to Scotland, and the recovery will be long enough to prevent our return before the end of the Season. This pile of stones will be vacant. You might as well put up here."

"I have my own place, Philip. My rooms may not be lavish nor extensive, but they are more than sufficient."

"Do as you wish." Philip stopped in front of a mirror and straightened his blindingly yellow waistcoat. "But it's a deuced shame to let the old place sit empty."

"My gratitude for the bit of charity," Jason drawled.

"*Charity?*" Philip's mouth quirked up at one corner. "I never knew I was doing good works by simply having brothers and an empty home and the presence of mind to piece together how very fortunate that combination truly is. A regular philanthropist, aren't I?"

Jason bit back a frustrated retort. Philip dressed ridiculously. He acted like a mindless popinjay. It was not what Father would have wanted from his heir. He'd have expected hard work, the respect of peers, intelligence, and the ability to be solemn for one moment.

"I understand you are bound for Corbin's estate," Philip said, apparently done studying his reflection because he turned to face Jason.

Jason nodded silently. He meant to travel to his twin's home in a few days.

"See if you can't ferret out this widow with whom he is so enamored, the one Layton told us about," Philip said. "Seems promising."

"I don't care to stick my nose in my brother's business," Jason answered with his characteristic forthrightness.

"Implying, then, that *I* do?" Philip raised an eyebrow but did not show any other sign of offense or irritation.

Jason shrugged his reply. Philip couldn't seem to stop nosing about in Jason's concerns.

"Perhaps Sorrel and I will stop by Corbin's on our way to Scotland." Philip directed a footman who carried a piece of luggage. "Thus I'll have ample opportunity to stick my nose in his business. Seems that's one of my duties as eldest brother."

"At least you would be seeing to *one* of your duties," Jason muttered under his breath.

"Perhaps you'd care to repeat that comment in a more discernible voice." Philip's tone grew suddenly so cold and clipped that Jason didn't doubt his mumbled remark had been heard, understood, and not at all appreciated. "Even a barrister can find himself brought up for libel."

"Are you threatening me?" Jason asked, his hackles instantly raised.

"I am *warning* you." Philip spoke in much the same tone Miss Thornton had used just before she'd asked him if he was "simple." Jason was utterly tired of being patronized. "*I* am accustomed to scathing criticisms," Philip said. "But not everyone is able to overlook baseless accusations. First and foremost, a gentleman must act like a gentleman." Philip almost looked and sounded like an earl for the most fleeting of moments. In an instant, however, he was back to swinging his quizzing glass on its ribbon and looking as though he hadn't a single lucid thought rattling around in his brain box.

"Put that thing away before you decapitate someone with it," Sorrel, Philip's wife, said as she entered, leaning heavily on her cane.

"Indeed, dear," Philip answered foppishly. "Imagine if the French had discovered such a use for their quizzing glasses. The aristocracy might have been able to fend off their executioners."

"You are intolerable at times," Sorrel said. "But you know that, of course."

Does he? Does Philip even care that he drives people mad?

"If you had seen me in my dark-blue waistcoat this morning before I changed my mind and donned this one, you would have declared me beyond intolerable," Philip answered. "'Twas a very plain, ordinary, boring blue, not to mention very unexceptionally cut. To make matters far worse, the color did absolutely nothing for my complexion, not nearly as stunning as the yellow."

Sorrel shook her head with palpable patience. "I imagine the blue actually looked respectable."

"Which would be the reason he chose to eschew it," Jason offered.

"How very right you are, Jason." Sorrel nodded firmly. She moved with such obvious pain and difficulty. The surgery she was facing would, as far as Jason understood it, alleviate some of that suffering.

Jason liked her. He liked that she didn't put up with Philip's nonsense. Perhaps she would prove enough of an influence to turn him back into the Philip Jason still remembered from his childhood: the brother he'd most admired, not this dolt who postured to the world.

"Philip hasn't been pestering you to look after Lampton House, has he?" Sorrel asked.

"Of course he has."

"Pay him no mind," Sorrel said. "He has for some inexplicable reason become convinced that the house will simply crumble into a heap of dust if there is not a Jonquil in residence at all times. I, for one, firmly believe the servants are breathing a collective sigh of relief at the prospect of being left in peace for once."

"Are you, Jeffers?" Philip asked Lampton House's long-suffering butler. "Sighing, that is? If so, I should very much like to know. I would be pleased to tutor you in a more effective and dramatic method than is generally employed."

Jason thought for just a moment that he saw Jeffers smile. Jeffers had been the London residence's butler since before Jason was in short pants, and he didn't remember ever seeing him smile.

"I assure you, my lord," Jeffers said, all pomp and dignity, "any sighs emanating from the servants' hall shall be executed with utmost drama and effectiveness."

"Very good, man." Philip nodded. He turned back to Sorrel. "Shall we, my dear?"

"I think we had better. I, for one, do not wish to experience a dramatic sigh several dozen people strong."

"Very wise of you, darling," Philip answered. "And there is the added benefit of seeing all my sartorial splendor during our carriage ride to Nottinghamshire."

"You should have settled on the blue and left it at that." Sorrel took Philip's arm, the look of pain forever etched in her features easing a little as his support lessened the weight on her badly crippled leg.

"Ah, but the yellow doesn't wrinkle like the blue," Philip pointed out. "And it is a very long trip to Havenworth. Should I have chosen the blue, I would, perforce, have been required to sit in my own little corner of the carriage rather than being more snugly situated beside my wife."

A blush crept across Sorrel's cheeks, surprising Jason quite thoroughly. She didn't seem the type to color.

"Of course, if you would prefer, I could take a moment and switch back," Philip offered.

"The yellow will be just fine," Sorrel said briskly. Then, head held high, she urged Philip forward and down the front steps of Lampton House toward the waiting carriage.

She wasn't one to suffer fools gladly, and yet she appeared entirely smitten with Jason's peacock of a brother. Jason watched the Lampton traveling carriage as it trundled up the street. Sorrel apparently saw something in Philip she liked despite the fact that he appeared a babbling fool to the rest of the world.

Whereas Jason, who was liked and respected by his colleagues, appeared to Miss Mariposa Thornton to be . . . well, a babbling fool.

He scolded himself for even thinking about the exasperating female, something he'd been doing more of than was advisable, especially considering he'd been in company with her only once.

Miss Thornton was pretty, yes. Beautiful, if he were being entirely honest—which he always tried to be. She was also frustrating and empty-headed and entirely confusing.

He would do well to answer her very straightforward legal question and be done with the entire thing.

Chapter Three

VERY LITTLE UNNERVED MARIPOSA—SHE'D seen and experienced far too much in her nearly twenty years to find herself daunted by life—but Mr. Jason Jonquil's arrival at her doorstep exactly one week after she had underhandedly secured his legal assistance shook her composure more than she would ever have admitted.

Day after day she'd waited for word that he had perused the documents she'd left him. No correspondence had arrived. Part of her had wondered if she'd offended him, if he'd realized she'd been playing a part in order to all but force his hand into agreeing to take her on as a client. His demeanor upon arriving, however, was one of wary condescension, much as one would assume when dealing with an unpredictable simpleton. Perfect.

"Good morning, Mr. Jonquil."

Mariposa saw that Black took immediate note of the name. Mariposa nodded subtly and motioned for him to take himself off. One word from him and all her efforts would be for naught. Keen as always to his duties, he left just as she'd hoped he would, though he took the opportunity to study Mr. Jonquil first.

Mariposa took a moment to study Mr. Jonquil as well. He was tall, something that would not necessarily have been readily apparent to her, she being barely over five feet tall in her thickest-soled shoes. Everyone seemed tall to Mariposa. But Mr. Jonquil must have been a foot taller than herself. He was lean but by no means scrawny. His hair was golden enough to have seen a great deal of sunlight but his complexion not nearly tan enough for that to be the case. She could come to no other conclusion than that his hair was naturally light, just as his eyes were almost unnaturally blue. And those eyes were, at that moment, focused directly on her.

Realizing she had been essentially staring the man out of countenance, Mariposa collected herself and covered the tactical error with words. "Have you finished reading the will already, Mr. Jonquil?" She kept her tone and expression light and somewhat vacuous.

"I have, indeed, Miss Thornton." That same look of exasperated confusion that had taken up permanent residence there during their initial meeting surfaced in his eyes.

"Good for you." Patting his hand would likely be taking things too far, so she refrained.

"Yes, I'm certain my colleagues are all very proud of this accomplishment." The dry response spoke of humor, but his austere expression hadn't changed in the least.

Mr. Jonquil's air did not ring entirely true. His mouth was continually pressed closed, as if holding back some word or another. He appeared to all the world to be quite calm and collected, yet she sensed a subtle but unmistakable tension.

She had spent so much of the past few years studying people, searching out the small clues they offered as to their character, finding those things about them that they kept hidden. Doing so had kept her and her family safe during the long years of war. Thus, she knew precisely what she was seeing in Mr. Jonquil. He was hiding some aspect of himself, though what or why she could not say.

Underneath the exterior he put forth, who was he? Was he angry or amused? Harsh or lighthearted? Though she did not know for certain which it was, she truly hoped to discover that he was jovial and charming and pleasant.

"Have you a room with a table or a desk where we might review the documents you left with me?" he asked.

"We have a book room." She didn't move in that direction.

Mr. Jonquil watched her expectantly.

She remained in place, hoping the ridiculousness of the situation would pull a smile from him.

"I would be very much obliged if you would lead the way, Miss Thornton." Mr. Jonquil's jaw clenched tight enough to affect his words.

How long could she tease him before his carefully constructed façade crumbled? And, more to the point, would he break into a grin or simply break her neck?

Mariposa's heart skipped at the challenge ahead of her. Settling her own dilemma was, of course, her first priority. In the meantime, however, she would see if she couldn't discover what kind of man Mr. Jonquil truly was.

Miss Thornton addressed her butler as she led the way out of the sitting room, "Black, do send word to my grandmother to join me in the book room."

"Your grandmother?" Jason struggled to imagine a termagant such as Miss Thornton having something as sweet and homespun as a grandmother.

"*Sí*. You met her at your office."

"Ah. Yes." Jason nodded, a few puzzle pieces falling into place. "The lady who twitches."

The slightest of smiles passed over Miss Thornton's face. "The poor dear is rather sensitive about her condition, so you would do well not to mention it."

"Do you expect her twitching to resurface this afternoon?" Jason made a mental note to keep a safe distance.

"I can guarantee her twitch will be frequently present." Miss Thornton sounded almost amused at the idea.

Strange. He followed her inside a small room with several shelves of books and an old, weatherworn desk.

"Abuela—that is, Grandmother—should be here momentarily." Miss Thornton pulled back a curtain to let in what little sunlight penetrated the heavy cloud cover outside.

Jason began laying out his paperwork. "Your grandmother wishes to hear the details of your father's will?"

"No," Miss Thornton answered. "She is coming so that I am not forced to marry you."

Jason dropped every last sheet of paper in his hand. After quickly recovering the breath her words had robbed him of, he said firmly, "Do not even say such a thing."

She gave him one of her nursemaid smiles. "Your concern for me is quite touching, Mr. Jonquil."

"Concern for *you?*"

"Oh dear. You are repeating things again."

Jason clamped his jaw shut and began collecting the papers. Concern for *her*? Did she think he objected to the idea of marriage on *her* account? Then again, perhaps Miss Thornton had reason to be concerned for herself. Jason knew full well he'd throttle the harridan within moments of any union between them.

"*Mi* abuela will be here in a moment, so there is no reason for worry. She will prevent any whisper of scandal."

"But can she prevent me from strangling you?" he said under his breath.

A fleeting look of amusement passed through Miss Thornton's brown eyes. The unexpected sight caught him up short. The only way she would find his comment amusing was if she herself realized how exasperating she was. He looked more closely at her but saw nothing in her eyes other than her usual look of innocent vacuousness.

Mrs. Aritza hobbled in a moment later. Her eyes, nearly identical to her granddaughter's, shifted between him and Miss Thornton. A quick exchange in Spanish passed between the ladies before they both sat.

"I have read your father's will, Miss Thornton." Jason assumed his most professional air. He still wasn't entirely sure why he'd agreed to take Miss Thornton on as a client; barristers rarely handled matters of inheritance and wills.

"And were you able to recognize all of the words, Mr. Jonquil?"

Before Jason could even begin to reply, Mrs. Aritza's foot smacked into her granddaughter's leg with such force that Jason actually heard the two make contact. Miss Thornton gave her grandmother a frustrated look as she rubbed at her shin.

"You have inherited a portion of your late father's estate." Jason preferred seeing to the matter quickly so he could go on his way. "Also named are Angelina Thornton, whom I assume to be your mother, Marcos, and Santiago Thornton."

The expressions that flitted across his client's face were intriguing, to say the least, a strange mixture of sadness and longing. These insights passed so quickly Jason hardly had time to register them before she spoke again. This time, her tone was more subdued.

"My older brother, Marcos, was killed during the Battle of Albuera," she said. "My mother and younger brother, Santiago, were lost during the war. My father and grandfather died near our home, close to Albuera. So, you see, I am all that remains of my family, other than my abuelita and her twitch." She waved her hand as if to dismiss the heaviness of the words she had only just spoken, but a look of sadness remained in her eyes.

"I offer my condolences for your losses." Jason felt the inadequacy of his words. He'd heard much the same sentiments after his father's death and knew how insufficient they truly were.

Miss Thornton shrugged off his proffered empathy.

He returned to the subject at hand, feeling remarkably uncomfortable with the unbidden surge of empathy he had momentarily felt for the exasperating lady. "A portion of your late father's estate reverts to his birth family, to any siblings he may have had. You have some property and funds to claim from his estate as well, enough to see you comfortably settled."

She listened, silent for once.

"In order to claim it, you will need to contact the solicitor employed by your father's family."

Miss Thornton sighed. "Ah. A solicitor. *Por supesto.* I knew I would need to set my sights higher. A barrister is simply not adequate."

Why did the infuriating woman continue to insist that a solicitor was a step up from a barrister? It made absolutely no sense.

Jason stopped himself from rolling his eyes. "If you will give me the name and, preferably, the direction of their solicitor, I can make inquiries on your behalf." Why had he made that offer? He might have been able to wash his hands of the troublesome Miss Thornton.

"I do not know who this solicitor is." Miss Thornton shrugged a shoulder again. "That is why I have you, no?"

"No," Jason answered. "A barrister does not fetch solicitors."

"Oh dear." Miss Thornton rose to her feet, a certain wobbliness to her tone that made Jason wary. "I had so hoped I wouldn't need to fire you again. Not when you have been doing so well." She began a fluttery pacing in front of the desk Jason had commandeered. "You have hardly repeated yourself at all since you have been here. I thought that so very promising. But I certainly do not have any connections in the world of law—I could never locate this awe-inspiring solicitor of whom you speak. It seems I must find someone who can."

"Miss Thornton, locating this solicitor would be a simple matter of inquiring of your father's family."

"Oh." She turned her large, innocent eyes on him. Too innocent, in fact. "Do you know where my father's family is?"

"Do you not?"

She shook her head.

That would make her quest difficult indeed. "Do you at least know *who* they are?"

"The Thorntons, I would think."

One corner of Jason's mouth twitched without warning. He immediately clamped down the unexpectedly amused response. Miss Thornton, after all, was not jesting. She needed help, and he had agreed to offer it.

"There could easily be dozens of Thorntons in England," he warned. "Can you not at least identify their home county?"

"I could tell you my home county," she offered.

"Is it in England?" he asked doubtfully.

"No." She answered with that same lack of understanding he'd come to expect.

"Then that information will likely not prove helpful," he said. "Unless the Thorntons have relocated to your home in Spain." He spoke the last word almost as a question, though he was relatively certain he had guessed her homeland correctly.

"Spain," she confirmed. "But they will not be there."

A falling out between families? Did the late Mr. Thornton's family disapprove of his marriage? The late Mr. Thornton's will had been rather boring, truth be told, but here was an intriguing mystery. Jason had never been one to walk away from a puzzle. No true student of the law lacked curiosity. "If you know your father's parents' names, I should be able to identify his family," Jason said.

"I know his birthdate," Miss Thornton said. "And I believe he was born in northern England."

"That is a start, at least."

"I do not wish to overtax you, Mr. Jonquil," Miss Thornton said, facing him straight on. "I would hate for you to revert to repetitions and blank looks again."

Jason merely raised an eyebrow at such a ridiculous remark.

"And I would dislike firing you when you are beginning to show so much promise."

"Send to my office any information you have about your late father and his family, and I will look into it," Jason said, hurriedly gathering his things.

"I will come by and give you all the information I have—"

"*Send it*, Miss Thornton," Jason insisted. "Send it to my office. You need not come in person. A simple letter will suffice."

With his almost desperate instruction hovering in the air, Jason quickly made his way from the room and, with any luck, Miss Thornton's vexing presence for good. Solving a mystery was only worth so much aggravation.

As he approached the front entryway, he could hear someone singing an off-key tune in a voice made loud with enthusiasm. "We despise your sullen thinkers, and fill the tavern with our noise."

The song stopped abruptly as Jason reached the front entryway and the butler finally took note of him there. He gave Jason a curious look. A well-trained butler would have opened the door, perhaps handed him his top hat and walking stick, and would have done so silently. He certainly wouldn't be singing a soldier's ditty in the doorway. What else should he expect in an establishment Miss Thornton oversaw?

"Are you any relation to Lieutenant Jonquil of the Thirteenth?" The man's brow creased, his one-eyed gaze not shifting in the slightest. Apparently the question was an important one to this odd butler.

"He is my younger brother," Jason said. "He was made a captain just over a year ago. You are acquainted with him?"

The butler puffed out his chest, stuck his left thumb—it being the only thumb he possessed—into his chest, and said with the deepest pride, "Served under him, I did. Fine lieutenant, he were. Served under him till Orthez."

"He was injured at Orthez," Jason acknowledged. Stanley had been badly injured, in fact, seriously enough to require that he be sent home to recuperate.

"Was injured then, m'self," the butler said, no lingering sadness or regret in his tone, merely a statement of fact.

Jason wondered which of the man's maimings had occurred in that onslaught. Perhaps all of them. Stanley, though left with significant weakness in one arm and recurrent fevers, had at least emerged intact.

"Your brother's the best lieut—cap'n in the whole deuced army," the butler said. "Best blasted man I ever knowed. Owe 'im my life, I do. A fine, fine genl'man."

"Yes," Jason drawled, plopping his hat on his head. "They all are."

Every last one of them. Jason had six brothers who were the best blasted men anyone had ever known. And it was a deuced nuisance at times. He heard them praised to the skies at each and every turn.

He worked hard. *He* had distinguished himself in his profession. *He* was a fine gentleman. But who noticed?

"Next time ye see old *Cap'n* Jonquil"—*Old* Captain Jonquil was a decidedly ironic way of putting it. The butler must have been on the other side of forty years old, and Stanley was not even four and twenty—"tell 'im Jake Black offers a shake of his hand."

"Captain Jonquil is preparing to embark for the Continent with his regiment," Jason said.

"Still with the Thirteenth?" the butler asked.

Jason nodded.

"Fighting them blasted, cussed French, is he?" The butler seemed to approve.

Someone needed to tell the unfortunate man that, if he did not curb his somewhat vulgar tongue, he might just find himself out of work. Not even the odd Miss Thornton would approve of such lower-class expressions in the doorway.

"Fine genl'man. And he'll be a fine cap'n."

It was praise, indeed, and came from someone Stanley had worked on behalf of, someone he'd led in battle. And what did Jason's clients, the people he worked on behalf of, say of him?

That he was *simple*.

And repeated himself.

Well, Miss Thornton would eat her words. Just see if she didn't.

Chapter Four

MARIPOSA WALKED THE FLOORS OF her bedchamber long after the darkness of night had descended upon London. Her circular path never varied. Neither did the topic foremost in her thoughts.

"What am I to do, Papá? Nothing is working as it should."

The empty room offered no response.

She stopped at her closed bedchamber door and leaned her weight against it. "I did what you told me to do," she whispered. "But everything is falling apart."

With perfect clarity, her father's voice repeated in her mind the words she'd long ago committed to memory, instructions he'd given them all as Napoleon's blood-filled conquest of her homeland had descended upon them. "If we are separated or if we find ourselves in danger, we must make our way to England, individually if necessary. We will reunite at the home of my family."

She was trying to obey his directive. Heaven knew she was trying.

"You never told me how to find them." She'd never imagined having to make this journey on her own, so she hadn't thought to ask him for more information. "I can't find them. I am misleading an unsuspecting gentleman, attempting to trick him into finding your family's solicitor. What if that can't be done? What if these lies don't work?"

Of course there was no answer. She'd been surviving more or less on her own for years. Coming to England had not changed that.

Mamá had never been entirely convinced the plan would work. "Will we be safe there?" she had asked. "What if England falls to the Corsican as well?" Years of warfare had only deepened the worry that had been etched in every line of her face.

"*Mi amor*," Papá had said. "Napoleon may wrest control of the entire Continent, but he will never conquer England. And we will always have a place with my family there. Far from war. Far from danger. On England's shores, we will finally know peace."

But they'd waited too long. War and danger had found them in their tiny corner of Spain. Thousands of French soldiers had descended on Albuera, only a few short miles from their home. Vengeful French soldiers had murdered her father and grandfather. The rest of the family should have fled—Mariposa should have insisted—but Mamá had been overcome with grief, spending her days staring out the windows of their home. Abuela, in the wake of losing her own husband and son-in-law, had been in no better state of mind.

"I was only fifteen," Mariposa whispered to the dark room. How often she had tried to convince herself that her struggle to assume control of her family had been understandable in one so young and untried by the world.

Hooves clomping and the press of wheels on cobblestone echoed up from the gas-lamp-lit street below. Mariposa had come to know the sound well, having spent a great many long nights awake and pacing since her arrival in London. Too many nights had found her still awake when the delivery wagons had begun making their earliest morning stops.

She crossed slowly to her window, forcing slow breaths, trying to clear her mind. The more tired she became, the more forcefully her most difficult memories pressed on her heart.

Her current view of the street below gave way in her mind to rows and rows of British army tents erected on the acres surrounding her childhood home. The occasional sounds of movement outside didn't overshadow the long-ago voices of the officers who had used the front parlor as their headquarters.

She dropped onto the window seat, turning her back to the window. She rubbed at her weary eyes. Too much had happened. There was too much worry and pain. She needed something to restore her hope.

"If only Mr. Jonquil can find Papá's family."

She'd heard his abilities praised so often by his brother, and Stanley would never mislead her. He'd shown himself a good-hearted and reliable companion, a friend in the truest sense of the word. He'd helped her and supported her through the aftermath of the battle of Albuera, a battle from which her brother had not returned alive.

Lieutenant Jonquil, along with a great many of his fellow dragoons, had helped her tend to the wounded and dying who were brought to her home to receive care, including Frenchmen left behind by their fleeing comrades. He had done a great deal to boost Mariposa's sagging confidence in the wake of so much loss. He, of all those around her, had seemed to understand how lost she'd felt and the enormous weight of responsibility she'd carried for her broken and grieving family.

"You must do what you feel is best," Stanley had said. "My father always told me it is in those moments when we are tested to our limit that we discover the person we truly are. You have it in you, Mary"— he had always called her Mary, claiming it was easier for an Englishman to pronounce—"to save your family. You are not one to quit when circumstances grow difficult. Use your strengths. Do all you can. And most important of all, cling to whatever hope you can find."

"Is that what you do?" Mariposa had asked as they'd moved amongst the most severely wounded, checking for those who had breathed their last. She'd tried to sound braver than she was. He believed in her so much more than she believed in herself. An almost overwhelming need to prove herself worthy of his trust swept over her.

"I search out every ray of hope I can find," he said. "I think if I didn't, this war would drive me mad."

"What if I lose the rest of them?" Mariposa asked, biting down on her lips to stop her sudden rush of emotion from escaping. "I have so little of my family left."

Stanley stopped his perusal and returned to her side. He took her hand in his, patting it in precisely the way her father had been wont to. That gesture alone nearly undid her, bringing every suppressed, painful memory to the surface. "When my father died," Stanley said, "I looked around at my family and wondered, *What if the rest of them die too? What if I lose them all?* But then I realized something."

"What did you realize?"

"I was only a little mite, thirteen, in fact. But I could help them. My mother—we call her Mater—she needed comfort, and I could do that." He nodded as if reliving that moment of resolve. "I could hold Mater's hand when she was teary or fetch her wrap if she grew cold—little things that helped her feel loved. And Philip, my oldest brother, was so overwhelmed. I could help him by keeping my younger brothers out of his hair. I looked for things I could do, no matter how small, and I did them."

"What if my family needs more than I can give?"

"You are all they have," was his answer.

And so, when the British army had packed up to move on to the next battle, Mariposa had gathered her family, along with their necessities, and left their ancestral home, uncertain they would be safe if they remained. They'd slept at times in barns, traded their belongings for food or funds, hidden from any and every sign of danger.

She'd quickly learned to assume anything and anyone might be a threat. She'd learned to play roles to keep her family fed and safe. She'd learned to lie.

She'd done her share of lying to Stanley's brother. What would her dear friend think of that? Would he understand? She needed to find the Thorntons' solicitor but could not hope to do so without help. Mr. Jason Jonquil was in the legal profession; he could search out another member of the legal profession without raising anyone's suspicions.

She could not risk drawing attention, not when a very real and worrisome threat hung over them all. Her efforts could not be kept quiet without some level of deception. The lies were justified.

She told herself as much over and over again. Any person would do as much to save their family.

The reality of their perilous situation could not be dismissed. She had received a note shortly before her mother and brother had disappeared, one that haunted her thoughts. Though she had not been present when the missive had been left for her, she knew who had penned it.

In the course of her survival, she had made the acquaintance of many people whose true identities were hidden, as hers so often was: invaluable allies she knew only by such names as The Bear and The Daffodil, as well as terrifying threats, like this man from France, known only as Bélanger. The notorious Frenchman was known for his brutal and vengeful nature, and she, by virtue of having shared with the British army information she'd stumbled upon about his plans for a covert crossing of the Channel, had made herself his enemy.

"A butterfly's wings are easily clipped," his note had declared. "Wingless and alone, she will die."

Wingless. That threat had been leveled at her. *Alone.* A threat made against her family.

"The young and the old are easily disposed of," he'd added. "The addled dispose of themselves."

Her younger brother, Santiago. Her aging abuela. Her mentally fragile mother. The threats had been too pointed to ignore. The man who had penned the chilling warning was precisely the sort to carry out such heartless acts. She knew him to be a murderer. And he knew she had full knowledge of his crimes.

From that day forward, she'd never stopped looking over her shoulder. She'd never let her guard down. Now two members of her family were missing, and she very much feared the ruthless Frenchman was responsible.

"On England's shores, we will finally know peace," her father had said.

Oh, Papá. I very much fear you were wrong.

Chapter Five

MARIPOSA LEANED BACK INTO THE questionable comfort of the less-than-elegant squabs of her rackety hired conveyance and smiled at how confused Mr. Jonquil would be when she stepped into his office. She had not yet sorted him out, but the attempt was proving excessively diverting. She needed the distraction and the bit of joy it brought.

What mischievous imp had convinced her to bring the information to him directly when he had so specifically instructed her to send it to him? The confounded man had hardly left her thoughts in the days since she had met him, he being such a mystery.

What reason could he possibly have for never smiling? Stanley had smiled and laughed with her even while surrounded by the horrors of war—at least he had early on. She herself had enough sorrow pressing on her heart to excuse a lack of levity, and yet she found reasons now and again to smile, to laugh, to find some joy in life.

"Such a handsome man really ought to smile," Mariposa mused aloud. *Such a handsome man.* She'd not intended to make that observation. "Well, no woman who saw him could possibly think otherwise," she defended herself. "Even if he is something of a gloomy cloud and will likely throttle me the moment I step through his door."

She sat alone in the hired hack. Abuela had remained at home, leaving Mariposa in the reliable hands of Will Williams, a veteran of the war against Napoleon. He was as large as a bull and looked every bit as intimidating. Mariposa, however, had discovered him to be as softhearted a man as she was likely to encounter. She felt as close to safe with him at her side as she likely ever would.

Will had spent a good deal too much time during his stint on the Continent within close range of the massive canons employed in countless battles and, as a result, could hardly hear a thing. He wasn't likely to give her away during their visit to Mr. Jonquil. Abuela was not so dependable; she'd taken to "twitching" whenever Mr. Jonquil was mentioned.

"Miss Mariposa Thornton," young Mr. Hansen announced precisely as he had the last time she'd come to Mr. Jonquil's office. Even the inflection was the same.

Does Mr. Jonquil not allow even the slightest bit of spontaneity? Mariposa looked around the room at the extremely symmetrical layout and perfectly organized papers and myriad books, no doubt organized on multiple tiers. She had an almost overwhelming urge to tip the painting behind Mr. Jonquil's desk and leave it hanging horribly askew, simply to see if Mr. Calm and Collected would show some emotion in response.

"Miss Thornton." Mr. Jonquil addressed her the moment his secretary left them. Mariposa recognized his tersely patient tone and very nearly grinned, which would, of course, have ruined everything. "I believe I told you to *send* your information to me."

"Yes." She opted for a tone of voice thoroughly infused with pride, as though pleased with herself for so closely following his directions. "And here it is." She pulled a small, folded stack of papers from her reticule. "I have sent it to you."

"No," he countered. "You have *delivered* it. I asked you to *send* it, Miss Thornton."

"And so I have." Mariposa kept her eyes wide and extremely innocent. "I have sent it from my house in my carriage to you. Personally."

"But that is not *sending*. That is *delivering*."

"You did not say you did not want the information *delivered*. You only said to *send* it to you. And I have. See?" She laid the folded papers on his desk. "It has been sent and has arrived." She smiled as sweetly as humanly possible.

"You have misinterpreted my words." Mr. Jonquil's exasperation became more obvious by the moment.

Mariposa sighed and gave him a look of overly sympathetic understanding. "At least you have not yet repeated yourself. That is something to be proud of, even if you still cannot seem to make yourself understood."

His jaw began twitching, and Mariposa judged it best to stage something of a strategic retreat. She wished to see his mask slip a little, not cause him apoplexy. She left her papers and wandered to the first set of bookshelves, eyeing them with an appearance of casual interest but, in all reality, entirely determined to identify Mr. Jonquil's method of organizing his many hefty tomes. She was certain there was a scheme and that it was overly complicated and clung to with a viselike grip.

What are you hiding, Jason Jonquil?

"Now that you have delivered these papers—"

"*Sent*," Mariposa threw back over her shoulder, unable to resist baiting him just a little more.

He didn't correct his word choice. "I am certain Hansen could summon your carriage so you can be on your way."

"Oh, I do not have a carriage here," Mariposa answered, successfully sounding offhand.

"No? How do you plan to return home?"

To Mariposa's surprise, Mr. Jonquil sounded concerned. She turned to look at him and very nearly exploded with laughter. It was not concern that had tinged his voice but outright horror. The poor man was deathly afraid he would never be rid of her.

"Why would I wish to go home, Mr. Jonquil?" she asked. "You have not yet read the papers. Do you not remember, that is why I have come?"

She patted his hand, knowing that would only add to the almost ridiculous role she played. But instead of exasperating *him*, the gesture momentarily overset *her*. A tingle of pure anticipation shot up from her hand to her arm and seemed to permeate her entire body in a matter of seconds. His was certainly not the first male hand she had touched—there must have been hundreds amongst the wounded and dying at Albuera and Orthez—nor was he the first handsome man she'd ever encountered, but never had she become so suddenly aware of a gentleman's mere presence.

She didn't at all like it. Her strategy depended upon being in control of their encounters, of keeping him upended. She simply could not allow herself to be unsettled.

Before she could pull back, Mr. Jonquil grasped the hand she still had pressed to his and pulled her the rest of the way around the desk until she stood close enough to hear his every breath.

"Now listen here, Miss Thornton," he said, his jaw tense, his words clipped. "I have been as patient as can be expected of any gentleman. But there are a few ideas you have tossing about in that otherwise empty head of yours that need straightening out."

She stood frozen, both by a sudden wariness at his authoritative and extremely annoyed tone and by a certain captivating quality he had about him.

"I am not incompetent," he insisted. "Neither am I an imbecile, nor do I repeat your words because I have none of my own. I do not take kindly to being treated condescendingly." He held her barely at arm's length. His grip on her hand was unrelenting but not at all painful, as if he made certain he did not hurt her, despite his obvious anger. "I will read through your papers, but I will not sit idly by while you insult me. Is that understood?"

For a moment, she was tempted to drop her pretense entirely, to simply confess her act and her reasons and ask him to forgive her. But it was too soon, and she did not know him well enough. The best way to survive in an often violent and uncaring world was under the protection of masks and armor and pretense.

Oh, why couldn't life have remained simple? Why hadn't Napoleon and his marauding soldiers remained in France? Why hadn't Papá and *Abuelo* simply remained at home that horrible day? Why hadn't Marcos been spared? Why had Mamá and Santiago been taken from her as well?

To her mortification, her chin began to quiver and not, she was certain, indiscernibly. He was too near to not notice. In fact, his expression softened. As he looked into her face, his tense posture relaxed ever so slightly.

Mr. Jonquil closed his eyes for the slightest of moments. A sigh escaped his lips. He released her hand and held out to her a folded handkerchief. "You are the most exasperating female I have ever known," he said quietly.

Pain radiated through her at his words. *Exasperating* was precisely how she had intended to appear. Still, it was hard knowing he thought of her that way.

Why should that bother me? She hadn't survived years of warfare by making friends. She'd survived by being careful and distant, by hiding behind the very mask he was commenting on.

"Is this gen'leman hurtin' you, Miss Thornton?" Will asked, his voice a little louder than necessary. The man didn't hear well, after all.

"No, Will," Mariposa answered, shaking her head to aid his understanding. She dabbed at a single tear that managed to escape her eye.

Through years of terror and difficulty, she had almost never broken down, not since that emotional conversation with Lieutenant Stanley Jonquil amongst the dead and dying of Albuera. A single unflattering comment from his brother and suddenly she was fighting a surge of emotion.

I must be tired. She had been up quite late the night before, after all.

She commanded herself to focus once more. The information she had delivered would help Mr. Jonquil find the Thornton solicitor, who would, in turn, help her find her family. She was too close to allow herself to fall apart now.

Her protective cocoon settled into place once again. "Will you require long to read through the papers I sent you?" Her voice was quieter than she would have preferred, but at least it was steady.

"Sent," he muttered. A hint of amusement hung on that single syllable. Amusement?

She had hoped to see indications of precisely that in him. It was enough to restore her spirits a little. "Excellent," she said. She had to look up, *far up*, to see his face. He had the most magically blue eyes. "I am so pleased to not have to fire you. I have heard it said that the third time is the charm, but I do not think that particular saying would apply in this situation."

"Certainly not," he answered dryly.

Someday, Mr. Jason Jonquil, Mariposa silently said, *I* will *see you smile.*

He led her to an empty chair opposite his desk and, summoning absolutely impeccable manners, offered her a seat before returning to his chair and unfolding the papers she had left on his desk. A fraction of a moment later, he looked up.

"Miss Thornton?" Mr. Jonquil asked.

She smiled in precisely the way she'd taught herself to, looking vague and untroubled despite the innumerable heavy thoughts swirling in her brain.

"Who recommended my services to you?" Mr. Jonquil looked as though he very much wished to know.

She opened her mouth to answer but was cut off.

"And do not answer 'a close acquaintance.' You provided that invaluable nugget already."

The perfect reply surfaced in her mind, one certain to frustrate the poor gentleman. She met his gaze and smiled sweetly. "Your brother."

Chapter Six

YOUR BROTHER, JASON REPEATED SILENTLY.

He had *six* brothers, and any one of them was capable of playing him such an underhanded trick. "Highly recommended," she'd said. One of Jason's own brothers had *highly recommended* she seek him out. But which one?

Not Charlie. He was only seventeen and probably entirely unaware of what his brothers did with their lives.

Corbin was unlikely to have sent him the exasperating woman. He was Jason's own twin, and the two had always understood each other on a level above and beyond any of the other brothers. Besides, recommending legal council to any person would require a conversation, and Corbin rarely spoke to his own family, let alone anyone else.

Philip. Jason tensed at the mere thought of his eldest brother. Philip had likely suggested Miss Thornton seek out Jason simply on a whim. Or, more likely still, because he knew she would drive him absolutely mad.

Yes, Philip was the obvious answer. And as fate would have it, Philip was on his way to Scotland with his wife and not nearly close enough to receive the kind of retribution Jason owed him.

Miss Thornton turned slightly to the side, her eyes studying the view from his office window. Despite the fact that she was a troublesome creature, Jason couldn't help admitting that she had an enchanting profile with her dainty mouth and tiny, pert nose. And, good heavens, that hair. Thick. Abundant. The most intriguing shade of deepest brown. There wasn't a man alive who wouldn't notice.

She is an aggravating prattle box, Jason reminded himself. He forced his eyes to return to the papers in his hands. He could still smell the breezy scent of her perfume from those few moments when she had stood directly beside him. It reminded him somehow of the seashore.

He concentrated harder on the reasons he disliked her. She misunderstood his words, twisted everything he said to make him look like a fool. And she did it so well that either she was a complete featherhead or a very gifted actress. There had been something in her eyes as she'd condescendingly patted his hand that had looked infuriatingly like laughter.

Jason hadn't lost his temper since he was at Eton and Corbin had been sent home for beating the tar out of George Finley. It had been unfair, unjust. Corbin had been defending Stanley from Finley's unrelenting torture. To be sent down for stopping a bully was insupportable. Jason had railed against the unfairness of it until he, himself, was very nearly sent home as well.

"One does not fight injustice by creating chaos if there are more productive ways of doing so," Father's letter had said. "I am certain you can think of many ways to address this miscarriage of justice without my having to fetch you home as well. Corbin is fine. You need to be also."

He had taken Father's words to heart. Righting wrongs and helping the helpless had become Jason's passion, eventually leading him to a career in the law. He'd learned to keep his temper and his calm and solve problems logically. He'd learned the value of honesty, which brought his thoughts to Miss Thornton once more.

Was she playing a game with him? He couldn't be certain. His sharp reprimand had brought tears to her eyes, along with a genuinely pained look. The emotion that had broken her voice had seemed real enough.

Which was the real Miss Thornton? The empty-headed, overly talkative version? Or the sensitive, self-aware one? She could not be both—they were too vastly different—meaning Miss Thornton was inherently dishonest, something Jason could never countenance.

"It is a somewhat long list," Miss Thornton's voice broke into his thoughts. "I suppose it will take time for you to read all the way through it."

Ah yes. The list she'd given him. Jason began concentrating with determination.

Instructions. Miss Thornton had headed her paper with that single word.

First, read the information I have sent you.

Second, review anything you did not understand.

Was it possible she had actually delineated how he was to do his job?

Making note of the most useful things might be helpful as well.

Next, begin making inquiries based on these useful things.

The list continued, outlining every conceivable step. He was even instructed to make certain he ate regularly and slept at night.

Jason lifted his eyes to see if Miss Thornton was laughing. Surely she meant the list as a jest. But her eyes were focused away once more, her features as vacant as ever. Featherhead or actress?

Jason flipped to the second sheet. Here she had begun her list of information about her father. She knew a birth date but not a specific location, nor the names of his family members. A marriage date was included, but the ceremony had taken place in Spain, which did not make identifying the Thornton family any easier.

"You have very little information to offer," Jason said. "Though your *instructions* were particularly detailed." He couldn't be certain, but he thought he saw a twinkle in her eye that belied her vacuous expression. Jason studied her the way he did when interrogating witnesses. His unwavering and fierce evaluation had never failed to break an opponent.

Miss Thornton simply smiled back, unshaken, unperturbed. Perhaps it was not an act, after all. Jason rubbed his mouth and chin with his hands, hating that he was the first to break eye contact.

"I thought the instructions might prove helpful," Miss Thornton said sweetly. "In case you forgot something."

"In case I forgot something," he muttered.

Her face took on that look of concern once more. "Oh dear—"

"I am repeating again," Jason finished for her. For just a moment, he could have sworn she fought back a laugh.

"How much time do you think will be required to find this mysterious solicitor?" Miss Thornton sounded a touch impatient.

"How long do *you* expect such a search to require?"

"Your brother would have already completed such a small task," she answered with a wave her hand.

"Yes," Jason drawled, "my brothers are all fine, fine gentlemen. Admirable in every way. Paragons of proper upbringing."

A look of confusion and surprise flashed momentarily across her face. "You say that as if you do not mean it."

"Oh, I mean it." He heard the sarcasm in his tone and silently reprimanded himself for his loss of calm. He had worked hard over the years to perfect the demeanor expected of a barrister and the son of a well-respected earl.

"I happen to know, sir"—suddenly her tone turned cold, even as she rose with almost palpable dignity—"at least one of those 'fine, fine gentlemen' does not deserve your mockery. He is indeed an admirable and good-hearted man."

"Then perhaps you should ask him to help you," Jason answered, stung into a sharp reply.

"I am certain he would not require being fired three times." Miss Thornton waved three accusing fingers in the air, her tone entirely serious. Something flashed in her eyes that Jason had never seen there before, something decidedly like anger.

"You have only fired me twice," Jason pointed out a little smugly, somehow pleased to have unsettled her.

"Then this will make three." She spun on her heel, fairly marching to the door. "Good day, Mr. Jonquil. You may add, 'Learn to appreciate your brothers' to my list of instructions. You have apparently neglected to do that." Her enormous footman closed the door behind her.

"Appreciate my brothers . . ." Jason's mutter trailed off as he pushed out a frustrated breath. How was it that she managed to undermine his calm so entirely? Who gave her leave to evaluate his family? To dictate what he did with his life?

He crumpled up her "instructions" and tossed them into his wastepaper bin, eyeing his tidy office with utter dissatisfaction. His gaze settled on a painting hung ever so slightly askew on the wall. He shook his head, rising to set it to rights.

Miss Thornton seemed impressed enough with his brother— Philip, no doubt. Why were so many women taken with dandies and fops? "Appreciate your brothers," she had said. Did they appreciate him? Did they admire him? No one ever referred to him as a "fine gentleman." No one ever sang his praises or defended his good name.

"Drat that woman."

The door opened once more. He spun, ready to confront Miss Thornton. He found, however, Mr. Pole and Mr. Thompson, two of his colleagues, standing in his doorway, skewering him with looks of disapproval.

"Gentlemen?" he inquired.

Pole led in Miss Thornton. She dabbed at her eyes with a handkerchief—*his* handkerchief. Jason wasn't entirely convinced the tears were real.

"Miss Thornton is distressed, Jonquil," Pole said. He didn't sound too pleased with Jason. "She says she is seeking legal council as you are no longer willing to advise her."

"No longer willing to advise her?"

"He repeats himself sometimes," Miss Thornton whispered to Thompson.

"It is not like you to abandon a client," Pole continued. "Especially one so obviously in need of your assistance."

"He said he was unequal to the assignment," Miss Thornton said.

So help him, Jason felt sorely tempted to shake her.

"Mr. Jonquil is an extremely talented barrister, Miss Thornton," Thompson assured her with gentle concern. She certainly had them fooled. "He would be equal to any assignment you could possibly hand him."

"Then, perhaps he simply does not wish to help me," she said despondently.

Jason narrowed his eyes on her. She knew precisely what she was doing; he knew that now for sure and certain. How much of this act was meant to goad him, and how much was actual innocence?

"Jonquil." Pole closed the distance, leaving Miss Thornton in Thompson's care. He patted her hand reassuringly. Jason very nearly muttered an uncouth observation. "It is not like you to mistreat a gently bred young lady."

"I have not mistreated her at all," Jason said. "She has a tendency to misunderstand things. Most things, in fact."

Her eyes widened momentarily at his words, further convincing Jason that she was not so vacuous as she made herself out to be.

"She seems to be a sweet-natured young lady who is genuinely distressed," Pole said.

"She is a thorn," Jason muttered and saw Miss Thornton's eyes narrow at him.

"If you are unwilling to continue serving as her legal council," Pole continued, oblivious to the interplay around him, "I am certain there are many others who would take up her case."

Jason balked at the suggestion. Was he to simply let her run roughshod over someone who lacked the ability to deal with her? Hardly.

"As I said," Jason answered, "she has simply misunderstood. I never withdrew my services."

"You see, Miss Thornton." Pole turned back to address her. "He was not dismissing you. If Mr. Jonquil says he will continue as your legal council, you may depend upon his word. Indeed, he will serve you quite well."

"What if he sends me off again?" she asked, the slightest quiver in her voice.

"Then you simply come to either of our offices," Thompson answered on behalf of both men. They watched Miss Thornton almost worshipfully. The infuriating woman was beautiful, there was no denying that, and that head of hair could be mesmerizing, but *worshipfully*? Had the two turned entirely daft? "We would be happy to be of assistance."

"Oh, thank you both so very much," she answered, flashing a watery smile in their direction. Beneath the emotion, though, the gesture seemed forced, rehearsed even. The woman grew more indecipherable by the moment.

She was offered two elegant bows before her newfound champions left her in Jason's office with only her burly footman for protection.

The door closed. Jason refrained from offering a mocking round of applause. "That was masterfully done, Miss Thornton."

"Yes, they are both quite accomplished at bowing," she answered with her usual empty smile.

Jason knew better. Without uttering a word, he walked to where Miss Thornton stood. A momentary flash of wariness in her eyes told him she understood she'd pushed him nearly to his limit.

"I warned you, Miss Thornton," Jason said, calling upon his legendary patience to keep from barking at her, "that I do not tolerate being patronized. I dislike condescension. However, I absolutely will not be made to look a fool in front of my colleagues."

"Does that happen often, then?" she replied, too much innocence in her eyes to be anything but feigned.

"I humble myself for no one."

Their eyes locked in a battle of wills. He had looked away first the last time; he would not again.

"Your arrogance, sir, is astounding," she replied. Jason noted with satisfaction that her façade had begun to crack.

"As is your incivility," Jason returned. "I believe I would be hard-pressed to find a lady of good birth with a greater lack of manners."

She opened her mouth, most likely to voice a protest, but he continued speaking before she could utter a single syllable.

"Perhaps that is simply the Spanish way." Jason thrust another barb. "Here in England, such ill-bred behavior is likely to get you throttled."

"Are you saying a self-respecting Englishman would lay his hands on an innocent female?" Miss Thornton asked with a doubtful raise of her eyebrow.

"No. Not on an innocent female," Jason said, making his way to the door, "but maybe on you."

Miss Thornton moved silently toward the door. Just as Jason felt a surge of triumph at leaving her speechless, he noticed a deep, humiliated blush spread across her entire face.

"That weren't very nice," Will declared in his booming voice from very near Jason's position. "Miss Thornton oughta be talked to r'spectfully. Ought not be implying she ain't no better'n—"

"Never mind, Will," Miss Thornton replied, her color still high. "It is of no importance." She turned toward Jason, not quite looking him in the eye. "Good day, Mr. Jonquil. I will send your handkerchief back to you."

She slid from the room—silent for once—without even a momentary glance backward.

Too late Jason realized that in his temper, he'd allowed his mouth to run rampant and had, however inadvertently, quite thoroughly insulted a gently bred young lady. He'd meant his remark about her not being "innocent" as a reference to the charade she'd been enacting. But the word carried an implication he'd not thought of. He had, without meaning to, cast doubt upon her morals.

His father, he knew with absolute, horrifying clarity, would have been utterly disappointed in him.

Chapter Seven

"Señorita Thornton," Black greeted as Mariposa stepped inside the house after her less-than-pleasant trip to Mr. Jonquil's office at Lincoln's Inn.

"Good afternoon, Black." She handed over her bonnet before tugging in frustration at the buttons of her pelisse.

Black and Will exchanged communicative glances. Her moment of indignity would, no doubt, be retold in excruciating detail the moment both men were below stairs.

"Not on an innocent female. But maybe on you." Mr. Jonquil had spoken loudly enough for even Will to overhear.

Will had immediately recognized the possible double meaning. Mariposa hoped Mr. Jonquil hadn't meant the insinuation. To even offer the insult was a slap in the face. To have meant it would be unendurable.

She tugged harder at the stubborn buttons. One flew off her pelisse with significant force, a clunk resounding through the small entryway as it struck the opposite wall. Heat stained her cheeks once more, and she scolded herself for being so easily affected.

She had remained strong and determined in the face of danger, deprivation, and even death, but embarrassment had always been her undoing. The taunting and degradation from the soldiers had been particularly disconcerting each time she had made the journey into Orthez during the French occupation. A single demeaning comment and her face would flame red. This outward expression of her inner humiliation had served only to fuel their enjoyment of her suffering.

Black retrieved her button before holding his hand out for her pelisse.

"Would you see that Fanny receives those?" Mariposa asked. Her abigail was truly a wonder with needle and thread. She would repair the damage with little difficulty.

"'Course." Black nodded, his lone eye focused on her with a level of concern that only further mortified her.

"Is Señora Aritza in?" Mariposa asked, knowing very well that her grandmother would not have left the house. She simply needed to take Black's attention off herself.

"She's napping in her room." Black's gaze remained too penetrating for comfort.

Mariposa nodded. They stood a moment in awkward silence. Will watched her with the concerned guard-dog expression he wore so often. Black's expression bordered on paternal. Mariposa half expected to see Abuela shuffle down the stairs with a lap blanket and a bedtime story.

These were people for whom *she* was responsible. She had pulled Black off the street, England having turned its back on so many of its returning soldiers. Black had, in turn, rescued Will from a similar state. Mariposa had kept Abuela alive during countless days and nights of toil and struggle. Seeing them so obviously convinced she was breaking down or falling apart proved excessively lowering.

"Was this morning's *Times* placed in the book room?" Mariposa asked, summoning her best tone of authority.

"Yes, miss," Black answered.

She nodded once more and moved with forced confidence from the entryway. Her determined posture did not slip in the slightest as she made her way to her destination. Playing a part was a necessity not reserved exclusively for fending off ill-intentioned soldiers or gleaning information from unsuspecting barristers. She pretended for her family, letting them think she was worthy of their trust when she actually felt entirely unequal to the responsibilities she carried.

Her true self lay so deeply hidden beneath her layers of disguises that she often felt like a stranger even to herself.

Mariposa dropped into the chair behind the book room desk and opened the newspaper, searching the Society column as she always did. She carefully checked for any mention of a "Thornton" family, though she had not in all the time she'd been in London seen a single reference to them.

She scanned the column, reading each *on-dit*. "Lord G, who has been quite a favorite among this Season's young debutantes, has left Town for an extended visit with his sister. No doubt the new Marquess has left behind many a broken heart and a few disappointed mothers."

That wasn't helpful.

"The Dowager Duchess of K___ hosted her annual mid-Season dinner party last evening. As always, invitations were scarce, those attending being the very cream of Society. It is not yet known if any of the guests were challenged to a duel by the infamous Duke."

On and on the column went, recounting the goings-on of people Mariposa neither knew nor, compared with the whereabouts of her family, cared a great deal to learn about. Her frustration grew with each entry. Not a single paragraph mentioned the Thorntons. The closest she came was a mention of a "Lord T." The Thorntons were firmly ensconced in the landed but untitled gentry. No lords or ladies to speak of.

Another pointless perusal.

Mariposa shoved the useless paper from the desk with an exasperated expulsion of breath. She rubbed her face with her hands.

"Oh, Papá, I cannot find them. You never told me how."

As always, she was answered by silence. She had not a single soul to help or guide her. She'd survived a seemingly endless war by sheer luck and the unreliable sufficiency of her wits. Such an accomplishment came at a price—during war, one learned that a pained conscience was far preferable to a pained everything else.

She'd traded her ability to trust and the right to be trusted for her family's well-being only to lose them in the end.

"Papá is not coming back, is he, Mariposa?" They'd been in France a year when Santiago had asked her that question.

"No, he is not." She'd managed the reply with matter-of-fact steadiness, though her heart had broken, realizing the little boy had lost another piece of his childlike innocence. She had tried to shield him as much as possible.

She'd wrapped her arm around his shoulder as they'd sat side by side watching the sun set over the French countryside—a rare moment of peace in their war-shattered lives.

"Papá didn't forget me," Santiago had said. "Everyone else does."

Abuela had still been very absentminded at that point, Mamá debilitatingly so.

"I will not ever forget. That is a most solemn pledge."

Not a single day passed without her thoughts turning to Santiago. Thoughts of him and Mamá pushed her onward in this increasingly frustrating search. Concern for him kept her from making her efforts known, despite the dishonesty required to do so.

She had not forgotten her beloved brother, and she would never stop searching for him.

Chapter Eight

JASON ENJOYED THE OCCASIONAL JAUNT through Hyde Park but only ever in the earlier hours of morning when hardly a soul was about and London was as close as it ever came to being quiet. The vendors setting up their carts and the street sweeps beginning their day's work took little note of him. He could allow himself a measure of lightness unbefitting a barrister in his office or speaking before the court. He even whistled a tune now and then. During those early walks, the tension he carried with him the rest of the day eased and lessened. He felt more like the carefree boy he'd once been, indulging in larks with his brothers and getting into mischief at Lampton Park. Though those years were far behind him now, he needed the reminder once in a while. He needed that brief taste of home.

But even a second chorus of "Early One Morning" did not ease his thoughts today, filled as they were with his father's words: "If I ever hear you've mistreated a lady, young or otherwise, I'll box your ears until you cry like a little girl."

He had said that to each of Jason's brothers in turn every time they'd left home for school or to spend a short holiday at the home of a friend or relative. Father had never permitted any unkindness toward a female, be that treatment deserved or otherwise. He would have entirely disapproved of Jason's final encounter with Miss Mariposa Thornton.

Jason felt heartily ashamed of himself over it. He had clearly seen her embarrassment at the implication of his words. Why he'd said such an unfeeling thing, he couldn't say, except that she frustrated him excessively. He knew she was baiting him, playing him for a fool, but he didn't know why. She seemed to have no qualms about humiliating *him*. But, he scolded himself once more, that did not give him leave to belittle her.

He maneuvered around two older women shuffling their way down the park path and paused just long enough to tip his hat to them. He continued on, his thoughts still on Miss Thornton.

The sight of a small flower vendor attempting to wave off a very determined terrier captured his attention almost immediately.

"These aren't yours," the young boy kept telling the tenacious pup. "Off with you."

The dog's tail wagged with unmistakable excitement, as if his nemesis were actually encouraging him. Jason shouldn't have chuckled, but he couldn't help himself.

The poor beleaguered boy turned pleading eyes on him. "He'll not leave the flowers be, sir. I'll have nothin' to sell."

He attempted to summon the little dog with a whistle. The animal looked at him but did not give up his quarry.

"Off with you, dog." The boy's command emerged too desperate and overwhelmed to be truly effective.

Jason scooped the mutt into his arms. "You seem to have found the only dog in all of London who likes flowers more than foxes."

"Not too bright, is 'e?" Some of the boy's worry had fled.

Jason turned the dog enough to look it in the eye. "Is that true, you troublemaker? Are you not too bright?"

The flower boy smiled as he quickly began lifting his flowers onto the waiting cart. "I usually get m' flowers on the cart before he can get to 'em. I was too slow this morning."

"What is your name?" Jason asked.

"Benny," he said, carefully straightening his flowers.

Jason addressed the dog again. "Benny is a man of business with a right to his inventory. You stop tormenting him." The dog responded by licking his face.

Benny laughed. "You're talking to a dog, sir."

"Have you never talked to a dog?"

"Yes, but I'm a li'l boy."

Jason chuckled. "I was a little boy once too, you realize."

"Did you talk to dogs then too?"

He nodded as he set the troublesome mutt on its paws once more. "My brothers and I did a great many silly things."

"Do you still?"

No. No, they didn't. He didn't spend a great deal of time with his family now that they were mostly all grown. Their days of laughter and larks were far behind them. At times he deeply regretted that. But his professional reputation, his attempts to counteract Philip's embarrassment to the family name required solemnity and unfailing dignity. Only during these early mornings did he allow himself any indulgence in frivolity.

"I'll take a posy," he said to Benny, slipping his fingers into the small pocket of his waistcoat where he had a few coins.

"Thank you, sir."

He nodded, paying for the handful of violets. "Best of luck with your flower dog."

Benny dipped his hat, and Jason did the same. He added the boy to his mental list of street children he meant to keep an eye out for.

"Buy an eel pie, sir?" a cockney voice asked from somewhere near his elbow.

Jason turned in that direction. A young girl, likely not more than nine or ten years old, her clothes little better than rags, her face dirty and her hair disheveled, watched him with heartbreaking hopefulness. She held a pie up for his inspection, though he was a bit too distracted by the filthiness of the hand in which she held it to take much notice of the offering itself.

"Only a ha'penny, sir. It'd be a fine bite for you, guv'nuh." Her eyes pleaded with him. "A ha'penny."

He had intended to buy the pie even before she'd begun begging. The street vendors could sometimes be very pushy, almost threatening. Everything about this poor child spoke of desperation.

Her circumstances were clearly far worse than her flower-selling counterpart.

"How many pies do you have in your basket, child?"

She peeked into it. "Six, sir."

"I'll take them all."

Her eyes pulled wide. "Truly, sir? You're not funnin' me?"

"Not at all."

"It'll come to three pennies, sir." So much doubt still filled her expression, as if she felt nearly certain he'd change his mind once he knew the total. "Do you still wan' 'em?"

He nodded firmly.

"I could wrap them up in paper for you."

"That would be fine." He didn't intend to eat them either way. Too many vendors sold items that left a person ill for days on end.

The girl dropped to her knees and meticulously wrapped up her six questionable pies. "If you're one to be walkin' about here often, I sell my pies every morning, sir. And sometimes I make oyster jellies too, if'n you're liking that more."

She had determination, he would give her that. And if she could make a living at selling her foodstuffs, she'd not need to begin selling herself, a fate that awaited far too many girls and women in London.

"What is your name?" He asked that question a lot during his morning walks.

"Fanny Smith."

"Do you like to cook, Fanny?" he asked as she wrapped up another pie.

She nodded emphatically. "And I'm good at it, or I'm trying to be at least. Someday I want to own a cart to sell from. Customers buy more from carts, thinkin' it's better food."

She had an eye for bettering her situation as well. He liked that. "If you could cook in a pub or an inn or a great house, would you prefer that? Or is your dream truly to have a vendor's cart?"

She looked up at him through her loose strands of brown hair. "I could never work in a great house. I don't talk proper like."

Then that was where her ambitions truly lay. "Refined speech isn't necessary in the kitchens, at least not when one is beginning.

By the time a girl like yourself reached the level of a cook, she'd likely have learned to speak more properly."

She sighed as she finished wrapping the last pie. "It's all just smoke though, ain't it? I'd never find a position like that, no how."

"Are you willing to work?" he asked.

"I ain't never been afraid to work, sir."

Precisely what he'd hoped to hear. He pulled from his case one of his calling cards. "I want you to deliver those pies to Lampton House." He explained to her how to find it. "And bring this card with you." He handed it to her. "Ring at the servants' entrance and tell them I am requesting they give you a chance to prove your worth in the kitchens."

"No trickery, sir?"

"No trickery. This is my brother's home. He and his wife treat their servants well. If you work hard and prove your worth, you might just manage to have a job cooking in a fine house someday."

"Oh, sir!" The girl was fairly shaking.

"I mean to ask Cook how you're getting on," he told her. "I hope to hear good things."

"Oh, sir. Thank you, sir."

He didn't at all expect she would be anything but a welcome addition to the household. Fanny would not be the first street imp he'd sent to Lampton House, though there hadn't been a great many. He now and then crossed paths with children like this Fanny Smith or Benny with his flower cart, children who hadn't yet been destroyed by the harsh realities of life on London's streets, who had dreams and a willingness to see them through.

Cook and Mrs. Jeffers, the housekeeper at Lampton House, knew Jason well enough to accept this oddity in him. He couldn't save every child in London, but he could help some. And he meant to do just that.

Fanny actually ran from the park toward Lampton House, her basket of newly wrapped eel pies swinging on her arm. He felt certain she would be a good addition to the household, but adding a new body to the kitchen would cause at least temporary upheaval.

"I should probably send Cook a handful of daisies in apology."

"Daisies are more of a 'good day to you' flower. Violets make better apologies."

He didn't have to turn around to know who spoke. Miss Thornton's accent, though subtle, didn't precisely blend in amongst the crowds of London.

He looked over his shoulder at her. "Violets?" he asked.

She nodded, her sincerity punctuated by the unmistakable amusement in her eyes.

He turned fully. "Such as these?" He indicated the violets he had purchased from the flower vendor only a few minutes earlier.

"Precisely like those, though I do not think Cook will be overly upset with you."

A kind word from Miss Thornton? That was entirely unprecedented. "You must believe she has a high opinion of me."

Miss Thornton waved the idea away. "She will be pleased with Fanny. The girl is here every morning. I've eaten dozens of her eel pies."

"Dozens?" He widened his eyes as if in shock. "And you're still alive?"

She smiled. "You are in a pleasant mood this morning, Señor Jonquil."

"I am in a pleasant mood most mornings."

Miss Thornton made a sound of pondering. "You are good to give little Fanny a job, señor."

Jason shook his head. "I've given her an opportunity. What she makes of it depends on her."

"*Sí*. But most would not do even this for someone small and unimportant."

"No one is unimportant."

The smile she gave him in return was bright and filled with approval. Though he'd not gone in search of her good opinion, he found himself warmed by the thought that he might have secured a small piece of it.

"You are very like him," she said. "I had hoped you would be." As usual, she spoke in riddles, not actually giving him any solid information.

She once more wore that same vague expression she had during her visits to his office. He knew it was not genuine—the mask had slipped during that very conversation—yet he couldn't say why she affected it.

Reminders of her visits to his office brought firmly back to his thoughts the apology he yet owed her. He didn't imagine it would ever be a comfortable undertaking. He might as well take care of that now. "Miss Thornton, before we go our separate ways, I wish to offer my apologies for the unintentional insult I offered you when last we met."

A deep blush immediately heated her face. She obviously remembered and had indeed caught the accidental slight to her character.

"I apologize for what I said," he continued. "I ought not to have allowed my temper to cloud my judgment."

Her dark brows angled downward, and her gaze studied him. Though his apology was sincere, it seemed the effort was proving insufficient.

"And," he added, "because I have it on excellent authority that violets are a crucial part of any expression of remorse"—he held the flowers out to her—"with my deepest regrets for speaking unkindly."

She accepted his offering with surprising graciousness for one who had shown herself to be dishonest and, at times, insulting. She had also interrupted what ought to have been a very peaceful and calming walk.

He meant to reclaim his morning. "I bid you a good day, Miss Thornton." He offered yet another quick bow.

He took only two steps before stopping. She was alone in Hyde Park. He couldn't simply leave her so utterly unprotected. While this was not the worst area of Town, he still couldn't countenance a young lady being there on her own.

He turned back, even as a sigh of frustration escaped him. "May I summon you a hired hack, Miss Thornton, to return you to your home? I cannot like the idea of you being here alone."

She smiled as unconcernedly as ever. "I am not alone." She motioned behind herself. "Will is here."

Her enormous footman was, indeed, not too far away, keeping a close eye on everything. He could certainly look after her. But Jason knew his father would never have been satisfied with such a slight effort.

"My offer yet stands. I would be happy to summon a hack. You are a good distance from your home."

She shrugged. "I crossed Spain and France on foot, señor. London will be"—she snapped her fingers—"no challenge for me."

And yet she was a challenge to him. "Well then. Once again, I bid you good day. Do send along any further information you can find about your father's family."

"I will."

"But *send* it. *Send.*"

She gave him a small wave. "Until we meet again, Señor Jonquil."

Meet again? He, for one, wasn't holding his breath. She had shown herself to have a good heart—she'd been buying eel pies from Fanny for weeks, after all, and had not been unforgiving in the face of his insults—but she was also deceptive.

Thank goodness he was headed to Corbin's estate at the end of the week. Miss Thornton could continue wreaking havoc on London. He would be safely tucked away in Nottinghamshire.

When Jason arrived at Havenworth, he found very nearly all of his family members there. Last he had heard, only he and his mother had been expected. Corbin would not be happy about the company. He was a quiet and withdrawn sort of person. He had been known to go days at a time without talking even to his closest family, and that was when they had all lived at home.

"What has brought everyone to Corbin's home?" Jason asked his brother Harold.

In his characteristically pious tone, Harold said, "Mater did not wish to leave Charlie or Caroline at the Park, as both have been giving her difficulties of late."

"And you have come to . . ."

"Spend a little time with my family," Harold said. "We are not together often anymore."

That was quite true. With Stanley on the Continent, they were never all together. Even before their brother had returned to his regiment, the Jonquils had not been together in quite some time.

They were all shown into the sitting room to await the arrival of their host. Jason took his customary spot at a tall window that overlooked a large stretch of lush grassland. It was his favorite prospect at Havenworth. His brother's home was peaceful in a way few places were. Lampton Park was too full of memories of Father. Lampton House in London was Philip's realm, and that alone made it a place of discomfort.

Havenworth was one of the only things any of Jason's brothers had that he truly envied. Not the estate, specifically, but the sense of contentment he saw in Corbin at having land of his own, doing what he loved, and being respected for it.

Jason enjoyed the law, but it never seemed like enough. Philip certainly wasn't impressed. Miss Thornton wasn't. Would Father have been? At times, Jason wasn't sure.

Corbin arrived and looked as nervous in company as he always did. *Poor Corbin.* What must it be like, being uncomfortable even with one's own family?

Mater immediately launched into another of her recitations of their youngest brother's many misdeeds. Charlie was going to be a handful. Jason sincerely hoped Philip was equal to the task. Father had been gone for ten years, and Charlie, unlike the rest of the brothers, hadn't had the benefit of his wisdom during his most difficult growing-up years. Jason hadn't been fatherless until he was fifteen years old.

How old was Miss Thornton when her father died? Jason wondered silently. *Sixteen. Perhaps even younger.*

He quickly dismissed all thoughts of the aggravating woman. He was on holiday. He would entertain only peace-promoting thoughts, which eliminated anything related to his most frustrating client.

Jason moved to where Corbin stood holding little Caroline, their niece, in his arms.

"You're the best uncle in the whole world," Caroline told Corbin.

Jason chuckled. "That is a rather bold declaration for a young lady with seven uncles." Crispin, a family friend of long standing, was always included in the uncle count. "Aren't I your favorite uncle?"

"You're my favorite uncle in London," Caroline clarified.

Jason shrugged. "I suppose I'll have to be satisfied with that." Somehow he'd hoped to hear something more flattering. At least she hadn't told him he was simple and repeated himself. "How are you, Corbin?"

Corbin nodded but communicated more in that small gesture than most people would have guessed. Jason saw weariness and an underlying frustration in Corbin's eyes. That would bear looking into. With Corbin, however, a less direct approach was always best.

Caroline had already tired of her uncles and was bouncing around the room.

"What did you do to earn the title of favorite uncle?" Jason asked.

"Invited children—"

"For her to play with," Jason finished for him, knowing precisely what Corbin intended to say, as well as recognizing when he didn't wish to finish his thought out loud. Were all twins that way, or had he simply developed that talent because Corbin's reticence required it?

"Genius." Jason acknowledged Corbin's answer. "The only thing I brought from London was a bag of toffee and a monumental headache."

"Difficult case?" Corbin asked in a tone that indicated he knew the answer already.

"A difficult *client*."

"Is she?" Corbin asked.

"Despite the fact that I am her legal council, Miss Thornton is convinced she knows better than I do on every matter. She descends on my office unannounced and expects immediate and undivided attention. She is a harpy of the first order, but my secretary as well as every other barrister in the entire building is practically falling at her feet. And—" Jason stopped abruptly, something only just occurring to him. "How did you know this client was a she?"

Corbin smiled at him, a hint of laughter in his eyes. Jason had to smile the tiniest bit himself. Corbin knew him too well, and he seemed a little too familiar with the telltale signs of an exasperating female.

"Are you dealing with a difficult woman too, Corbin?" Jason's mood lightened a little. Corbin had that effect; he was peaceful, like Havenworth.

"Not difficult. Just—"

"Elusive." Jason nodded his understanding. "Is she a harpy?" He wanted to be sure Corbin wasn't about to entangle himself with a female who would take advantage of his quiet nature.

Corbin shook his head. That was a good thing. He needed a woman who respected him and didn't see his quietness as a sign of weakness or lack of intelligence.

"Does she order you around?"

Corbin chuckled and shook his head again.

Jason nearly sighed with relief. Perhaps this woman wasn't a disaster waiting to happen, unlike—He refused to finish the thought.

"You're having trouble winning her over?" he asked. Concentrating on Corbin's troubles instead of his own might clear his thoughts.

"She doesn't notice me."

That wasn't entirely surprising. Corbin blended in, didn't capture anyone's attention long enough for them to realize he was more than worth knowing. "That's your problem. You have to make an impression."

"Philip said . . ." His words trailed off as he nodded.

Philip. Precisely the person Corbin didn't need advice from. "You haven't been listening to Philip, have you? He probably told you to dress like a fop and simper about. No lady is interested in a gentleman who wears brighter colors than she does."

Corbin would look even more ridiculous dressed like a peacock than Philip did. Over the next few hours, Jason found ample time for chewing over Corbin's difficulty. If his brother had managed to meet a woman who was not exasperating and confusing and entirely impossible to keep out of one's thoughts, then Jason would see to it that Corbin had all the help he could possibly want.

One of them ought to enjoy some degree of good fortune in matters relating to women.

Chapter Nine

"THERE WAS ALSO A TIME when your father and I found all of the tin soldiers from the nursery on top of the garden shed." Mater laughed, shaking her head. "Your father and I spent many long hours attempting to sort out how Philip and Layton managed that. They weren't nearly tall enough. We realized after a time that a brother sitting on another brother's shoulders would likely be enough height for their bit of mischief."

Jason bit his lips shut to hold back his own amusement. He remembered the soldiers on the roof lark. He had sat on Philip's shoulders and Corbin on Layton's while Stanley had stood guard. They had been so certain that the groundskeeper would think a ghost had placed the toys on the roof. Lud, they'd embarked on a great many ridiculous pranks when they were children.

"And did they really replace all the ink in the nursery inkwells with tea?" Charlie asked. "Philip told me that once."

Jason rubbed his fingers over his mouth to hide his grin. Those long-ago tricks had been almost acceptable in a boy influenced by his mischievous older brothers, but he was a grown gentleman, and such things ought not to still make him laugh. This family had enough ridiculousness to endure from Philip. Jason's role was to add some degree of dignity. That, of course, was difficult when

Mater was regaling his youngest brother with tales of their most diverting larks.

"Jason, I remember," Mater very pointedly did not look in his direction, "had an incredible talent for acting a part, no matter how ridiculous."

"Jason?" Charlie looked and sounded shocked.

"Jason," Mater confirmed. "One time, he convinced a newly hired grounds worker that he was the knife boy from the kitchen who had been sent to determine how sharp a knife needed to be to quickly cut through rhubarb. It was, of course, merely a diversion to allow his brothers to slip into the orangery to steal fruit."

Jason could not hold back his grin at that long-forgotten deception. "Heavens, I'd forgotten about that."

"I'm not surprised," Mater said. "You have . . . outgrown such things, haven't you?"

Why did Mater sound nearly disappointed? Of course he had outgrown such things. He was no longer a child. He was a well-respected barrister and a credit to the Jonquil name.

"I could not pretend to be a knife boy whilst assisting my clients, could I?" he answered.

Mater's eyes twinkled. "I would pay a year's pin money to watch that."

Charlie jumped in. "How much would you pay to watch him climb on Philip's shoulders? That is the sight I want to see, especially since they'd probably end up in a bout of fisticuffs."

"I do not indulge in fisticuffs," Jason replied, very much on his dignity. "Neither do I undertake mischief or larks or any other such childish things."

Charlie slouched in his chair and hmphed. "I wish I'd known my brothers back when they weren't boring."

Boring. Apparently he needed to add that to his list of recent complaints he'd received. *Simple. Repetitive. Incompetent. Boring.*

While Miss Thornton hadn't offered the same denunciation as Charlie, he wouldn't be at all surprised to discover she agreed with him. The looks she gave him, even during his apology a few short days earlier, had spoken loudly of amusement at his expense.

Jason met the woman Corbin was pining for and was struck by the way that quiet, gently spoken lady looked at his brother: with trust and confidence and respect. There was no mockery or dismissal. How had his nearly silent brother managed to claim her good opinion?

As if fate meant to undermine Jason's conclusions, Corbin stepped inside the room in the very next moment, sporting the beginnings of a decidedly black eye and a hint of discoloration covering one side of his face. What had happened? Had he been thrown during a ride? Jason hoped that at the very least, Corbin was taking care of his injuries.

"Have you put a cold cloth on that bruise? It looks awful."

Corbin looked back at him, his angry glare directed solely at him.

"What?" Jason asked warily.

Corbin's butler interrupted any response, speaking three words Jason would never have expected to hear at Havenworth. "Miss Mariposa Thornton."

"What the bl—" Corbin's elbow stopped Jason's words.

Miss Thornton! There had to be some kind of mistake, a mispronounced name, a sudden onset of dementia in Corbin's butler— anything! But then, Miss Thornton herself walked inside, eyes dancing as she surveyed the room.

Jason's fists tightened at his side. The source of complete chaos and upheaval in his life and, lately, his thoughts now stood in the middle of the Havenworth drawing room. *Havenworth.* The place to which he retreated for peace and calm. The place where his family was assembled.

"Well. *Ahí estás,* Mr. Jonquil," Mariposa's vibrant voice declared to the room at large. "You, señor, are a difficult man to locate."

"What the bl—"

"Language, señor!" Miss Thornton cut him off. She wore one of her extremely innocent expressions.

"You were instructed to direct all correspondence to my secretary," Jason said. He had told her so specifically, wishing to avoid any conversations between her and his colleagues. She had belittled him before them. Did she now mean to insult him in front of his family?

"If I wanted a correspondent," she said as she walked past him, still smiling sweetly, "I would write to my abuela."

"Your abuela lives with you."

"So you can see how pointless letter writing can be." Miss Thornton nodded and looked almost grateful, as if he'd agreed with her or confirmed her observation. She addressed her next observation to his mother. "And you must be Mater."

He didn't recall telling her the family's pet name for their mother. Mater apparently wondered too. "How did you . . . ?"

"Your son speaks of you often."

"Jason?"

Miss Thornton laughed, dismissing the idea with a wave of her hand. "Not that one. The *capitán*."

Stanley? All this time, Stanley was the weasel? Stanley, who had always been the nice one? Drat the man, sending him such a whirlwind of chaos.

"You know Stanley?" Mater grasped Miss Thornton's hands, a break of emotion in her voice.

"*Sí.*" Miss Thornton smiled at Mater. "When the fighting was in *España*. Our *casa* was used by the British. I knew him then. And again at Orthez. He is a good man. Not useless like that one." She waved her hand toward Jason.

Jason felt certain his face was twitching. *Not useless like that one.* She had indeed come to speak ill of him, and to his own mother. This after they'd had a relatively civil encounter in Hyde Park not many days hence. Was there no end to her willingness to ill treat him?

"Corbin, may we use your library?" Jason asked, his jaw tight. "I believe Miss Thornton has some business to discuss."

Corbin silently agreed. Miss Thornton did not, however, make her way from the room. She crossed to Corbin, offering him a genuinely pleased smile.

"You are Señor Corbin?" she asked. She did not seem bothered nor surprised that he did not respond but continued talking as if in the midst of a friendly conversation. "As you see, I have met your evil twin."

Corbin smiled. He actually looked almost at ease, something Jason had rarely seen. Miss Thornton was weaving her spells again.

"Come, Miss Thornton." Jason waved her toward the door.

"It was wonderful to meet all of you." Miss Thornton smiled at the rest of the room but didn't move so much as an inch.

"Now," Jason snapped. He would discover precisely how she'd located him, what errand could possibly have sent her so far from London, then send her back to Town with a few choice words to chew on.

If any person had ever taken such a long time to cross a room as Miss Thornton did at that moment, Jason was unaware of it. Behind her empty-headed expression, he saw laughter in her eyes.

That laughter would not last long.

Things were not going at all the way Mariposa had envisioned. She had discovered, thanks to Mr. Jonquil's secretary, that he was visiting "a brother." It had been the work of a moment to decide which of the Jonquils that would be. Stanley had made clear, probably more than he had realized, that Jason and Corbin shared a bond exclusively their own.

A few well-placed questions in the most innocent of tones saw her furnished with directions to Havenworth, which, as fate would have it, resided not terribly far from the town of Copperton, where she had learned a family by the name of Thornton resided. Her tightly guarded funds were beginning to dwindle, and this journey had required that she further deplete her accounts. The prospect of meeting yet another member of the Jonquil family had helped her justify the expense, especially after discovering the Thorntons she had found were not *her* Thorntons.

She had fully expected to find some comfort and reassurance and joy at meeting Corbin, the soft-spoken brother. But entering the drawing room to find so many members of the Jonquil family present had nearly overset her. Mater had been in the room. Mater, of whom Stanley had spoken with such tenderness. And little

Charlie, who was not at all little any longer. And Corbin had been just precisely as she had imagined him—a more serene version of Jason, who was not his physically identical twin but with whom he noticeably shared facial expressions and gestures.

She had wondered about this tightly knit family for years. Mariposa had thought many times how pleased she would be to someday meet them. She had always imagined herself doing so with happy dignity. Instead she had rambled on and on, probably not even entirely in English—she had the unfortunate tendency to mix languages when nervous—and had, no doubt, made a complete cake of herself.

Mr. Jonquil ushered her through the open door of what proved to be a library, a look of forced forbearance on his face. His obvious frustration with her only increased her guilt.

"You have a wonderful family, señor." She shook her head to dispel the sudden, intense longing she felt for her own loved ones.

"Why have you come here, Miss Thornton?" A subtle layer of anger laced his words.

She pulled a precisely folded square of linen from the reticule dangling at her wrist. "I have sent you your handkerchief."

Mr. Jonquil's jaw clenched further, his eyes snapping. "Your grasp of the English language is not the least bit lacking, Miss Thornton. You most certainly understand the difference between *send* and *deliver*. Your pretense of confusion is both unnecessary and insulting."

He saw through her. She knew he did. Panic began to bubble inside. Her pretenses had only ever been found out once before, by the murderous French spy Bélanger. She had been fleeing from him ever since and, in that flight, had been separated from Mamá and Santiago.

Horrible things happened when her secrets were discovered, and Mr. Jonquil had just uncovered one.

She repaired the chink in her armor the only way she knew how—with a thick layer of misdirection. "I happened to be in Nottinghamshire—"

"One does not accidentally travel from London to Nottinghamshire," he countered. "The journey requires more than one day."

"It was not *un accidente*." She could not, however, explain that she'd come looking for her family. Admitting that discovering the location of her extended family was imperative enough that she would spend the time and money necessary to make the journey to Nottinghamshire on the slight chance that they were there would raise more questions. Answering those questions would only further reveal her perilous situation. She simply could not risk it. "I had your handkerchief and wanted to send—"

"Try your hand at the truth, Miss Thornton."

"But I have been—"

"Enough." His gaze narrowed. "I held out hope that I had misjudged you or at least that you had decided to change your tactics in light of our affable conversation in Hyde Park. It seems, though, that was feigned as well."

"I do not understand."

"Allow me to be clear, then." He stalked across the room toward her. "You have denigrated me before my colleagues."

Mariposa backed up as he drew closer. Her heart pounded in her ribs, the panic inside bubbling more by the moment.

"You have treated my time with utter disregard and repeatedly insulted my professional abilities."

Her back hit the wall, trapping her where she was as he came closer, tension showing in every line of his face.

"You have been patronizing and insulting from the moment I met you." Mr. Jonquil stopped directly in front of her.

Mariposa managed to breathe, though she couldn't say how. He was intimidating, unnerving, and obviously livid. She didn't feel that she was in danger, not physically, but every sense was on edge.

"Señor Jonquil—"

"Now you have pushed me beyond bearing. I will not allow any person, including your exasperating self, to ill-use my family, continuing your deceptions here in my brother's home and tainting my mother's concern for Stanley with your feigned sincerity."

"*¿Su familia?* I would not hurt your family. No. *¡Jamás!*" Her pulse thrummed in her ears.

"You, Mariposa Thornton, are a liar." His lips curled, and his nostrils flared in disgust. "I doubt a single truthful syllable has passed your lips since first we met. I do not work with clients whose word is worth less than the soot that covers London."

Soot? Did he truly think so low of her?

"And be assured," Mr. Jonquil added, "I will take whatever steps necessary to warn my colleagues against your deceit should you choose to inflict yourself upon any of them."

"*¿No me vas a ayudar?*" Mr. Jonquil's look of momentary confusion told Mariposa her English was slipping, a sure sign that she needed to escape before she completely fell apart. "You won't help me?"

"I do not feel you require my legal services any longer," Mr. Jonquil answered, giving her a look of frigid civility. "Indeed, you would do well to consider the entire legal establishment beyond the reach of your dishonesty. Good day to you, Miss Thornton."

Tears of mortification poured from Mariposa's eyes as she lay in a cramped room of a roadside inn that night. She had brought her chambermaid with her on this ill-conceived journey for propriety's sake but wished to heaven she could have been alone with her grief. Instead, she kept her face turned toward the wall and away from the cot where Jane made her bed.

The disgust that had twisted Mr. Jonquil's mouth as he'd declared her a liar had cut a deep and painful wound in her heart. A liar. That was all she was to him.

In the early days after she'd led her family from their home, producing gross fabrications had been difficult. She'd struggled every time. Lies now came so very easily.

She wiped at more tears with Mr. Jonquil's handkerchief. In her distress, she'd forgotten to leave it with him. He would likely think she'd made off with it on purpose. What reason had she given him to think well enough of her to not assume she was a thief as well as a deceiver?

Papá had taught her to be honest and true and trustworthy. He had taught her to value integrity above all else. She had traded her honor for food and shelter and for her family's safety. The war had changed her, and not for the better.

Mr. Jonquil considered her word worthless. She couldn't help but agree with him. Her father would have found very little in her conduct of which to be proud.

"A contract is not worth the ink with which it is written if the signers have no honor," Papá had said when the Peace of Amiens was brokered. He didn't feel Napoleon could be trusted. That had proven true time and again. And Papá had denounced him many times over, nearly as much for his lack of integrity as for his efforts to pull down the nations of Europe.

Oh, Papá. Her tears picked up their pace. *I am ashamed of what I have become, and I know you would be as well. But it is all I know anymore. I don't have any idea how to change.*

Chapter Ten

JASON WALKED ARM IN ARM with Mater around the back garden at Havenworth. He would be in Nottinghamshire only another hour and meant to spend it with his beloved mother.

"Your brother has truly made a fine life for himself here," she said.

"He has, indeed."

"Though Harold would, no doubt, wax long about the vice of conceit to hear me say as much, I am inordinately proud of Corbin." Mater glanced back at the house. "I worried a great deal about him, about all of you boys, truth be told. Without your father here these past years—"

Jason guided her around a puddle in their path, keeping his gaze straight ahead while Mater regained her composure.

"I miss him, Jason."

He rubbed her arm with his hand. "I miss him as well. At times I can still hear his voice as clear as if he were standing next to me."

Mater took a slow breath. "Charlie has very few memories of him. It breaks my heart."

"Oh, Mater." He slipped his arm free of hers and pulled her into a one-armed embrace.

She leaned her head against him. "Philip has told Charlie about your father again and again, hoping to give him some idea of the man he was."

"Then Philip does remember him?" Jason ought not to have spoken so sneeringly, but discussions involving Philip never failed to feed his frustrations with his oldest brother.

"You once idolized him," Mater said. "What changed that?"

"He did," Jason answered. "He changed."

Mater motioned Jason to a stone bench set beneath the intertwined branches of two trees. "I have not failed to notice your irritation with Philip. I have simply chosen to allow the two of you to sort out your difficulties on your own. Until now."

He eyed her sidelong.

"Tell me your grievance with your brother."

And burden Mater with the view Society had of her oldest son? "I would rather not—"

"Jason." He hadn't heard that scolding tone from her since he was young. "Argue with me all you like; I have more than sufficient patience to sit here until you spill your budget."

"'Spill my budget?' Who has been teaching you Town cant?"

"That particular phrase I learned from Charlie, though I suspect he first heard it from Philip." Mater shook her head in apparent weariness. "There is that look of disapproval again. Talk to your mother, Jason."

"Father was a remarkable man."

"I will not argue with you on that point."

How would she feel about the rest of his points? He stood, unaccountably nervous yet surprisingly anxious to speak the frustrations that had weighed on him for years. "Father bore his title with dignity. He was a credit to the family name, respected by Society and his peers. Selfless. Upright."

Mater nodded. "Again, I agree."

"Philip has taken all of that, the legacy he inherited, and has rendered it a farce." Jason paced a few steps in each direction. "The Lampton title has become a byword. He is laughed at and the family with him."

"You are upset with your brother because he embarrasses you?"

"No. Because Father's memory deserves better."

Mater patted the bench beside her. Jason obeyed the unspoken summons.

"Do you know what my opinion of your father was when I was a young girl?"

He knew his parents had spent their lives on neighboring estates, but this part of their history he had not heard.

"I thought him arrogant, obnoxious, and an embarrassment to the neighborhood."

"Father?" He could not believe that.

Mater laughed lightly. "Yes. And if he were here, he would tell you I was not entirely wrong. But he would also insist that I was not entirely correct either." Her expression turned wistful and nostalgic. "I see a lot of him in each of you boys, but one trait you all share with him is a tendency to hide the person you truly are."

"I don't understand."

She took his hand in hers. "You all keep yourselves tucked safely behind various masks and walls, whether it be isolation or playing the fool or"—she eyed him more pointedly—"clinging to the appearance of impeccable respectability."

"Respectability is not a bad thing."

"Being your full self is a *better* thing, my dear." She patted his cheek. "Give your brother a chance to be his full self before deciding who he is. You might both be surprised by what you discover."

Chapter Eleven

"MISS MARIPOSA THORNTON," HANSEN ANNOUNCED from the door of Jason's office a few days after his return to Town.

He couldn't have been more surprised if his secretary had announced the emperor of China. Jason rose to his feet, bracing himself. How would she insult him this time? He'd had more than a week free of her exasperating company, though the reprieve had been filled with enough difficulties to last a very long time, not the least of which was the conversation he'd had with Mater. His thoughts were in enough of a jumble without Miss Thornton adding to it.

But the lady who entered his office was noticeably different from the one he'd last seen at Havenworth only ten days earlier. Gone was the sunny smile and eyes sparkling with mischief. No aura of confidence surrounded her. Miss Thornton looked nervous. She kept near the door as Hansen stepped out and closed it behind him.

"What is it you want, Miss Thornton?" Jason asked sharply. "I believe I was quite clear about no longer serving as your legal council."

"*Sí*—Yes, sir."

The uncertainty in her voice sent off warning bells in Jason's mind. She wasn't looking at him. That was decidedly odd. Miss Thornton was not one for timidity and reserve.

"I will not permit any of my colleagues to be badgered into service either," Jason reminded her.

"*Lo sé*," she said quietly. "I did not come *aquí* in order to obtain new legal council, Señor Jonquil."

Miss Thornton's English was slipping, very much as it had at Havenworth. "You have determined to try a different Inn of Court?"

"No, sir," she answered. "*Estoy segura de que usted conoce—*" She cut off her own words and started again. "I am certain you know a sufficient number of your colleagues to make any attempts at obtaining council a fruitless effort."

There was no censure in her tone, nor any self-pity. And why wouldn't she look at him? Her eyes never rose much above her clasped hands.

"I did not come here to regale you with my difficulties, señor," Miss Thornton pressed on. "I neglected to leave this *en la casa de su hermano*," she said, her words suddenly rushed. She stepped swiftly forward and deposited a handkerchief on his desk, the matching double *J*s in one corner declaring it his own. "And to . . . to apologize. I should never have lied to you. I know I treated you *horriblemente* and *usted no se merece* to be misled nor disrespected before *sus* colleagues, nor embarrassed before *su familia*. It was wrong of me. Very wrong, and I apologize. *Perdóneme*."

Perdóneme he could sort out. The rest of her lingual slips were beyond his understanding, though he felt relatively certain it was all part of a very jumbled expression of regret. He wanted to trust that she truly was sorry but couldn't be certain. A liar could never be completely trusted.

"Your words *de censura* were difficult to hear, but you were correct. About me. *No estoy*—I am not truthful as I should be. And I have been unkind."

Jason couldn't help watching this almost heartrending apology with something akin to shock.

"If you wish me to confess my underhandedness to your colleagues, señor, I am prepared to do so. And to . . . to your . . ." Was her chin actually quivering? "And to your family." Her voice broke as she made the offer. "I will confess that I was unkind to you and that they would be well advised not to pay me any heed."

She would declare herself untrustworthy to his family as penance? That was unexpected, as were the tears clinging to her eyelashes when, for the first time since stepping into his office, Miss Thornton met his eye. The pain he saw in her expression struck him deeply. Miss Thornton's mask had slipped. Instead of the spoiled young lady he had expected, he saw one who looked entirely defeated, as if she bore a weight far too heavy for her shoulders. There was no cynical triumph in her expression, only torment and heartbreaking humility.

Jason was too shaken to even respond. And Miss Thornton was not done with her unexpected soliloquy.

"Only, please . . ." One of those lingering tears slipped down her cheek. "Please don't tell Stanley. After everything he's done for me, after all his kindnesses, I couldn't bear it if he despised me. Please. I—"

Miss Thornton stopped abruptly, her face going even paler, her eyes lowering once more. Something of Jason's surprise must have shown on his face.

"Forgive me," she whispered. "I have no right to beg favors."

This was far too much self-castigation. Something, Jason knew, was decidedly not right. His words of chastisement could not be the only source of Miss Thornton's obvious pain; he had not been that harsh.

How did Stanley, of all people, factor into it? Did Jason's younger brother and Miss Thornton have an affection for one another? That seemed unlikely. Stanley had been markedly attentive to Miss Marjie Kendrick up until the day he'd returned to his regiment only a few short weeks earlier; though to Jason's knowledge, there was no formal understanding between them.

"I am determined, Señor Jonquil, to be honest and forthright from now on," Miss Thornton said, discreetly inching toward the door. Hasty retreat hardly seemed her style.

Jason found himself following, completely baffled by her seeming change of character and oddly wishing to reach out and pull the poor creature into a reassuring embrace. Jason was not generally one for an outward show of emotion, but she seemed to so desperately need it.

"I will not give *mi familia* or yours any further reason to be ashamed of me," Miss Thornton added.

"Miss Thornton," Jason said, stopping her even as her fingers gripped the doorknob.

She looked back at him, and her red-rimmed eyes made his heart thud uncomfortably. Her suffering was so obvious and so unexpected that he simply stood in shock, hoping he hadn't been the cause of such pain.

He searched his brain for something, anything, to say. "What of your legal difficulties?" he finally managed. "I was not able to identify your father's family's solicitor. If you do not locate him, you will not be able to claim your inheritance. What will you live on?"

A small, sad smile flashed momentarily across her face. "I will address my problems on my own, señor."

"You have very little information to go on. Without someone in the legal profession assisting you, you aren't likely to be successful." Though, he admitted in the back of his mind, he had given her little choice, declaring he would denounce her to any barrister or solicitor she sought out.

"I will do my best," she said. "And that will have to be enough." Miss Mariposa Thornton slipped from Jason's office, leaving him entirely bewildered.

Jason couldn't say just what brought him to Lampton House that evening. He must have made his way there out of habit, though he'd had his own place for more than half a decade.

"Welcome, Mister Jonquil," Jeffers greeted, completely unruffled by Jason's unannounced arrival.

The knocker had been taken off the door, a clear indication that the staff understood, even if Philip hadn't, that Jason didn't intend to leech off his eldest brother. Yet there he stood in the front entry of the family's London home, allowing a footman to divest him of his outer coat, hat, and gloves.

"At what time would you like dinner, sir?" Jeffers asked.

"That won't be necessary." Jason shook his head, wondering again what had propelled him to come.

Instead of accepting Jason's pronouncement, Jeffers offered a warning reply. "Cook's feelings will be hurt if you refuse."

"Seven o'clock will be fine," Jason heard himself relent.

In the back of his mind, he wondered just what Philip had done to change the austere butler Jason remembered from his childhood into this smiling, friendly man. He couldn't decide whether or not he approved of the change. That alone was odd. He generally disliked anything Philip did different from Father's way.

Lampton House was eerily quiet. Only his vivid memories filled the silence with the robust laughter of a houseful of young boys.

"Someday, my love," Jason could hear Father's voice echoing across the years, "they will all be grown and gone, and we will stand in the silence and miss all the noise they make."

But Father was the one who was gone, and Jason stood in the empty house, fighting the tug of memories and the pain of loss. How Jason missed him, longed for his guiding influence. Speaking of Father was difficult, but remembering him so clearly pained Jason almost beyond bearing.

A flash of unexpected clarity struck with such force that Jason stopped halfway up the stairs. He had avoided Lampton House in London and Lampton Park in Nottinghamshire for years but had never admitted to himself the reason. But this was it. Father was everywhere in both houses, the pain of his death made fresh by both the memories of him and his glaring absence. Being in either place forced him to remember.

Jason had been at Eton when news of Father's death had come. He'd not had the opportunity to say good-bye. The whole world had felt unstable from that moment on. He'd seen Philip sag under the weight of responsibility. He'd watched Mater, pale and sobbing, age years in a matter of days. Layton had looked lost. Corbin had stopped talking, even to Jason. Stanley had turned almost desperately helpful. Harold had retreated into his books. And Charlie, only seven years old, had spent weeks asking where Father was.

Jason had been numb. By the time the truth of what had happened had sunk in, he was back at school, Philip was answering to their father's title, and nothing was ever the same again.

Keeping away had been his only defense. With distance between him and those places he most associated with Father, he could almost pretend he didn't still grieve in the deepest parts of his heart.

His feet carried him automatically to the bedchamber that had been his and Corbin's in their youth. The space didn't look at all the same, and yet there was a calming familiarity there that he'd needed. He'd felt oddly upended since Miss Thornton's call.

Jason had expected to find haughtiness behind the mask she wore but had seen only vulnerability. He had anticipated denial but had received an apology. He had assumed his words would simply bounce off her unnoticed. Instead, his censure had landed her a jarring blow. Piercing her armor had brought pain into her eyes, and it was eating away at him.

You feel guilty. He dropped into the chair near the window. *You feel responsible for bringing her pain.*

But why should he care? She was infuriating and aggravating. She was also suffering.

"Seeing one's own flaws is painful," Father's voice echoed in his mind. "But it is vital if one is to smooth the rough edges of one's character."

Right on the heels of that reassuring declaration came the reminder of Father's annual threat to box their ears should any of his sons mistreat a female.

"Oh, Father." Jason sighed, slouching in his chair. "Where are you now when I have so many questions?"

Chapter Twelve

JASON SPENT TWO DAYS AT Lampton House. Though he still felt the weight of memories walking its empty halls, he found a degree of comfort he hadn't felt in years.

He mulled over the contradictory picture he had of Miss Thornton. Try as he might, he couldn't reconcile the contradiction she presented. Yet Mater's words returned every time he attempted to make sense of Miss Thornton. "You all keep yourselves tucked safely behind various masks and walls." She might just as well have been speaking of the confusing young lady. Miss Thornton was hiding, but from what and why?

He sat at his desk, accomplishing nothing despite having been at his office for more than two hours. The door opened, and Hansen stepped inside, that look on his face that always indicated he was about to announce a client.

"Mrs. Aritza to see you."

Mrs. Aritza? "Show her in." Why would Miss Thornton's grandmother come to see him? How were they supposed to communicate? Jason quickly ran through his mind those barristers whose offices were near his, searching his memory for any who spoke Spanish.

"I do not interrupt?" Mrs. Aritza asked, her accent heavy but her words distinguishable.

"You speak English." He should have known Miss Thornton hadn't been forthright about that either. How could one person be so thoroughly dishonest?

"*Un poco*," was the reply, accompanied by a gesture indicating a minuscule amount. "Enough," she added with a shrug.

"Please, be seated." Jason motioned to a chair, wondering just how much "*un poco*" was and whether or not they would be forced to communicate entirely in gestures.

Mrs. Aritza seemed to understand his offer and shuffled to the chair he had indicated. Only when she was seated and had turned her deeply wrinkled face up to him did Jason notice the panic hovering in her expression. The intuition that had led him through more than one difficult case pricked at him again.

"What has happened, Mrs. Aritza?" Jason sat in the chair beside her.

"*Mi nieta*," she said, tears suddenly swimming in her eyes.

"I do not speak Spanish," Jason said, feeling the lack acutely.

"I am needing your help," she pleaded. "She, *mi nieta*, found *el nombre de su familia* in a book and is to see if *que son sus parientes*."

Jason was having difficulty following the perplexing sentence. "*Parientes*? Parents?"

"Family," Mrs. Aritza clarified, her hands gesturing rather more wildly than before. Jason could see she was becoming ever more distressed.

"Señora"—Jason remembered that word, at least—"please help me understand."

A flicker of hope appeared in the poor woman's eyes. Jason felt all the more anxious to help her. When was the last time he'd truly been useful to someone on a *personal* level—for this didn't seem like a legal matter.

"Mariposa is searching for her *familia*—"

"Her family?"

Mrs. Aritza nodded.

"She is not looking for her family solicitor?" he pressed.

Her brow creased a moment in thought. "No. For her *familia*. Not *un* solicitor."

Why, then, had Miss Thornton sent him looking for one? She had been very specific about that. Why lie about such a commonplace thing as wanting to claim an inheritance? Why not simply tell him she was in actuality looking for her family?

"She is gone," Mrs. Aritza said.

"Mariposa is gone?"

Suddenly the woman crumbled, weeping into her hands. "She is gone. *¡No está aquí!* She is gone."

"Where has Mariposa gone?" Jason's heart pounded, despite himself.

"*A Escocia.*"

Where in the world was that?

"*Al norte,*" Mrs. Aritza added through her sobs.

"North?"

She nodded.

North. Escocia. "Scotland?"

Another nod.

"Please tell me she had the sense to bring that enormous footman with her."

Mrs. Aritza clearly didn't understand him.

"Is she alone?" Perhaps a more direct sentence would be better understood.

"*Sí.*"

Yes. Mariposa had gone alone, then.

"She says she must not burden others anymore," Mrs. Aritza said.

I will solve my problems on my own. Mariposa had said just that with a look of utter defeat in her eyes. Lud, had *he* pushed her to this?

"Her money, it is very little. She must not pay for un *carruaje.*"

"When did she leave?" Jason asked. The poor woman could do naught but cry. "Please try to speak to me. I cannot help her if I do not know where she is." He laid a comforting hand on her own tear-dampened one.

"I no *sabía* if you would help me," Mrs. Aritza said. "Stanley, he spoke *mucho* of you. He made us think to trust you."

"Of course you can trust me, señora. Only tell me by what route Mariposa has traveled and when she departed. I will try to catch her carriage."

Mrs. Aritza turned her deep-brown eyes, so very much like her granddaughter's, to him. "We have no carriage."

"Then how is she traveling?"

"*El correo.*"

"I don't know that word."

"*Las cartas,*" she tried. "The letters."

His heart stopped altogether. "She's traveling by post?"

"*Sí.*"

He leapt to his feet on the instant, muttering further curses under his breath. A young, beautiful, unprotected woman alone on a mail coach? Had the aggravating creature taken complete leave of her senses?

"I searched her clothes," Mrs. Aritza said through her tears. "She has taken those she wore when we were crossing *España*. She will look to you to be poor."

She was traveling in disguise, then.

Mrs. Aritza continued. "Her post wagon"—that wasn't quite the right word, but Jason knew precisely what the woman meant— "left this morning at six hours."

"The Great North Road," Jason said to himself. That was the way the post would travel. He had made the trip north from Town many times and knew a faster way. He turned to Mrs. Aritza, belatedly offering a handkerchief. "You must allow me to place you and a small number of the Lampton staff on the road to Nottinghamshire," he said, holding her trembling hand in his. "My mother lives there, and I would feel easier knowing you had someone with you to offer comfort and company."

"Mater?" Mrs. Aritza asked, the light returning to her eyes.

"Stanley mentioned her too, did he?" Jason smiled a little.

Mrs. Aritza nodded. "He spoke much of all of you."

"Then you will be comfortable with Mater?"

After a moment to sort out the words, she nodded once more, putting Jason's mind at ease.

"Let us not delay," he said.

They did not waste a single moment. Within the hour, Mrs. Aritza was comfortably ensconced in one of the Lampton traveling carriages headed for Lampton Park adequately provided with a maid and footman. Jason rode northward on one of Corbin's prize mounts from Philip's stables.

He sincerely hoped Miss Thornton hadn't embraced her vow of honesty too entirely. Her very safety depended on creating an inconspicuous façade. Should any of her fellow travelers suspect she was a well-born lady, alone and unprotected, more than her reputation might suffer.

How had she come to be in such a coil? Mere days had passed since Mariposa had sworn to no longer be a teller of half-truths and outright lies. She glanced at her wear-worn brown dress, thrice-repaired boots, and heavily mended cloak and winced. Her very appearance was a deception.

Only by refusing to talk had she avoided telling an entire string of plumpers during this most uncomfortable of journeys. The other travelers in the mail coach had learned only that her name was Mary and that she expected to be joined on her journey at a future stop by a male member of her family. She'd simply referred to the nonexistent relative as He.

In a few short hours, she'd amassed three more lies to her name. Mariposa refused to add to the list. She had other troubles.

A man sat directly across from her, not a gentleman by his appearance but not lower class either. Mariposa supposed him to be a clerk or a shopkeeper. Two things about him were obvious: he was rather large compared to her, and he was showing an inordinate amount of interest in her.

She avoided making eye contact and refused to speak with him. Still, he smiled at her with alarming regularity.

"So your *brother* is meeting you down the road a bit?" the man asked, the question an obviously leading one. He was trying to determine if she was unprotected.

Blast! She *was* unprotected but didn't want him to know that.

You are a liar. Mr. Jonquil's scathing voice echoed in her mind. She wanted so badly to not deserve that criticism.

She assumed her most bashful look and turned her eyes more determinedly to the window and the passing landscape, avoiding the lie by simply not answering. An unnerving though quiet chuckle met that gesture. A chill radiated through Mariposa's entire body. She'd heard laughs like that, sounds that instantly set one on the alert. The soldiers occupying Orthez or stalking the roads of Spain and France had laughed in precisely that way. Staying hidden had saved her in the past. Hiding was not a possibility in a closed mail coach.

"So will he be at the next stop, do you suppose?"

Mariposa gave a tiny smile. Let him make of that what he would.

He apparently saw it as a sign of encouragement. Before too many more miles passed, he orchestrated a change of seats, much to the displeasure of his fellow passengers. Positioned like he was, his knees brushed Mariposa's with every jolt of the carriage.

She pulled her legs in as much as possible, tucking herself into the corner. The man slouched more, his legs jutting farther from his side of the carriage. She took a quick covert glance only to find a predatory smile on the man's lips.

She swallowed down the thick lump that materialized in her throat. Dozens of incidents flashed mercilessly through her memory. Vulgar laughter at a tiny inn in eastern Spain. Coarse comments echoing from a not-distant-enough French army encampment. Huddling with her family as quietly as possible amongst the hay in the back corner of a barn, hoping the discontented mob out scouring the countryside didn't find them and exact ill-aimed revenge for years of warfare. She'd feared for her life again and again. She'd trembled with terror more than once.

But England was supposed to be safe—Papá had told her so countless times. All the fear and danger would be left behind. War would be a distant memory. She would be safe.

England was supposed to be different.

A chuckle reverberated through the carriage. Mariposa muscled down a sob.

Please, she silently prayed, *please send someone to help me.*

But the heavens, she feared, didn't answer the pleas of a liar.

The mail coach pulled into the yard of an inn some three hours after that desperate prayer. Mariposa was a breath away from panicked tears but knew from instinct and experience that such vulnerability would, to the cad who was tormenting her, be an open invitation to further his campaign.

She would be afforded a scant ten-minute break while the horses were changed and the coachman given a fortifying tankard of ale. Mariposa sprung from the coach, hoping to find a hiding place to huddle in until the time came to board once more. With any luck, she could secure a seat as far from her tormentor as possible.

Not five steps from the coach, someone grabbed her wrist. Mariposa did not have to look to know who held her so painfully firm.

"You cannot tease for so many miles and then simply slip away." The grip on her wrist tightened further. "We have a few minutes, sweetheart."

Despite knowing it would only add to his view of her as a challenge, Mariposa instinctively pulled on his grip, trying to free herself.

He laughed.

She cast her eyes around the inn yard, looking for anyone who might come to her aid. Only the kind-eyed but obviously intimidated older woman who had given her numerous commiserating glances even noticed her predicament. There would be no help, no rescue.

She had saved her family, kept them safe and protected. For years she'd borne their burdens without complaint. Why, in her hour of most desperate need, was there no one to help her?

Her assailant tugged at her wrist with such force that she had no choice but to stumble after him. He was moving away from the inn and into the more secluded yard around back. Her fierce attempts to free herself proved futile.

"Stop," she insisted. "Let me go."

He didn't appear to hear or care. She fought him still, the struggle becoming more pronounced and more conspicuous.

"So you have a little fire." The man chuckled ominously. "I like that."

"Release me!"

He tightened his grip and gave a sudden jerk. Mariposa very nearly lost her footing, barely managing to keep from stumbling to the ground.

He spun her around, and she found herself nose to chest with the man accosting her.

"None of that, missy. I've been wanting to see that hair of yours. Drives a man mad, it does. But you probably know that."

She flinched when he reached for her. Her continued struggle did no good. She was no closer to freedom than she'd been moments earlier.

"I'll be seeing it down, I will."

"I rather think not," a second voice replied, unmistakable authority in its tone.

"Scuttle off," her captor snarled. "This is none of your concern."

"It absolutely *is*."

Mariposa felt a pair of hands rest lightly on her shoulders. Her wrist was immediately released, even as she felt herself gently set aside. She barely registered a tall, lean figure step past her before a well-placed fist leveled her would-be attacker, who slumped rather pathetically and slid to the ground.

Mariposa raised her eyes to her rescuer and could not, upon looking into his face, keep back a sob. His clothes were not those which befitted his station. His accent, obviously assumed, lacked the refinement she knew was naturally there—indeed, she had not even recognized his voice. But there was no mistaking him once she looked.

Without a second thought, she threw her arms around him, burying her face in his jacket front. Her voice came out as little more than a whisper. "Oh, Jason!"

Chapter Thirteen

"ARE YOU ALL ABOUT IN the head?" Jason demanded, probably more harshly than necessary. Mariposa's unexpected and almost desperate embrace had caught him off guard, nearly as much as his heart-thumping reaction. "Do you have any concept of the fate that might have befallen you, traveling unprotected?"

She lifted her face at his words of criticism, and Jason could see by the starkness in her eyes that she knew precisely what could happen to a lone woman. His stomach clenched. Had the cad done more to her than he'd thought?

The look in her eyes, though, was too deep-rooted to have been planted there only in the past few minutes. She had learned to be wary long ago. The idea was not reassuring. Had there been others who had eyed her like a starved dog would eye a cut of beef? Jason had to restrain himself lest he kick the still-prostrate reprobate. He chose, instead, to guide Mariposa across the inn yard and move away from the scoundrel.

More than a little unnerved at the surge of protectiveness he felt, he put some distance between himself and Mariposa and gave her his most reprimanding look. "Have you any idea how worried your grandmother is?" he demanded. "She was beyond distraught when she came to my office."

Mariposa's entire countenance softened. "I thought perhaps your arrival was coincidence. You truly came for *me?*"

"To save you from yourself," Jason muttered the correction, for the first time questioning why he'd hied to the rescue so quickly. "And to ease your grandmother's concerns." Which brought another grievance to mind. Jason crossed his arms over his chest and gave her an evaluating look. "She, by the way, speaks surprisingly good English, and I detected not a single hint of her previously frequent twitching."

Mariposa looked appropriately ashamed, but Jason felt no triumph in seeing it. Rather, he felt a strange urge to embrace her again. Aggravating woman! To mask his confusion, he paced away a few steps.

"I should have included that in my confession, Mr. Jonquil." she said.

He inexplicably found himself disappointed that she hadn't used his Christian name as she had in the moment of palpable relief that had followed his flattening of her attacker.

"She does speak English, though not as well as I do," Mariposa admitted. "She also speaks French. And Portuguese." She sighed. "And Abuela—she does not twitch."

When he'd first realized she was prevaricating, he'd wanted nothing more than to force her to admit it. Finally getting what he'd hoped for did not prove nearly as satisfying as he had anticipated.

He turned the uncomfortable feeling into frustration and continued his interrogation. "Perhaps now would be a good time for you to explain just why you felt the need to deceive me so entirely," Jason suggested, though no one hearing him would mistake his words for anything resembling a request.

Mariposa certainly didn't. "I needed your help," she said with a quiet desperation. "But I couldn't—There was too much . . ." She shook her head, her forehead creasing, her eyes closing. "I am determined not to lie, Mr. Jonquil, as I told you before, but I simply cannot tell you the truth."

"You don't trust me?" Jason asked, the possibility more disconcerting than he would have guessed.

"I don't trust anyone," she whispered. "*La confianza es la primera víctima de la guerra.*"

"I am afraid my Spanish does not extend beyond the most basic of greetings," Jason reminded her.

But she just shook her head again, unwilling, it seemed, to translate.

Jason let out a whoosh of frustrated air. He was growing more confused by the moment. Mrs. Aritza had offered very little information beyond her granddaughter looking for her family and not, as he had previously been told, a solicitor. What he did not know was just why finding them had warranted this mad dash from Town or why she cloaked herself and her search in such secrecy.

"I shall see if there is a hired hack available to return you to your grandmother." He turned to walk back to the inn, but Mariposa's hand shot out, taking hold of his arm.

"I must continue my journey," she insisted, her look implacable.

Jason raised an eyebrow, but she did not seem the least unnerved by his look of reprimand. So he allowed his gaze to shift to her would-be attacker, hunched on the ground, clutching his bleeding nose. Mariposa paled slightly, but her determined stance did not waver.

"I must continue," she said.

"Why?"

She hesitated only a moment. "I have to find my family. I made a promise."

"You intend to get back on that mail coach? Court the danger that would nag at your heels? Take such a monumental risk?" His voice rose with each question. She was mad! She must have windmills in her head, dust in her attic, cobwebs in her brain box.

"I have to find my family."

"You are repeating yourself, Mariposa," Jason pointed out dryly.

Then it happened. Her lips slid into a bright smile, her deep-brown eyes twinkling, the lines of worry around her eyes easing. Everything about her expression rang with sincerity.

"I shouldn't have said that to you so often." She sounded near to laughing. "But you do have the most diverting tendency to repeat things. Especially when you are caught unawares."

Jason had never seen a smile quite like hers before. The beauty of it, the glowing sincerity and pure joy of it momentarily knocked the wind from his lungs. She was enchanting.

She was also far too tempting to rogues like her former traveling companion. If she continued on unprotected, she would find herself in desperate circumstances, he had no doubt. He wasn't entirely sure he hadn't pushed her into this ridiculous plan by threatening to prevent her from receiving aid from any other quarter.

"You are determined?" he asked.

She nodded decisively.

Blast! He couldn't simply leave her to fate and the dangers of an unforgiving world. *If I ever hear you have mistreated a female . . .* As a gentleman, he was honor bound to assist her. They would need a great deal of ingenuity to manage the business without tarnishing either of their reputations. Even more than that, he would have to lie rather extensively. He sighed. "It is a very good thing you are an accomplished actress. That is one skill we are going to need."

"*We?*" she asked, obviously bewildered.

"Stanley is not the only principled gentleman in my family, Mariposa." He took determined hold of her hand and marched her back to the front of the inn. The post would be departing soon. "No gentleman of honor would abandon a gently bred female to the cruelty of the world, regardless of whether or not she had placed herself in that position."

"Everyone else did." Her voice was hardly loud enough to be heard.

Jason ignored the pang of compassion that stirred in him. He was helping her only out of a sense of duty and responsibility. Her history was irrelevant.

"Step up," he instructed once they had reached the coach. "I believe there is an empty seat for me." He smiled, picturing the cad they'd left behind in the stable yard.

An older woman with a careworn face but kind eyes looked at Mariposa with something akin to relief. Mariposa smiled back at her.

"You have found your—" The poor unknown woman seemed at a loss to identify Jason.

He took a deep breath. Only one course of action would keep them both inconspicuous during their trek north. They must pretend to be poor, unimportant, and something else far more uncomfortable.

He finished the woman's sentence with as much conviction as he could muster and with what he hoped was a convincing lower-class accent. "Her husband."

Mariposa—when had he begun thinking of her by her given name?—allowed the smallest of startled gasps, but when Jason looked down at her, she had diverted her eyes in a look of utter bashfulness. Jason fought down an amused smile. For once, he was not on the receiving end of her trickery; he was benefiting from it.

"Oh, lands, ain't that just wonderful," their traveling companion declared. "Mary seems such a dear, sweet thing. And that bounder—" Her eyes darkened with suppressed anger. "I'd been prayin' for hours someone'd be at the next stop to protect her."

"So had I," Mariposa said.

Though Jason knew her capable of deception, he believed her. It was an odd feeling, being the answer to someone's prayers. He doubted it had ever happened to him before.

The mail coach jerked as it began the next leg of its journey.

"Seems that bounder didn't return in time," Jason observed, smiling conspiratorially at the woman who sat across from Mariposa and him.

"Good riddance, I say," another man dressed in the garb of a vicar said, lifting his nose momentarily from a book. "I'm right glad to see your wife has caught up with you at last."

Jason nodded.

"It is a sore trial to be separated from the person one loves." The older woman nodded her understanding and gave Jason and Mariposa such a look of fond approval he could almost hear her sighing. "Mary seems far more at ease with you here."

A wonderfully awful idea entered his brain, and holding back a chuckle of ironic satisfaction, Jason addressed their talkative traveling companion. "Mary is such a shy, quiet sort o' girl. I doubt you'll hear more than a few words out o' her this entire journey."

He felt Mariposa stiffen beside him. His words had essentially made her continued silence necessary for their ruse. That would grate, he'd wager. But, oh, how he had earned the right to ruffle her just a little.

An imp of mischief pushed him on, one he'd been ignoring for years in favor of—how had Mater phrased it?—the appearance of impeccable respectability. She had also declared him a dab hand at imaginative acting. Perhaps it was time to dust off that particular talent.

In an aside to the woman, he said, "Though she's my dear wife, I confess she ain't terribly bright."

"She *is* female," the vicar replied with a dismissive shrug.

That would rankle. Jason very nearly grinned. He didn't dare look at Mariposa lest he laugh out loud. She deserved this bit of turn-around, so help him. Not a soul who knew him would witness this lark; he need not worry about its impact on his reputation. He could simply enjoy being a little absurd.

"But I daresay she has a good heart," the older woman said, still looking at them both as fondly as if they were her own children.

"Oh, the very best," Jason acknowledged. "So you must forgive 'er if she's rather too quiet and if, when she does summon the courage to speak, she repeats 'erself." He tapped his temple with his index finger in a gesture meant to communicate she was missing a brick or two.

A sudden, unexpected pinch on his arm very nearly brought a startled yelp to his lips. Jason caught himself in time and covered her assault with his own smooth words.

"Of course, dear," Jason said, gazing at Mariposa with feigned adoration and using a tone that clearly indicated that he thought she had made a request with her pinch. He raised his arm and settled it snuggly around her, pulling her up against his side. He hoped she would be as uncomfortable with this arrangement as he had been facing down the accusatory glances of his colleagues weeks earlier and the insatiable curiosity of his family. Giving her back a little of her own proved far more enjoyable than he would have anticipated.

Mariposa untied and slipped off her bonnet, then she stretched enough to speak almost directly into his ear. "You are telling a lot of plumpers for someone who lectures about honesty," she said sotto voce.

"Turnaround is fair play, dear," he answered just as softly.

The older woman sighed. "Young love. So refreshing, Mr.—"

"Jones," Jason blurted the first thing that came to mind.

"I am Mrs. Brown," their companion answered with a friend-ly smile.

"Pleasure." Jason inclined his head. "And you 'ave my gratitude for looking out for my wife. She does wander about at times if she ain't looked after."

He nearly laughed out loud when he felt a jab in his ribs. Lud, when was the last time he'd been so entirely entertained? Likely not since the knife-boy episode.

He glanced at Mariposa, fully expecting indignation and flash-ing fire in her eyes. To his surprise, she appeared to be desperately holding back laughter.

He grinned down at her. As if to prove that he knew nothing about women, Mariposa's laughter died on the instant and tears sprang immediately to her eyes. Yet through her tears, she contin-ued to smile.

"What has upset you so suddenly?" he asked warily.

But she merely shook her head before laying it silently against his shoulder.

A sigh made its way across the coach. Theirs was apparently a convincing performance. That was, Jason insisted to himself, the reason he settled his arm more snugly around Mariposa as she leaned against his side.

It was relief, he further told himself, that made their relative positions so pleasant—that and the fact that she smelled far better than any person had a right to after an entire day in a closed-in mail coach. He certainly wasn't complaining over the view of her fascinating head of hair. It was unusually thick and, he would wager, silky as well.

He was once again fighting a smile for which he had no explanation. Unbidden to his mind came words Mrs. Aritza had said as Jason had escorted her to Lampton House: "Mariposa means butterfly. She was once light and happy. War made our young women old and hard. It injured their souls. I wish to see her fly again."

The little speech offered in halting English had seemed odd at the time. Now, sitting with Mariposa all but in his arms, Jason couldn't help agreeing with Abuela. He had seen the tiniest hint of happiness in Mariposa's eyes. It couldn't have been more obvious that she was meant to be joyous.

"Jonquils save people," Father had once said only partly in jest. "It's what we do. We can't help ourselves."

Jason had never managed that. He had never been anyone's hero or rescuing knight. He wasn't the earl, able to impact lives simply by existing. Nor was he a father as Layton was. Or a soldier or vicar. He was simply Jason. But he had only moments earlier come to Mariposa's aid. It was a feeling he could quickly grow accustomed to.

Chapter Fourteen

THE SIGHT OF JASON JONQUIL's long-awaited smile brought tears to Mariposa's eyes. His pensive aura had always felt forced and unnatural, but she had only ever seen the briefest hints of the lighthearted man she was certain lay beneath his tense exterior. How she'd longed to see him look happy.

It was almost enough for her to forgive him both for making a lack of intelligence and near silence an integral part of her role over the remainder of the journey and for indulging in an entire chain of lies after having scolded her so thoroughly for precisely that.

She'd been hard-pressed not to laugh out loud as he'd turned the tables on her. *The rogue.* Two could play at that game. If she was truly fortunate, she might even coax that elusive laugh out of him. If she could bring laughter to her irascible butler after all he had seen and experienced, surely she could manage as much for Jason.

She lifted her head ever so slightly and glanced up at him, keeping her expression vacuous and her tone simplistic. "You smell like turnips," she observed quietly but just loudly enough for the other occupants to hear her comment.

Jason's head slowly turned in her direction, surprise registering on his face.

"Mmmm," she added, holding fast to the role of clueless simpleton.

He must have seen the devilry in her eyes. His own expression slipped into one of patient adoration. "You 'ave always liked turnips," he replied, patting her shoulder, then resting his hand there. To Mrs. Brown, he explained, "She never had a doll as a child but came to enjoy the company of turnips. And radishes. She is very fond of vegetables, though it took many years for her to not cry when they were chopped up to be eaten."

Mariposa dug her knuckle into his ribs once more, biting on her lips to prevent a rare giggle. She laughed, chuckled at times, but she never giggled. Jason did little more than shift his position in response to her jab.

"How did the two of you meet?" Mrs. Brown asked. She regarded them as if they were the most romantic of couples. She had no reason to doubt their story, though Mariposa wondered if it was entirely fair of them to be so untruthful.

Jason looked down at Mariposa with an anticipatory expression. After not only taking her to task for lying but also declaring her a nearly mute, empty-headed nincompoop, she was not going to rescue him from his own hole.

She lowered her eyes in her most bashful expression, even pressing her hands to her cheeks as if covering a blush.

"Such a shy little thing," Mrs. Brown said.

Jason leaned closer and whispered in her ear, "Minx." But his tone was full of amusement.

"Do tell her the story, honeycomb," Mariposa smiled lovingly up at him.

"*Honeycomb?*" Jason mouthed.

Mariposa's look of featherheaded innocence didn't slip for an instant.

"Oh, now isn't that just precious," Mrs. Brown declared. "Do tell your tale, Mr. Jones."

Mariposa could see the wheels turning in Jason's mind as he desperately created a courtship story. She fought down a grin.

He proved more imaginative than expected.

"I first saw my Mary sitting in a mud puddle clutching an armful of filthy turnips. When I asked her why she was sitting there with those vegetables, she told me she was saving their lives. She cried an' cried as she pressed 'em to her cheek. And I said to myself, now that's a girl with a big heart—not too bright but a big heart. She couldn't bear to see a defenseless turnip suffer."

"Ah," Mrs. Brown nodded. "So you met as little uns."

"No," Jason corrected. "Just this year."

Mariposa had to bury her face in his jacket to hide her laughter. He'd described her as a full-grown woman crying over turnips. Their fellow travelers must think her completely daft.

"How does the girl feel about potatoes?" the vicar asked as if more than a little concerned about her state of mind.

"Can't bring herself to eat 'em, poor thing." Jason's shoulders rose and fell in an exaggerated sigh.

Mariposa bit down on her lips to hold back a grin. She had assumed he possessed some degree of humor underneath his starched-up exterior. She hadn't expected such an entertaining degree of mischief.

The arm he had draped across her shoulders slid slightly lower, very nearly into an embrace. Nothing could be more natural than to lean more fully against him. All across Spain and into France, she had been the one to offer reassurance. She had borne the weight of survival for all of her family, despite being little more than a child. No one had ever come to her aid when life was threatening and exhausting. But Jason, whom she was certain had never so much as liked her, had come to find her. He'd offered his aid and his support, and he was helping her still.

She felt him shift and lifted her face. He grinned down at her. Jason had a beautiful smile—masculine but beautiful just the same.

"Should I tell them any more stories, Mary?" Jason whispered, raising his eyebrow in obvious challenge.

She didn't answer. She was the mute, didn't he remember that? But she did smile back. And he didn't look away.

"Mr. Jones, I am so glad you took care o' that bounder," Mrs. Brown said. "He was fair tormentin' our little Mary."

"Was he tormenting you?" Jason asked her, his tone gentle and understanding.

The reality of what had very nearly happened washed over her. She felt her composure slip to a quiver and had to fight back the emotion that surfaced.

"Tears?" Jason looked genuinely concerned.

"I've had a difficult day," she whispered in reply.

"You have a few hours before the next stop." He lowered his voice too. "Try to rest."

"When I awake, you won't be gone?" How pathetic and desperate she sounded. She shifted, uncomfortable at having revealed so much.

Jason shrugged. "The coach is moving too fast for me to jump out."

She allowed a small show of amusement. He shifted beside her, and Mariposa found her head had little choice but to rest against him.

She'd spent years surviving on her own, not trusting a single soul. But there she sat, with a gentleman she had known only a matter of weeks, if one did not count Stanley's confidences regarding his brother, and she felt unexpectedly safe and protected.

The man didn't even like her. But he was helping her.

Perhaps England truly was different.

Mrs. Brown was asleep, leaning against the coach window, her mouth agape. The vicar was snoring. Mariposa's breathing had long since grown rhythmic with sleep. Jason seemed to be the only person in the mail coach still awake.

It was a shame to wake Mariposa, really, but it was imperative that he know where they were headed. He doubted the mail coach would let them off at the doorstep of whichever family member Mariposa was chasing down. Would she trust him with even that bit of information? She had insisted she trusted no one.

He bent closer to where she rested against his shoulder, whispering quietly enough to not wake their traveling companions. "Mariposa." He repeated her name again before she began to stir.

A look of confusion slid momentarily across her face before she seemed to piece the puzzle together. "I fell asleep," she said quietly as she sat upright.

"And, you will notice, I did not leap from the coach at the first opportunity." The quip earned him a smile.

When, he wondered, had he turned into a jester? He was not usually so quick to tease, at least not lately, provided one did not count London street children. Perhaps his veneer of solemn respectability was not quite as all-encompassing as he'd believed.

"I need to ask you a few questions while we do not have an attentive audience," he said.

Her gaze slid around the coach, taking note of the sleeping passengers, before returning to Jason's face. She fiddled nervously with the edges of her bonnet resting on her lap. She would simply have to find the strength to trust him at least a little if they were to accomplish her goal and do so without destroying both their reputations.

"Your abuela said you were bound for Scotland," he said, measuring his words carefully so as not to make her think he would be forcing confidences. "Will the mail take you as far as you need to go, or must you change routes at some point?"

"The directions I have indicate a location not far from Haddington," Mariposa said. "But I don't know the area well."

Haddington? He hadn't been there in years. "My"—Jason caught himself before saying *father*—"brother has a hunting box ten miles from Haddington. He is there now, in fact, with his wife."

"One of your brothers is married? This must be a recent occurrence."

Jason nodded. "Two of them are, in fact. Both very recently. Three, if Crispin is included in the count."

"I thought Crispin was *always* included in the count." Mariposa obviously understood that Crispin had long been an honorary member of the Jonquil family. "Which two were recently married? No, let me guess."

Jason leaned back a little, watching her. How well had Stanley described them all? Could she really sort it out on her own?

"Philip." She spoke with inarguable confidence in the accuracy of her first hypothesis.

"Correct," Jason answered. "And who else?"

Her brows drew in; her finger tapped against her lower lip. She looked entirely adorable. Reminding himself that she was also exasperating, Jason put a little more distance between them, trying to appear unaffected.

"Harold and Charlie are both too young," Mariposa said. "Stanley would not have married, knowing he was returning to war. That leaves only Layton and Corbin."

She seemed unable to decide between the two. Her knowledge of his siblings was impressive. Just how many conversations had she had with his younger brother?

"There was no mistress of Havenworth when I was there," she said. "And though there were many guests, there were not enough to indicate a wedding. The rest of your brothers would have been present if one of them was to be wed."

Jason nodded in appreciation of her logic. He had always suspected she was sharp witted.

"Then it must be Layton."

"It must be."

"He is healing, then." She pressed her hand to his arm, a look of earnest relief on her face. "Stanley said he had become a recluse after losing his wife—his *first* wife, I suppose I should say."

"He was fortunate enough to meet a lady who guided him through his grief. He is, I fear, almost nauseatingly happy."

The slightest reddening of her eyes gave Mariposa's emotions away. Heavens, was she on the verge of tears over a gentleman who was not even her own family, whom she had likely never before met?

"I am so very pleased to hear that." The slightest quaver shook her voice. "Your family must be so relieved."

"Stanley truly did tell you a great deal about us, didn't he?" Jason shook his head in amazement.

A haunted look entered her eyes. "He needed to talk, especially after Orthez."

"And you stood his friend."

"Stanley stood my friend as well. I lost most of my family in one way or another during the never-ending war. Somehow he knew how much I needed a family to belong to. He let me share his. He allowed me to pretend to be a Jonquil."

"Which explains why you took me to task for my lack of brotherly sentiment." Things were beginning to make more sense.

"Stanley needed far more than an army sawbones." Mariposa's gaze took on the vagueness of one lost in memory. "The war was destroying him in more than merely physical ways. I do not imagine that has changed. I had hoped he was receiving support from his family."

"His arm was still a little weak, but he seemed well enough." Jason found himself suddenly reviewing every moment he'd spent with Stanley during his months on English soil. Was he indeed unwell?

"Some wounds are not obvious, Jason," Mariposa said.

He sensed a pulling away, as if she once again protected herself against inquiry. *I don't trust anyone.* Her earlier words echoed in his mind. He would do well not to press her too quickly for confidences.

He decided to turn the topic. "You know that this journey cannot be accomplished in a day."

"The mail runs day and night," she said.

"Even so, from London to Edinburgh, the mail requires more than two days. A single day on a mail coach without even one member of your family would raise eyebrows. Two days *and* two nights would ruin you entirely."

"I am here with my husband. Is that not so, Mr. Jones?" Mariposa held his gaze.

"You are willing to go through with this? Force us both into further dishonesty? Not to mention there is always the risk of discovery."

She nodded firmly. "Finding my family is the most important thing in the world to me." The intensity in her tone grew with each word. "My mother needs me. And my little brother, my sweet Santiago—"

"I thought they were dead."

Mariposa paled instantly, swaying slightly as if she would faint dead away. Jason reached out a hand to steady her. He'd hit upon something, something she was hiding.

The sound of the guard perched on the back of the mail coach blowing his yard of tin woke the sleeping passengers, alerting all to the forthcoming stop.

He'd learned from the driver during their last brief stop, during which Mariposa had dozed undisturbed beside him, that this was to be a slightly longer stop than usual. Drivers would be changed, as well as the team. It was also the final stop for their current guard— another would take his place. There would be a rare twenty minutes between arrival and departure. Those passengers continuing on were advised to quickly obtain food before reembarking.

Jason intended to spend this time getting what information from Mariposa he could. There was a great deal she wasn't telling him.

Chapter Fifteen

JASON HANDED MRS. BROWN OUT of the carriage before offering his hand to Mariposa. She took it, surprised at the tingling sensation that traveled up her arm at that simple touch. The inn yard bustled as dusk approached. Jason pulled her closer to him as they navigated the crowd.

"We only have a few minutes," he whispered, his breath tickling her ear. "Are you hungry?"

"Starving," she answered, keeping her own voice low.

Mrs. Brown watched them with her ever-present look of misty-eyed approval. She, no doubt, found them quite romantic. Guilt began bubbling inside Mariposa. The kindhearted woman did not deserve to be so thoroughly deceived.

Mariposa moved ever closer to Jason as he led her into the public tap room. There were so many people. Suppose someone recognized Jason. Or decided to accost her. She'd only barely escaped the last scoundrel who'd taken such an idea into his head.

"A bite to eat, innkeep?" Jason kept his accent lower class, but the authority in his tone could not be ignored.

"Aye," was the reply, accompanied by a sharp nod. "My wife has a pot of potato stew simmerin'."

"Potato?" Mrs. Brown and the vicar both gasped, turning wide-eyed looks of concern on Mariposa.

She knew her part. Blast Jason for that. She buried her face in his jacket and did her best to appear entirely undone at the thought of potatoes being chopped and boiled. And, blast him, she could feel Jason shake as he fought down a chuckle.

"Not to worry, Mary." He patted her back like one would an unhappy child. "I am certain we'll find you a slice of bread or something."

Oh, he would not be allowed to skirt this new trouble so easily. She raised wide, puppy-dog eyes up to him and, just loudly enough for their traveling companions to hear, asked with a telltale break in her voice, "You wouldn't eat the sweet, darlin' *potatoes* in front of me, would you?"

"Oh, Mr. Jones, do not subject her to that," Mrs. Brown pleaded.

Mariposa kept her mouth turned down but allowed her eyes, visible only to Jason, to brim over with mischief.

Mrs. Brown's concern did not abate. "The good vicar and I will eat at a table removed so she'll not be upset."

"I'm certain we can find bread for both of us," Mariposa insisted.

"Of course," Jason answered tightly. She could see tension in his jaw. For a moment, she feared she'd pushed him too far. Then she saw a twitch at the corner of his mouth. He was fighting a smile.

Within a minute, they were settled at a small table in the far corner of the room with a large dinner roll apiece.

"You, Mariposa," Jason whispered, "are a chore. Do you know that?"

"You are the one who told that ridiculous story about potatoes."

"It was turnips," Jason reminded her. "The meddlesome vicar planted the idea of potatoes."

"*I* was the one attempting to be honest," Mariposa said with a pointed look.

He shook his head. "This has been a highly unusual day."

"I wish potentially dangerous journeys and run-ins with scoundrels really were so unusual."

Jason took hold of her hand. "Tell me," he said quietly, gently.

In whispers too quiet to be overheard, she told him of her home in Spain, of her family. She spoke of the war and her father's death. She told him of their desperate trek across Spain and into France, of struggling to survive, of supporting a mentally broken mother, an elderly grandmother, and a very young brother. She spoke of Orthez and the end of the war, or at least what they all had believed was the end. Napoleon's escape had changed that.

"Then your mother and brother did not die in the war?" Jason asked, whispering to her as they made their way back out to the inn yard.

"They disappeared."

Their conversation continued in low whispers.

"And your father's instructions to come to England brought you here to look for them?"

She nodded.

"But why did you not tell me this when you first came to my office instead of feeding me lies? If I had known your circumstances, I could have helped more. You had me looking for a solicitor."

Mariposa debated with herself. She hadn't told him about Bélanger, the man who had necessitated her headlong flight from the Continent.

"There is more, isn't there?"

She glanced up at him and saw frustration creasing his brow. Beneath the vexation was clear and unmistakable disappointment. If only he understood how difficult it had been to tell him as much as she had.

"Please do not press me, Jason," Mariposa said, stopping their progress to turn toward him, hoping he would understand. "I have already told you more than I have told any other person. Such confidences are extremely difficult for me."

"I have done my utmost to always be honest with you. Is that not reason enough to trust me?"

She wished it were. "I don't trust easily."

"I know."

They stood a moment, neither speaking, neither turning away.

"Well, Mary,"—Jason raised his eyebrows at the humor of that pseudonym—"we'd best climb in. We've a long night of travel ahead of us."

"You aren't going to change your mind and leave me to my own devices?" Mariposa had half expected him to turn tail after hearing her tales of woe.

"You have asked me that before," Jason said.

"Perhaps your tendency to repeat things is contagious."

He allowed something of an obligatory smile at her quip. In the next moment, however, his expression turned serious once more. "Do you truly think I am going to abandon you?"

Mariposa lowered her eyes when she heard the disappointment in his voice.

"But, then, plenty of others have, haven't they?" He took her hand in his once more. "We Jonquils have our failings, Mariposa, but we always keep our word."

With a sigh of relief, Mariposa closed her eyes. He would not desert her. For the first time since her father's death, she had someone to rely on.

"Seems a man ought to kiss 'is wife when she looks like that, guv."

Mariposa opened her eyes at the unexpected voice only to see a man climbing on top of the coach, probably their new driver. He was in his seat rather more quickly than Mariposa would have expected and turned to watch them expectantly.

"Oh, do give the dear girl a kiss, Mr. Jones," Mrs. Brown said from very near the coach. "She was so very brokenhearted about the potatoes."

Mariposa was grateful they'd conducted their conversation quietly. She'd been so engrossed in the discussion, she hadn't realized how quickly their privacy had disappeared.

"She didn't set to caterwauling in there," the vicar offered as he climbed inside the waiting mail coach. He somehow managed to make that sound like the veriest compliment.

"A man who refuses to kiss his wife will seem very odd," Jason whispered to Mariposa in warning. "And we do not want to attract undue attention."

"No, we do not," Mariposa agreed, her voice strangled.

Jason drew her slowly closer, his eyes studying her face as he did. Mariposa swallowed against the sudden moisture in her mouth. As the distance between them closed, she rested her free hand, palm open, against his chest. Even through his clothing she could feel his hammering heartbeat. It was every bit as fast as her own. But was that a good sign or bad?

"You don't have to do this, Jason," she whispered, even as his face descended toward hers.

"I absolutely have to do this," was all he said.

And with no more warning than that, he kissed her. She had always expected her first kiss to be enjoyable. She hadn't anticipated it being shattering. From the moment his lips touched hers, there was not another thought in her head beyond the magical feeling of Jason holding her, the solidity of him next to her, the clean, crisp smell of him. She spared not a moment's concern for the audience witnessing the encounter. All that mattered was that he continued to kiss her.

All too soon, however, he broke away. She was breathless, unable to do little more than simply gaze up at him. Jason did not, however, appear at all affected.

"Coach won't wait much longer," he said as calm as anything, then guided her inside the coach. No mention of their kiss, no look of surprise or pleasure.

Mrs. Brown smiled at them fondly. The vicar nodded, seemingly in approval. Jason settled in.

Mariposa felt her heart dislodge from her throat and drop to her stomach. It was all part of this lie they were living. She suddenly understood why dishonesty was so devastating. In that moment, she truly knew how it felt to suffer from a lie.

Something had upset Mariposa. Jason tried to convince himself it wasn't the kiss they'd shared. They'd been all but forced into it, but he'd found the undertaking more than pleasant. Indeed, if they hadn't had an attentive audience, and if he hadn't had doubts as to Mariposa's feelings on the matter, he'd have simply continued kissing her.

There was such a mixture of fire and innocence in her that had manifested itself rather beguilingly in that moment. He'd never felt his heart race as fiercely as it had. Only by calling upon every ounce of self-possession had he not let the impact of their kiss show. Their entire ruse would have been ruined otherwise.

But Mariposa had been withdrawn and distant ever since re-entering the mail coach. She no longer leaned against him as she had on the previous leg of their journey. She kept just enough of a distance that the others in the coach would not notice any change. But Jason noticed. Had he offended her with his attentions? The thought was decidedly lowering.

As the mail coach rumbled on, the passengers sitting in silence, watching the dimming landscape, Jason found his eyes straying to Mariposa more and more frequently.

Why had she felt the need to lie to him in the first place? Was it simply a distrust of strangers or something about him personally? There was more to her search for her family than she was admitting; she had said as much. But what? She did not need to hide the truth from him any longer. Why, then, was she still being less than open with him?

The coach slowed down. Mariposa's eyes met Jason's in the little remaining light, a question in their brown depths.

"We're probably headed uphill," Jason explained quietly. "They'll ask us all to step out of the carriage to take the strain off the horses."

"And *we* . . . ?"

"Will walk along behind."

"Lovely," she answered with an amused smile.

Yes. She is *lovely.*

The coach came to a stop, and all passengers were instructed, as he had predicted, to disembark and continue the uphill journey on foot. They would be permitted to climb aboard once the hill had been crested.

The tedious ascent gave Jason ample opportunity to think. What had happened to him in the last few days? He had ever been unflappable and serious minded, as his profession required. He'd been unwaveringly honest, even condemning those who embraced deceit of any kind. And yet, there he was, walking along a dark road, dressed more like a tenant farmer than a barrister, answering to an assumed name, teasing a young lady, and thoroughly enjoying every minute of it. He had left behind a desk full of work and a long list of clients, neither of which he'd even thought about in the hours since Mrs. Aritza's tearful arrival at Lincoln's Inn until now. He had a more pressing responsibility to Mariposa.

That responsibility had led him to this ruse. He was playing a part, dressing rather ridiculously, acting irresponsibly. He reminded himself forcefully of—

"Ah, lud," Jason muttered under his breath. *Philip.* He was acting precisely like Philip.

He had good reason, he reassured himself.

And Philip doesn't? a voice in his head demanded.

Jason stopped in his tracks. He'd never considered the possibility. He'd always known Philip was pretending to be a mindless fop. But he'd assumed it was irresponsibility and disrespect for his position and title. What if there was a legitimate reason for it?

"Jason?" Mariposa's cautious inquiry snapped him from his contemplation.

He turned to look at her, though she was little more than a silhouette in the dark, walking along beside him.

"If I make a confession, do you promise not to laugh at me?" She posed the question with a heavy dose of wariness.

"I give you my word," Jason said.

She took a quick breath, then spoke swiftly. "I am afraid of the dark. I have been since we crossed *España*. The danger was always highest at night, and I—"

Her confession sped up with each word. Jason reached out and pulled her closer to him, his arm around her shoulders.

"I used to lie awake for hours, waiting for something horrible to happen. I was the only one to keep *mi familia* safe, and at night, I could not see what might be coming. No one was there to help. Santiago would cry, and I could not comfort him—I felt no comfort myself. I still do not like being out at night."

Jason squeezed her shoulders. "You are not alone now, Mariposa," he whispered to her. "You are not alone now."

Chapter Sixteen

Jason could see that Mariposa was exhausted. Three times the passengers making their way north with the Royal Mail were required to brave the dark, chill night and walk behind the lumbering vehicle up rather steep ascents.

"While I am grateful the horses have been saved so much effort, I should like to have been spared myself," Mariposa had said under her breath as they made their way up yet another slope.

"Perhaps if you'd be willing to pull the mail coach to the next stop, the driver would consider allowing you to remain inside during our next climb."

Mariposa laughed, as Jason had intended her to. He'd discovered she was every bit as uneasy in the dark as she'd professed to be. During each outdoor trek, he had attempted to distract her by asking questions about her family.

Jason learned a great deal about his companion. Hers had been a gentle and nearly ideal upbringing before the war. The years since had brought almost unimaginable hardships. Yet she found things to laugh about as she recounted events in her life. One particularly poignant theme ran through her stories: her brother Santiago meant a great deal to her. She spoke of him almost as one would her own child. Mingled with her happy memories was an ever-deepening sense of desperation. The boy's fate weighed heavy on her.

Jason too recounted events from his own past as they made their way up the various hills along their route. He told her of moments he hadn't thought about in years: Philip and Layton declaring themselves the "Jonquil Freers of Prisoners" and taking it upon themselves to help their younger brothers escape punishments. The "battles" they had enacted along the banks of the Trent at Lampton Park. Father laughing rather uproariously at any number of absurd pranks the brothers played on one another. Mother sneaking ginger biscuits into her reticule so she and Jason could share them in secret behind the tool house not far from the river.

Long stretches of silence filled the night as they continued their trek north, both Jason and Mariposa lost in memories. He thought of his own brothers and how frantic he would be if any of them were missing. Her Santiago, however, was too young to care for himself, making his disappearance far more worrisome than that of a man grown.

Only he and Mariposa remained inside the coach as the sun began to peek over the horizon, the vicar having permanently disembarked in the middle of the night and Mrs. Brown having left them shortly before sunup.

Jason hovered somewhere between asleep and awake, bouncing and swaying with each movement of the coach. He had moved to the opposite bench after Mrs. Brown's departure, giving Mariposa room to lie down. She had been sleeping quite soundly but did shift and turn in her sleep until she'd managed to get comfortable. Having a smaller frame allowed her to lie on the bench curled into a ball without any gangly limbs jutting out at awkward angles. Jason had contented himself with leaning into a corner, his feet up on his own bench.

He stretched against the crick in his neck, twisting his back to relieve the stiffness setting in. Sitting up straight, he allowed his eyes to focus. He smiled when his gaze settled on Mariposa. He had learned more about her during the course of their uncomfortable journey than he would have in a year's worth of Society functions. And surprisingly, he liked what he'd discovered.

She was intelligent. She possessed a quick wit and a personality that couldn't help but lighten a person's mood. Further, she did not pitch herself into hysterics at the first sign of inconvenience. It was almost enough to make him forget her behavior when they'd first met. Almost.

He shifted his eyes to the window as he noticed Mariposa waking. He didn't dare risk being caught staring at her. She would not hesitate to take him to task for it.

She asked him a question in a sleepy tone. Unfortunately, she posed her question in Spanish. Before he had even a moment to remind her of his linguistic limitations, she corrected the oversight. "Have we been abandoned?"

"In fact, we have," Jason answered, looking back at her now that her question gave him an excuse to do so. "Our companions have, no doubt, gone in search of a bed that actually allows them to stretch out a bit."

Mariposa smiled a little. "That is one of the advantages of being small—the ability to 'stretch out a bit' even in cramped quarters."

"Yes, well, none of the Jonquils were blessed with shortness."

"No. You were cursed with being tall and handsome, poor boys. How do you endure it?"

Handsome? Did she really think so? She might very well have made the remark as a jest. That proved a thoroughly discouraging thought.

"You look tired, Jasón."

He very much liked her Spanish version of his name. He stretched out as much as the small carriage would allow. "I am tired, in fact. Two hours of sleep will do that to a person."

"Two hours?" She sounded appropriately horrified. "I did not realize you were that uncomfortable. You must be exhausted."

Pride won out over honesty. "Only a little." His stomach chose that precise moment to loudly proclaim its empty state. "And starving to death," he added for good measure.

"I am rather hungry myself," Mariposa said. "If only the inn last night had been serving anything but potatoes."

That had been an unlucky coincidence. "It could have been worse, I suppose."

She tipped her head, eyeing him with curiosity. "How so?"

He shrugged and assumed his most casual expression. "They might have been serving turnips."

A wide, laughing grin split her face, her eyes dancing. The effect was dazzling. When first he'd seen Mariposa, Jason had dismissed her as only passingly pretty, with a mouth too wide for true beauty. The smile she wore in that moment would have changed the opinion of even the most stubborn of people. Though he was not yet entirely sure what to think of her, he could not deny Mariposa was, at times, positively stunning.

"After that ridiculous story you invented about my dedication to vegetables," she said, "it would have served you right if the inn had had nothing but turnips."

"In the end, I had no dinner and very little sleep, so I think you have had your revenge."

The quip he'd meant to be humorous had quite the opposite effect. Her expression grew almost instantly somber. She slipped to his side of the carriage, watching him with heaviness in her eyes. "I never dreamed you would follow me nor insist on coming along, nor offer to ask your brother if I might stay with him and his wife in Scotland." Her brow creased with worry, her eyes never leaving his. "I know I have caused you a great deal of inconvenience and difficulty. That was never my intention. I have been a thorn in your side enough the past month or so."

Instantly he found himself torn between soothing her worries and allowing her to stew most deservedly in her own juices. She *had* been a thorn—more than a thorn, a *dagger* in his side for weeks. The Mariposa he'd spent the last few hours with had wriggled her way into his sympathies. However, the troublemaker Mariposa, whom he had to admit he still watched for warily, needed a moment or two of discomfort. His indecision rendered him entirely silent.

Mariposa either didn't notice his lack of response or continued on in spite of it. "I would not at all blame you if you wish to disembark at the next stop and seek out a meal and warm bed. You've been vastly more helpful than I at all deserve."

He could see by the earnestness of her expression that she was sincere. He remained uncertain of a few things, but there was absolutely no question of his abandoning her. "I do not intend to slip off."

She just shook her head. "I realize you feel obligated as a gentleman, but—"

"Resign yourself, Mariposa. I'm not jumping ship."

"But it is not fair of me to ask you—"

"You didn't *ask* me to come along," Jason pointed out. "I insisted." He would have done no less for any woman in her situation, regardless of how aggravating she might be.

"But only because Abuela begged you. You cannot be enjoying this."

Enough was enough. She would change his mind if she kept this up, and then he'd hate himself for the rest of his life. A gentleman did not abandon a lady in distress. "One more word of protest out of you, and the next passenger to join us on this journey will hear an endless stream of embarrassing stories about you, *Mary*."

She bit her lips closed. For the space of a moment, she was silent. Then amusement slowly began to replace the worry that had tightened her expression. "I believe you," she said with the slightest hint of a laugh.

"That is a very good thing. My threat, I assure you, is not an idle one."

"Even if it means sleeping another night in a mail coach?"

"Even then."

Mariposa sighed, though without the abundance of drama she'd once given that sound. "You make me rather ashamed of tormenting you so much when we first met."

"Ashamed?" He nearly laughed out loud. "You enjoyed every minute of it." His chuckle burst out at the sight of Mariposa struggling to hold back a grin.

"You were so easy to tease," she said. "I shouldn't have, but—"

"But you were having such a wonderful time," Jason finished for her. "I could not make heads nor tails of you and your seemingly inadvertent insults." The remembrance dimmed his enjoyment of the moment. He simply could not reconcile the two vastly different versions he'd seen of her.

She raised her eyes to his face once more. A hint of embarrassment lingered in her gaze. "I kept hoping you would see the humor in it all and laugh, or smile at the least."

"I was supposed to be amused by a constant stream of lies and aspersions on my character?" That seemed unlikely.

"I was not so awful as all that." Apparently she had a rather selective memory.

"You told my colleagues I was incompetent. Contrary to what you seem to believe, the experience was not one I found enjoyable." His lighter mood of a moment earlier was quickly dissipating.

Mariposa shifted to face directly forward, no longer turned toward him. "I am sorry," she said quietly.

"That doesn't particularly help, though, does it? Misters Pole and Thompson still think a client left my office convinced I am unfit for my occupation." His brother Harold would likely have lectured him on the saintliness of a forgiving nature. With the memory of her insults returning one after another, Jason was not particularly in the mood to offer absolution. "My family yet believes that I am, at least in your opinion, worthless. How exactly were those moments supposed to bring a smile to my face?"

Mariposa pulled her legs up beside her on the seat, leaning back against the squabs. She turned her face toward the dingy window. "I said I was sorry." Her voice barely carried across the foot that separated them.

"You said a great many things, and few, if any, were even remotely true." Jason wasn't sure what he'd hoped to accomplish by revisiting her actions those first few weeks. Perhaps he'd thought to receive another acknowledgment of guilt. He might have had the satisfaction of hearing her say she'd been wrong, that he was not the slow-top she'd made him out to be, that she'd come to see some worth in him. His efforts had gained him little beyond a coach filled to the ceiling with silence.

Nearly a quarter hour passed between them without a single word spoken. Only the sound of the carriage wheels grinding along the road broke the heavy, awkward silence. Jason wondered if, on the other side of her uninformative back, she looked unconcerned or conscience stricken. The Mariposa with whom he'd spent the last twenty-odd hours would likely be riddled with guilt. The termagant who'd frequented his office the past few weeks, however, would feel no such pangs.

Why must women be so blasted confusing? If she would act logically, perhaps he would react logically.

He turned in her direction. She still had her back to him. Was she angry? That made no sense. *She* had ill-used *him.* So why did he feel the urge to apologize? What would he even apologize for?

I am sorry you treated me like a worthless piece of mutton for weeks on end? Or *I am sorry that I cannot even decide if I can trust you to be honest with me?*

He rubbed at his stiff, sore neck, wondering when he'd so utterly lost control of his life.

The coach pulled into an inn yard. As it came to a complete stop, Jason didn't hesitate, didn't look back. He threw open the door and leapt out.

Chapter Seventeen

ONLY BY SHEER FORCE OF will did Mariposa keep the tears from falling. After everything she'd done, she deserved to be abandoned, left to her own devices in a mail coach at some unknown stop on an English road. She was hardly entitled to Jason's support, but losing it dealt her a blow from which she doubted she would soon recover. He had said he would remain with her, but there she was, alone. Just as she had promised Santiago she would not leave him, yet they were apart. Perhaps this was her punishment for failing her brother.

"You crossed Spain on foot," she whispered to herself. "You can certainly ride a coach to Scotland." She would survive. She always did. Survival, however, felt like a rather hollow accomplishment.

The coach door opened. Mariposa turned just enough to peek, doing her utmost not to let her hopes get too high. She did not recognize the man who entered, likely close to two decades her senior. Remembering all too vividly the bounder who'd accosted her only the day before, Mariposa kept her face turned away from this newcomer. She tied her bonnet firmly on her head and pulled herself into the far corner, determined that the man take little notice of her.

She closed her eyes and tried to fill her mind with thoughts of more pleasant times. When she was very little, her mother used to

sing to her a song about a butterfly in a field of flowers. If she concentrated hard enough, she could almost hear Mama's voice singing
it again. She had sung it to Santiago when his fear and confusion
had left him nearly inconsolable. There had once been a time when
she and her family had been happy. All she'd wanted since the start
of the war was to have those times back again.

She felt more alone than ever.

Mariposa heard another passenger climb in. It was the first stop
of the morning and the one most likely to see more travelers get on
board. Being unobtrusive was decidedly the safest approach. She
kept to her corner and, when she opened her eyes, did not allow her
gaze to stray from the window.

The coach lurched as it resumed its journey. With fresh horses pulling, their speed significantly increased from what it had
been on the last leg. The inn yard quickly disappeared.

Silently Mariposa bid Jason farewell and, in her heart, thanked
him for seeing her as far as he had. Not since her father's death had
someone taken the time to look out for her.

The other passengers were blessedly quiet. Perhaps everyone
would keep to themselves and the journey could be undertaken
without incident.

Mariposa nearly jumped out of her skin when something was,
without warning, laid on her lap. Her eyes darted in the direction
of the delivery. She could not say what she'd expected to see, but
the sight of two scones lying inauspiciously on a napkin caught
her entirely by surprise. Who had put them there, and why?

She raised her eyes enough to look at the passenger next to her
on the seat. Instantly, her heart leapt into her throat. Jason. He hadn't
left her.

His eyes darted in her direction. He didn't smile, didn't say a
word. In fact, he didn't look particularly happy to be back in her
company. He simply pulled out the folded newspaper he held under his arm and turned his attention to it, not sparing her another
glance.

Mariposa's heart sank. Only upon receiving Jason's silent
dismissal did Mariposa fully realize the change she had undergone

over the few short weeks she'd known him. She had sought him out, knowing from Stanley that the Jonquils were a family of trustworthy and caring individuals. She had at first thought of Jason Jonquil as a source of information and assistance but little beyond. Along the way he had become a friend, a confidant, and somehow more.

Mariposa could hear Stanley's voice echoing from the past as they'd talked of their childhoods and parents. "Our father raised us to be gentlemen," he had said. "We none of us can turn our backs on a person truly in need."

That Jason had remained with her out of a sense of duty could not have been more clear. For a fleeting, glorious moment, she'd thought he had come back because he cared, not in a benevolent way but personally, tenderly. But she was only another in a long line of Jonquil charity cases.

What right do you have to even hope for such a thing? she silently demanded of herself. *You, who so ill-used him?*

Even an entire night spent suffering from hunger could not make the scones taste like anything other than air. She ate but did not savor.

Though she repeatedly looked in Jason's direction, his focus never shifted from the paper he held. At such a distance from London, the paper could not have been any less than four or five days old. Having been in Town only two days earlier, nothing in the paper could truly have been news to him. That she warranted less attention than stale bits of gossip and outdated news items humbled her further.

He was willing to see her to her destination. The least she could do was cause him as little inconvenience as possible. Their fellow passenger sat directly across from Jason, reading a book. It would be some time before they made another stop.

She knew from experience how to blend in with her surroundings. The skill had proven lifesaving during their wartime travels. The execution of that skill, however, had always rendered her extremely lonely. Once again, she pulled herself tightly into her corner of the carriage and leaned her head back against the squabs to the extent her bonnet would allow. Perhaps she would be lucky enough to sleep and could pass the next leg of her journey lost in pleasant dreams.

Sleep was not so slow in coming as she feared it might be. The complete silence around her, coupled with the rhythmic swaying of the coach and her nearly overwhelming exhaustion, quickly did its work.

Through the haze of pending sleep, she thought she felt something touch her. When a moment later the sensation repeated itself, she became more fully alert. Years of necessary watchfulness, especially at night, jolted her awake.

She grabbed at the hand that had brushed her face and brought her eyes into frantic focus. Jason's apologetic expression did not, at first, register.

"I didn't mean to startle you," he whispered. "Mater says that sleeping in a bonnet is not very comfortable."

Her fuzzy mind could not fully comprehend what he'd said.

"I was attempting to take yours off without waking you."

Take off her bonnet? Mariposa nodded, awake enough to acknowledge that she had been uncomfortable wearing it.

She fumbled a moment with the ribbons but managed to untie them and slip her bonnet off. Jason took it, setting it on the seat across from her.

"Thank you," she said, still whispering.

He nodded but didn't speak. Somehow, that hurt as much as his earlier silence. Did he dislike the idea of talking with her so very much?

She glanced quickly at the man traveling in the coach with them. Seeing his attention remained riveted on his book, she quietly asked Jason the question that had lingered in her mind. "Why did you come back?"

"Come back?" He spoke as quietly as she had.

"At the last stop," she said. "I thought you had decided to leave me. Why didn't you?"

His brow knit, his eyes focusing on her. No anger or resentment touched his expression. He looked, instead, confused. "In all honesty, I am still sorting that out."

Her whisper broken by a push of emotion she hadn't expected, Mariposa offered yet another apology. "I am sorry for all I have put you through. I cannot think back on my behavior without feeling utterly ashamed and fully mortified. I—"

Jason pressed a single finger to her lips. Her immediate silence arose more from the overpowering sensation of his touch than from the unspoken command inherent in the gesture. If she had harbored any doubts as to the increasingly precarious state of her feelings for Jason, the impact of that simple, brief touch would have entirely convinced her. He saw her as a nuisance, and all the while, she was falling further in love with him.

"No self-recriminations," he instructed. "You passed a difficult night, and it would be best if you were to sleep."

She nodded but could not find her voice.

Jason grew almost instantly stiff and shifted back to his side of the carriage seat. For a moment, he'd been thoughtful and gentle and kind. Then he'd grown starchy and unapproachable again. How utterly confusing he was.

Mariposa wrapped her arms around her middle and adjusted her position until she was as comfortable as possible in the cramped confines of a mail coach. Perhaps a bit of sleep would do her good. If she were very, very lucky, she might even awaken with some idea of what she ought to do about her traitorous heart and its decision to grow attached to a gentleman who felt no such inclination toward her.

Life, at times, was exceedingly unfair.

Chapter Eighteen

JASON KNEW BEYOND A DOUBT that Mariposa Thornton was going to kill him. Not in the murder-him-in-his-sleep sense but in the drive-him-completely-mad sense. She could be absolutely infuriating, and yet he couldn't think of an experience in recent memory that had proven more diverting than the hours he'd spent with her in this confounded mail coach.

He had stood in the public room of the inn that morning, waiting for the proprietor to wrap up the scones he'd purchased, seriously contemplating his own mental state. No amount of effort had convinced him that he intended to continue on with Mariposa strictly for reasons of gentlemanly obligation and basic human kindness. His reasons were far more personal.

He could not have walked away. In fact, he had begun to suspect that his inability to leave her might easily turn into a permanent inclination to remain with her. The possibility did not prove at all comfortable.

Jason glanced at Mariposa. She looked different in her sleep. Only when the oblivion of sleep washed away the weight of her responsibilities did he realize how burdened and tense she was in her waking hours.

"My Mariposa, she was so sweet when a child," Abuela had said as Jason had helped her prepare for her trip to Lampton Park.

"She would tell to me her dreams. Her dreams, they are no more. They are gone."

How quickly he had condemned Mariposa—at first as empty-headed and managing, then, after her deception was revealed, as lying and manipulative—only to find himself regarding her in a very different light only a few short days later. She had survived more than he would ever endure. She had lost her father, her home, and her childhood all at once. Yet she had emerged a vibrant, strong, and determined lady.

So why did he find it so blasted difficult to decide what to think about her?

"*Excusez moi, monsieur.*"

Jason snapped himself from his rather consuming thoughts at the sound of his fellow passenger's voice. The man had not spoken a word prior to that moment.

"You and the young woman are quarreling, *oui?*" the man asked.

Falling back on the same lower-class accent he'd used the day before, Jason answered, "We are." That simple response seemed safer than any other explanation.

"She is very beautiful," the Frenchman said.

Jason's hackles immediately rose. Of what interest was it to this stranger that Mariposa was beautiful? What were his intentions?

The man smiled. "Fear not, monsieur. I have no designs upon your wife."

Jason didn't correct him. Let the man think Mariposa was married—married to a protective husband, no less. He kept his eyes on the stranger.

"I only ask," the man continued, "because the sorrow I saw in her face before your return touched me."

Sorrow? Had she been upset?

"When she saw that you sat beside her, she . . . her face, it lit up." The man opened wide the fingers on both his hands, like the spreading light of a candelabra. "She looked at you with so much joy and happiness. Then you opened your paper, turning her away, and I watched her die a little."

The French were generally known for their overly strong imagery. Yet Jason's conscience struck him. He had retreated into that paper because he could not decide how to reconcile the contradictions she presented him. News, however outdated, seemed safely neutral.

The still-unidentified man sighed. "My wife, she gave me that look each time we argued. I would not be ready to end our quarrel. She would see that in me, and her eyes would turn sad and dim."

Jason had also seen a measure of unhappiness in Mariposa's eyes. He'd been valiantly attempting to convince himself he hadn't put it there.

"You think I should apologize?" Jason knew the answer but asked the question just the same.

"*Oui.*"

"What if I told you this argument was not my fault?" Mariposa, after all, was the one who had begun their association with lies and deceit. Her harebrained scheme was the reason they were stuck in a mail coach for two days.

The man chuckled knowingly. "It does not matter who is at fault. Being right is far less important than a woman's tender heart."

Words of wisdom if ever he'd heard any. It was precisely the sort of thing his father would have said to him. Jason ought to have at least spoken to Mariposa when he'd entered the coach instead of retreating into a stony silence. They'd exchanged a few words when he'd accidentally wakened her, but she'd been so sleepy, he doubted she would remember.

He, on the other hand, remembered that moment quite well. He'd touched his finger to her lips. Gads, he hadn't expected the simple gesture to knock the wind out of him. For the slightest fraction of a moment he'd contemplated pulling her fully into his embrace and keeping her there for the foreseeable future. The strength of that impulse shocked him so very much that he'd needed to put immediate distance between them. Had she felt it as well? Or had he only made her uncomfortable?

"You said she was pleased to see me?" Only after blurting out the question did Jason realize how abrupt he'd been.

His companion smiled, obviously amused. "I have seldom seen a woman happier to find herself in a man's company."

Jason rather liked the idea.

"She seems a sweet-natured girl," the Frenchman added.

Jason actually laughed out loud. "She is a spitfire," he corrected.

The man's deep chuckle joined his. "Even better."

Mariposa shifted beside him, even opening her eyes a little. Apparently they were making too much noise.

"Now you have something for which you can apologize," the Frenchman said. "For waking her," he clarified.

Jason grinned. "Having a reason does make an apology easier to make."

Mariposa straightened, though she still looked half asleep. "I cannot find my bonnet." Her words emerged a bit slurred and slow.

Jason motioned to the missing article. "On the seat across from you, my dear." Had he just called her "my dear"?

She looked at her bonnet and nodded, saying something in Spanish. Her words did not sound like a condemnation. Either she was still very much asleep, or she was as confused by the inadvertent pet name as he was.

"Your wife, she is a Spaniard?"

All of a sudden, Mariposa was fully awake. She stared back at the Frenchman, not with a look of surprise or wariness but one of unmistakable fear. Without taking her eyes off their companion, she slid across the seat, not stopping until she had reached Jason's side. What could he do other than wrap his arm around her shoulders? The situation positively required it.

"Who is he?" Mariposa whispered, tipping her head up toward Jason, else her nearly silent words would not have reached his ears.

"I am sorry, sir," Jason said. "I do not believe I know your name."

"Jean Beauchene."

Jason turned back to his very comfortable armful and said, "He is Jean Beauchene."

"Are you certain?" she asked. Her voice shook, the sound making Jason aware of the fact that she was trembling.

"What is the matter?" he asked, suddenly quite concerned. "Are you unwell?"

Her terror-stricken expression took on an edge of pleading. "He is French." She offered no explanation beyond that.

"Yes, he is." There had to be more reason for her fear than merely his nationality.

In the next moment, he thought he understood. Though Mariposa had rather skimmed over the details, she had at least hinted during her confessional over their meager dinner the evening before that her few encounters with the French during the ongoing war had been hostile at the very least. Such experiences could easily prejudice a person.

So Jason pulled her closer. She leaned against him, burying her face in his jacket. He did not think she was crying; somehow, he had a difficult time picturing her weeping. Mariposa had ever presented herself as resilient and unbreakable. That something as innocuous as a French accent had rendered her so completely shaken spoke volumes of the terror she must have endured during the war.

His gaze fell on the Frenchman. To his credit, Jean looked concerned and empathetic.

"I would guess," Jean said, "that she experienced some of this war firsthand."

Jason nodded. "Far too much of it."

He did not know how many minutes passed as he silently sat with Mariposa beside him, his arm yet wrapped around her shoulders. She continued to tremble, her grip on his jacket iron-clad. Her fear was palpable and all-encompassing. Nothing about Jean as an individual should have created such an out-of-proportion response—clearly Mariposa hadn't even known who he was.

What, then, had brought on such immediate fear? Was she expecting to run into a Frenchman? Perhaps hoping to *not* run into one? Jason had a nagging suspicion Mariposa's worry stemmed from a particular Frenchman, one she was, for whatever reason, unable to identify on sight. He could only imagine the terror that must accompany such a situation: fearing something one could not recognize and might be entirely unable to avoid.

He leaned his cheek against the top of her head, aching for her. What kind of suffering she must have known! "You are safe now, Mariposa," he whispered.

"You cannot know that." Emotion thickened her voice.

"I don't think you need to be afraid of Jean."

The declaration did not seem to comfort her. She continued to shiver and not, he suspected, from cold. "But he could be—" She didn't elaborate.

"He could be *whom*?"

Mariposa only shook her head, still pressed to his side.

He had guessed correctly, then—she feared someone in particular. Jason truly did not believe Jean posed a threat, but he would not leave Mariposa's side until he was certain she was not in danger.

Chapter Nineteen

JASON KEPT A KEEN EYE on Jean Beauchene. Though he watched for any sign whatsoever that the man was nefarious, untrustworthy, or in any way dangerous, he found none. Mariposa must have felt some of her concerns ease as well. She slowly emerged from within the folds of Jason's weatherworn jacket and even occasionally glanced across the coach.

As the day wore on, they all grew more companionable, though Mariposa never entirely lost her edge of wariness. Jean, they learned, had enjoyed something of a Grande Tour before the Reign of Terror forced him to flee for the relative safety of England. He had, in fact, spent some time in the very area of Spain where Mariposa had grown up.

"I do not believe I saw your estate specifically," he said when she quietly asked him about it. "Though I did travel through Albuera and the surrounding countryside."

"And did you not think it the most beautiful place in all of Spain?" An almost dreamy quality touched her tone.

Jean smiled paternally. "Home is always the most beautiful place one can imagine."

She came very near to returning Jean's smile. Jason felt a surge of relief. He did not at all like seeing her as obviously unhappy as she had been of late. Though she no longer sat within the circle of his arms, she remained close by his side. For the briefest of moments, he was tempted to take her hand. The impulse passed, however. They were not, after all, actually husband and wife. Theirs was only a tentative friendship, in fact.

"Prado Verde is very beautiful," Mariposa said, still speaking almost exclusively to Jean. "But I think it was made more beautiful because my family was there."

Jean nodded. "I am not certain I could ever return to my home," he said. "I fear it would feel too empty without my loved ones there."

Mariposa leaned her head against Jason's shoulder, which made him feel almost smug. *Smug?* What had happened to his logical self of late?

"Does your family remain in France?" Mariposa asked.

"No." Jean filled that single word with decades of sadness. "They were all killed during the Terror. I alone escaped and only because I was away from them at the time."

"Does that ever make you feel guilty?" Mariposa's voice emerged much softer and far more uncertain than it had but moments earlier. "You are alive and well and they—" She took a shaky breath. "And they are not."

Jason could not say for which of her family members her heart ached in that moment—those who were killed or those who were missing. Such a burden she bore.

"I like to think," Jean said, "that even after all they suffered, they would be pleased to know I am well."

For a time, they all sat in silence, and then more neutral topics were introduced. Mariposa conversed more openly with Jean, something that at first pleased Jason but quickly grew inexplicably irritating.

By midafternoon, Mariposa had shifted to the far end of the bench seat they shared, and rather than feeling grateful for the added room to stretch and shift and generally make himself more comfortable, Jason had to stop himself from taking hold of her arm and pulling her back to where she had been. He kept his grumblings to himself, but only just. His ability to remain unruffled in any and all circumstances seemed to have evaporated.

"At the risk of offending one or both of you"—Jean eyed them with obvious curiosity, a fact Jason had been ignoring for at least three quarters of an hour—"might I ask what it is you are quarreling about?"

Mariposa's eyes immediately turned in Jason's direction. He cleared his throat, feeling decidedly uncomfortable. He'd forgotten to mention to her his earlier conversation.

"You told him we were having an argument?"

Why did he suddenly feel like a child caught stealing biscuits from the kitchen?

"*Oui*," Jean said. "But he would tell me nothing else, except that he was not at fault."

Mariposa crossed her arms and gave Jason a look that likely should have burned a hole right through him. So he shot Jean a look he hoped would have an identical end result.

No one in the carriage burst into flames. Jean did, however, begin laughing.

"You've been very helpful," Jason told him with as much dry sarcasm as he could muster.

"Then I shall add to my helpfulness and say this." If not for the empathy in Jean's expression, Jason would have immediately objected. "Though I do not know the source of your disagreement, I have watched the both of you throughout the day, and it is plain to see that you are miserable being at odds with one another."

"Perhaps we are simply miserable in general," Jason grumbled.

Though he was not looking at her, Jason had a feeling Mariposa's look had grown even more explosive.

"I said I was sorry." The vehemence of Mariposa's tone immediately pulled Jason's attention to her. Sure enough, she was glaring. "I have said it over and over again. I've done everything except grovel at your feet and beg. What's more, I didn't ask you to follow me. I never asked you to come after me."

"Whether or not you specifically asked for my company is entirely irrelevant," Jason said. "The situation demanded it. I couldn't very well let you run off like you did."

"You most certainly could have." She looked away from him, though her posture continued screaming her annoyance. "*Especialmente* if doing so is making you *mucho* 'miserable.'"

"I never actually said I was miserable."

"You could at least pretend like you don't hate me." With that declaration, Mariposa turned her back fully to him.

Hate her? "I never—" But what was the use in protesting?

Their history was difficult enough that nothing he said was likely to convince her that he did not, in fact, hold her in contempt. He hadn't even disliked her in a very long time. Rather, he'd come to like her a little too much for his own comfort.

"You think he hates you?" Jean asked.

"*Sé que él me odia.*"

Jean looked at Jason, a question in his eyes.

"She reverts to Spanish when she's upset," Jason said. "Probably because I can't understand a word of it. You have to admit it is a very effective way of letting me know she is not speaking to me."

Jean returned his attention to Mariposa. "*¿Por qué crees que te odia?*"

She spun around, amazement clearly written on her face. "You speak Spanish?"

Jean nodded and smiled. Mariposa's gaze flicked to Jason for the minutest fraction of a moment before returning to Jean. Without warning, she launched into a highly animated speech delivered entirely in her native tongue. Her hands waved about, gesturing broadly and expressively. He didn't think he'd ever heard so many syllables fly so quickly from a person's mouth.

As he sat mute and entirely unable to translate a word, Mariposa and Jean undertook a conversation, one which likely cataloged his many shortcomings. It did not take long for Mariposa to shift to Jean's side of the coach. Jason's mood only darkened. By the time the mail paused for its evening change of teams and drivers, he did not feel himself in charity with either of his fellow passengers.

Only out of a sense of civility did Jason allow Jean to pull him aside during their evening meal in the public room of yet another inn. Mariposa remained at the table, eating in silence.

"I realize I have thrust myself quite unforgivably into your affairs during our very brief acquaintance," Jean said.

Jason didn't bother to disagree.

"When I first boarded the mail coach and came across your lovely Mariposa"—Jean's use of the word *lovely* did nothing to improve Jason's spirits—"looking so forlorn, I was immediately put in mind of my dear sister."

"She reminds you of your *sister*?" Jason would not have predicted that.

Jean raised an eyebrow in censure. "Surely you did not suspect me of having romantic intentions toward a woman two decades my junior? Not to mention one married to another man?"

"Well, I—That is . . ."

Jean held up a hand, cutting off Jason's rambling attempt to excuse himself. "Your Mariposa spoke very vaguely of her trials before coming to England, though what she told me was enough to convince me she experienced absolute horrors."

"She did." The detailed explanation she'd given Jason only the day before left no doubt that her life had, on many occasions, been terrible.

"And she is much tormented by the loss of her younger brother. She cannot even speak his name without her voice splintering in agony. He haunts her thoughts and, I suspect, her dreams at night. Though she puts forward a brave face, I think your sweet Mariposa is breaking inside."

Jason felt certain Jean was right. "I do not know what I can do to relieve any of her suffering."

"Be her safe haven," Jean said. "War leaves wounds that too often go unseen. It changes people, and rarely for the better. Give her reason to feel secure and protected so she can begin to heal."

Those words remained with Jason throughout their brief stop. He felt thoroughly chastised. When one took into consideration all she had been through, a certain degree of understanding was more than called for. She had been dishonest when faced with a stranger she could not be certain would be an ally. She'd hidden behind the armor of an assumed façade when braving a world that had hurt her again and again. Were these such unforgivable actions?

He had been taught to be honest at all times, though even he acknowledged the necessity of the ruse they had enacted since embarking on this journey. How much more justified were her lies when faced with a man she did not know, in an unfamiliar country, with a lifetime of suffering and danger fresh in her thoughts?

Jason realized with a pang of regret that he had been too harsh, too quick to pass judgment. While he yet struggled to understand her, he knew Mariposa deserved a greater portion of his kindness and consideration than he had hitherto granted her.

They returned to the coach. Mariposa retreated immediately to her corner.

Jason swallowed his pride and slid over beside her. "Mariposa," he whispered.

She glanced at him but only briefly.

"This is not easy for me," he said. "So I would greatly appreciate any support you are willing to give."

That seemed to pique her curiosity. She at least turned her head in his direction.

"I have been insufferable and pompous." Jason pushed on despite his innate dislike of confessing all his misdeeds at once. "I have always considered myself not easily fooled, but you came along and pulled the wool over my eyes so entirely and with seemingly little effort. And in my pride, I condemned you out of hand for being deceitful. That same pride got in the way of my good sense and prevented me from forgiving you as I should. I held a grudge, and for that, I am sorry."

She faced him fully. "You do not hate me any longer?"

"I never hated you."

"You most certainly did." But a smile seemed to hover just below the surface.

"May we begin again, Mariposa?"

"I would very much like that."

Jean rejoined them only a moment before the carriage began its journey once more. The three of them rode quietly as night began to fall.

Mariposa leaned closer to Jason, something which had an immediate effect on his heart rate, and placed a brief kiss on his cheek. He sat frozen, shocked. A flattering hint of color touched her cheeks. He slid away from her, all the while attempting to look unaffected.

He had never been one to feel tempted to go beyond the most rigid bounds of propriety. But he found himself so powerfully drawn to Mariposa that he did not feel he could entirely trust himself not to kiss her quite thoroughly right there in the carriage. How had he gone so quickly from finding himself in charity with her to wishing to kiss her truly and deeply?

Distance seemed key. Jason shifted until his back pressed against his side of the carriage, as far from her as he could get without leaping out the window.

"You should probably try to get some rest." An innocuous subject would serve as a welcome distraction. "We'll reach Philip's tomorrow. He's exhausting even on a full night's sleep."

"I have been looking forward to meeting him," Mariposa said. "Stanley painted such an amusing picture of your eldest brother."

"I'll just sit over here." Jason slipped across the carriage to the empty space beside Jean. "So you'll be able to lie down."

"Won't you be uncomfortable sitting up all night?" Mariposa asked.

He shook his head. Sitting beside her with that unsettling kiss still fresh in his mind would be far more uncomfortable.

Long after Mariposa had grown quiet and relaxed with sleep, Jean broke the silence of the carriage. "I will be disembarking not long after we cross the border into Scotland. I should like to hear from you, if you would be so good as to write." He handed Jason a bit of paper with his name and direction scrawled on it. "Let me know how the young lady is doing."

"I will." Oddly enough, Jason had come to feel like Jean was an old friend, despite the less than twenty-four hours' worth of acquaintance they shared.

"Perhaps you will even be willing to someday tell me just why you are pretending to be of the lower classes," Jean added with a mischievous twinkle in his eye, "and just what your reasons are for acting as though you are married."

Before Jason could formulate any kind of reply, Jean turned his attention once more to his book.

The Frenchman had seen through their façade. But how quickly? What had given them away?

"A word of advice, monsieur, for any future masquerades."

Jason listened warily.

"When a man is kissed by his wife, that man generally does not run for his life."

Remembering all too vividly the very simple, very brief kiss that had sent him into rather immediate panic, Jason smiled, acknowledging the truth of Jean's statement. His amusement only grew, realizing how very obvious they'd been about their mutual unease in each other's presence. In a moment's time, he was laughing out loud. Jean joined him.

"Take care of your sweet butterfly, Jason."

"I intend to."

Chapter Twenty

Jason awoke the next morning, every bit as stiff as he'd been the morning before but far less conflicted. He had meant what he'd said to Jean—he would support Mariposa and care for her in whatever capacity he was permitted. Whether that meant assisting her as she searched Scotland for her elusive family or returning her unharmed to her grandmother, he meant to see it done.

They had passed the morning in relative silence. Mariposa's unease had grown by leaps and bounds. He'd come to miss the cool confidence of the young lady who'd walked into his office weeks earlier. Seeing her so upended made him feel rather helpless.

"Will your brother be upset that I am turning up unexpectedly?" Mariposa asked out of the blue, nervousness evident in her expressive eyes. "He doesn't even know me, and I wasn't invited."

"Philip, for all his show of being a dandy, is not at all high in the instep." Jason was surprised to realize that he meant what he said. He didn't generally have many compliments for Philip.

"Stanley could not understand why Philip began acting the way he does," Mariposa said, eyeing the passing landscape, her fingers wrapping around themselves in an unconscious gesture of discomfort. She likely had no idea how endearing it was. "He said the new Philip was very different from the old Philip."

Jason couldn't have agreed more. "He has always been light-hearted, the first of us brothers to enjoy a lark or share a humorous anecdote, but he didn't used to go to such lengths to be ridiculous."

"You believe it is an affectation, then?"

"I know it is. I simply don't know why he does it."

"All of us have reasons for the disguises we wear," Mariposa said quietly, leaning her forehead against the window and continuing to look out. "Some masks are meant to save us from the world around us. Others are meant to shield us from ourselves."

Jason tried to unravel what she'd said but found himself as confused as he was intrigued. "From *ourselves?*"

"Like Stanley." She shrugged as she spoke. Jason had come to recognize that as one of her signature gestures; it could mean dismissal, acceptance, rejection, and any number of things in between. He smiled at the sight of it, a sure sign that their days-long quarrel had come to something of an end. "He hides from his own pain and hides it from others as well."

Other than the painful injury he'd sustained, Stanley hadn't seemed to be suffering as acutely as Mariposa had believed him to be.

"He acts as though he is unaffected by what he has experienced, but his eyes give him away." She turned to look at Jason. "He hates being a soldier. He has spent half a decade surrounded by death and inhumanity and endless suffering, and it is destroying his soul." Those were heavy words and an enormous declaration, but Mariposa seemed convinced. "Stanley is not suited to the life he is living," she said. "He can't close off his heart. He can no longer shield himself from the pain."

"Stanley has never said anything about—"

"Because he is a gentleman of his word. He will fight so long as he is able and needed, but I worry about the price he is paying. He is dying inside."

Those words brought to mind similar ones Jean had spoken, that war left wounds unseen. How many of those same wounds did Mariposa bear, scars beyond even those she had revealed to him?

Mariposa's stomach tied into a rather intricate knot as they waited at the front door of a cozy cottage surrounded by lush vegetation. Jason had managed to secure them a seat on the back of a delivery wagon for eight of the ten miles required to reach the Lampton hunting box. More than fifty hours of nearly nonstop travel had taken its toll, however, and Mariposa knew she looked a positive fright.

The door opened, and a woman of indeterminate years and a decidedly piercing gaze skewered the two visitors with a dismissive sweep of her eyes before beginning to close the door once more.

"Now, Mrs. Dunbar," Jason said, a smile in his tone that stood in sharp contrast to the overbearingly serious gentleman Mariposa had once known. "You wouldn't close the door on one of your meddlesome boys, would you?"

"Why, Master Jason! As I live and breathe!" The woman's eyebrows shot up, her mouth falling open. "His lordship never said ye was coming to see him."

"Probably because he doesn't know yet."

"Well, come in. Come in. Both of you." She ushered them in without batting an eyelash. "Don't you look a sight." She tsked. "What've you been doing to yourself to come here looking like a beggar boy?"

"I've been riding the Royal Mail," Jason answered with a mischievous smile.

"Don't tell me you've gone and lost all your money on a card game." Mrs. Dunbar gave him a reproachful look.

Jason just laughed. "Not at all. Is Lord Lampton in?"

"Of course he is," Mrs. Dunbar answered. "Where else would he be with his wife still off her feet, I'd like to know."

In the next moment, they were led down a corridor toward what Mariposa assumed was either the drawing room or the sitting room. Her heart beat harder. She was about to meet Philip, the brother Stanley had more or less idolized, the brother she had heard the most about, the enigma. She knew herself entirely dependent on his forbearance. If he was put out by her presumptuousness in calling upon him unannounced, she would be in rather dire straits.

"I am certain Philip will not eat you," Jason whispered beside her, quite startling her. She had all but forgotten he was with her.

"You'll intervene if he begins to look hungry?" Mariposa pressed, managing to make her concern sound lighthearted.

"My word as a gentleman." Jason had been in happier spirits since their reconciliation the evening before. The thought that her friendship had come to mean so much to him touched her deeply.

She felt herself relax. Jason would watch over her.

After a few short moments, the Earl of Lampton entered the room, a look of mingled amusement and curiosity on his familiar face—familiar because all the Jonquils bore a striking resemblance to one another. For herself, Mariposa thought Jason the more distinguished looking of the bunch.

She studied Lord Lampton rather too acutely for her scrutiny to go unnoticed. He was, indeed, every inch a dandy. She'd never seen so many fobs on a single watch chain. He wore a waistcoat of tartan beneath a form-fitting, bottle-green jacket. His neckcloth was the very model of flamboyant extravagance. Yet there was unmistakable intelligence in his eyes as he surveyed the two occupants of his sitting room.

"Welcome, Jason," he greeted his brother, swinging his quizzing glass on its ribbon as he sauntered to where Jason stood. "No doubt you heard of the dashing new wardrobe I have acquired and have come to bask in the artistry of my attire."

"Very . . . festive, Philip," Jason answered. Mariposa was certain Jason held back one of those smiles she so dearly loved.

Philip—Mariposa really couldn't think of him formally after hearing so much about him through Stanley—seemed taken aback for a moment. "Indeed," he managed to say, one golden eyebrow quirked upward. "And do you plan to add something less complimentary once you have recovered from your initial shock? Or shall I assume I have finally left you speechless?"

He still used the tone of a mindless fop, but Mariposa sensed a degree of truthfulness in his voice. Jason, she deduced, was generally quick to belittle Philip's chosen attire. Stanley had always said Jason and Philip were too much alike for an easy friendship, their personalities both being quite forceful but their means of expression conflicting. It was fascinating to see the clash firsthand.

"On the contrary." Jason shook his head in obvious amusement. "I cannot help but remark that you have quite outdone yourself. I never thought to see a waistcoat that surpassed the shocking appearance of the yellow you wore upon quitting Town."

"I am flattered, brother, that you recall my traveling wardrobe in such detail," Philip replied, a twinkle in his eye. "Perhaps you really do care."

"Perhaps." Jason shrugged.

Mariposa grinned at that. He had begun to shrug like a Spaniard. She, no doubt, had played a role in that.

"And you truly do not mean to berate me for my unbearable elegance?"

"I mean, as a matter of fact, to overlook it, to the degree such a feat is possible," Jason replied.

The smile disappeared immediately from Philip's face, his brows snapping together in concentration. "Are you feeling unwell, Jason?"

Jason chuckled. Philip stared.

"May I make known to you Miss Thornton." Jason slipped into the appropriate introductions, the smile on his face not lessening. "Mari—Miss Thornton, this is my brother, the Earl of Lampton."

"My lord." Mariposa made her best curtsy.

"Miss Thornton," Philip returned with a dazzling bow, his watch fobs clanging as he did so. When he straightened again, he wore a most mischievous smile. "I cannot begin to express how anxious I have been to make your acquaintance."

"Indeed?" Mariposa answered, feeling a laugh bubbling inside but unable to account for the reaction.

"My mother is, I must tell you, quite inordinately fond of you."

"She is? But I have only met her on one occasion."

"And made quite an impression." Philip took to swinging his quizzing glass once more.

Mariposa felt her lightheartedness vanish. She could only imagine the impression she'd made that day at Havenworth. She had belittled Jason and had, no doubt, earned the censure of his family.

"Banish the long face, Miss Thornton," Philip instructed. "Mater had nothing but praise for you."

Mariposa kept her eyes lowered to hide her confusion. Praise? She had long hoped to earn Mater's good opinion but couldn't reconcile the result with her behavior.

"I have, I fear, been most backward as a host." Philip interrupted her reflections. "Do be seated, Miss Thornton."

She obeyed automatically, taking a seat on a nearby sofa. She was heartened when Jason sat beside her. In her confusion, she had felt her confidence slipping.

"Perhaps one or both of you would be so good as to tell me the reason for your most welcome visit," Philip suggested, only to continue in a most unexpected vein. "I have my suspicion it is not I you have come to visit but rather my not-too-distant neighbors."

"Neighbors?" Jason asked.

"You're repeating again," Mariposa whispered to him only to receive a bright smile. She returned it with marked enthusiasm. How she'd missed his playful side during the tense hours they'd passed the day before.

"Yes, neighbors," Philip continued. The look in his eyes told Mariposa he had not missed the exchange between her and Jason. "Not five miles east of here is a quite well-respected family. Mrs. Douglas's maiden name, I understand, was Thornton."

Chapter Twenty-One

JASON SAW MARIPOSA PALE, AND he instinctively reached for her hand. He squeezed her fingers in what he hoped was a reassuring gesture.

"You know Mr. and Mrs. Douglas?" Mariposa asked, her voice uncharacteristically shaky.

"I do, indeed." Philip maintained his lighthearted air. "Fine couple. Their children are all grown now, and they, I believe, have cast themselves in the role of surrogate parents during our time of difficulty and hardship."

Mariposa looked confused, and well she might be. Jason had not mentioned Sorrel's operation, the reason for Philip and Sorrel's trip to Scotland.

A new voice, that of Philip's wife, entered the conversation. "Can you not abandon the theatrics for one conversation, dearest?"

The only thing Philip abandoned faster than his seat was his dandyish mannerisms.

"Sorrel." Concern added an edge to Philip's tone. "You are supposed to be resting. *Off your feet.*"

"As interesting as I find the bed curtains I have stared at for days on end, I would far rather visit with—" She leaned on her cane and looked around the room, momentary surprise registering in her eyes. "With Jason and his guest."

"Sorrel." Philip clasped his hands on either side of her face, studying her quite acutely. "What if you have done damage?"

"With this monstrosity strapped to me?" she replied dryly, indicating her leg. Though her dress fully covered that limb, there was something in the hang of her dress that indicated her leg was encased in something large and cumbersome.

"MacAslon said it was no guarantee," Philip said in a warning voice. Jason listened in awe. There was no trace of the mindless fop about his brother. If that persona were his true character, could he drop it so easily and so entirely?

"Would you feel more at ease if I told you Willy carried me down?" Sorrel asked.

"Willy takes far too much pleasure in carrying you around," Philip grumbled, but there was more petulance than true displeasure in his tone, almost like a young child pouting over a lost treat.

"Summon your flawless manners, dear." Sorrel gently caressed her husband's cheek. "Introduce me to this young lady."

A look passed between the couple that made Jason instantly feel like an intruder on a very private moment.

Mariposa, he noted, watched the scene with a look of complete wonderment, a contented smile touching her lips. "They truly love each other," she whispered.

"You sound happy for them."

"I have thought of your family as my own for a very long time. Of course I am happy for them."

After the appropriate introductions were made and all had resumed their seats, with Philip sitting quite close to his wife, her hand held securely in his own, the conversation resumed. Philip relayed what he knew of the Douglases without relinquishing his hold on Sorrel. Indeed, Jason found himself quite fascinated by the picture his brother made. He was attentive, caring, absolutely besotted, and not at all frivolous.

"Mr. and Mrs. Douglas live alone?" Mariposa asked.

"Quite," Sorrel answered. "Though I have not been to their home, I understand from many conversations with Mrs. Douglas—

she has kept me company quite a few times since my surgery—that she and her husband live alone."

"They have had no visitors?" Mariposa pressed.

"Did you expect them to?" Philip asked. The perceptiveness of that response immediately caught Jason's attention. Here was a glimpse of the intelligent, quick-witted brother he had once admired.

"I admit that I did." Mariposa's spirits noticeably sagged.

"Perhaps they do," Sorrel said. "With my indisposition, we have not been able to visit them at their home. If their visitors were disinclined to call upon the sick and afflicted"—she grimaced in a humorous display of self-deprecation—"we would not have met them."

The tiniest flicker of hope returned to Mariposa's eyes.

Jason took her hand once more. "It is possible they have visitors who prefer to keep to themselves."

"Just as they would," she said to him, her look significant enough to indicate just who *they* were.

"Precisely." Jason did not pull his eyes away from hers. How he wished to see her expression light and teasing once more.

"I will send around a note asking if we might call upon them for tea tomorrow, if you wish," Philip offered, his keen eyes not missing a bit of the exchange.

"Could we not call today?" Mariposa asked in her characteristically energetic way.

"I suppose it wouldn't hurt to ask." Philip rose to his feet. "If you ladies can bear to be separated from my sartorial masterpiece"—he tugged at his overly bright waistcoat—"I shall pen a note immediately."

Philip had assumed the mask again. Jason was no closer to discovering the why of Philip's disguise but found he was no longer so deeply bothered by its very existence.

"Jason," Philip said almost under his breath, motioning Jason to follow him across the room to a writing desk.

Jason looked into Mariposa's face, not wanting to abandon her if she needed his continued presence. But she smiled reassuringly. Jason squeezed her hand one more time, then rose to follow his brother.

They stopped just short of the writing desk. Philip gave Jason a searching look. "Mater wrote to me about Miss Thornton. The entire family was convinced within minutes of her arrival at Havenworth that she could do you a world of good."

"Which is odd," Jason answered, "seeing as how she spent the entirety of that interview insulting me."

"Ruffled your feathers, did she?" Philip smiled.

Jason nodded emphatically.

"That is a trait a gentleman ought to seek out in a lady, you know." Philip's gaze slid to where Sorrel sat conversing quietly with Mariposa across the room. "She doesn't allow you to be complacent. She'll make you want to be better."

The tenderness in his brother's eyes belied every unflattering assessment Jason had made of Philip over the years.

"How is Sorrel?" Jason asked, as concerned for his sister-in-law's well-being as he was for Philip's mental fortitude should she be laid low by her ordeal.

Pain immediately flashed through Philip's eyes. "It has been horrible." He closed his eyes then and let out a tense breath. "MacAslon rebroke her leg in three places." He shook his head as if to remove the memory. "I was not even in the room, but her cries of agony filled his home. I think I will hear that sound in my nightmares for the rest of my life."

"But is she faring better now?" Jason asked, horrified by the details of a surgery he had only vaguely understood before. "Was it worth it?"

"The breaks are healing far better than the original injuries did." Philip opened his eyes once more, though his expression remained troubled. "We will not know for some time if the improved alignment will lessen any of her pain. Most of her difficulties are in her hip. So even all this suffering will likely not entirely alleviate her dependence upon her walking stick."

"But she will be in a better state than before?"

"We hope so." Philip smiled a little, his eyes once more on Sorrel. "I am already investigating options for improving her hip, though all I have learned so far indicates it is beyond the scope of medical science."

"But you will keep trying." It was not a question. Jason could see Philip's determination. It was a Jonquil trait. They not only jumped to the rescue with alarming fervor and frequency but were also ferociously loyal to those they cared about.

"I cannot bear to see the pain in her eyes every moment of every day," Philip said. "I would do anything to see her made whole."

With that one statement, the years of frustration and resentment Jason had felt toward his brother began to dissipate. Philip quite suddenly had the bearing, the demeanor, the sense of responsibility of their father. In fact, Jason could not recall seeing any of his brothers more closely resemble their sire than Philip did in that moment.

Mariposa fought a surge of light-headedness as the family housekeeper opened the door to the Douglas's sitting room.

"Why, Lady Lampton!" A woman, no doubt Mrs. Douglas herself, exclaimed. "Are you recovered enough to be making a call?"

"Precisely what I asked," Philip said sotto voce.

Sorrel—Mariposa and the young countess were on a Christian-name basis almost immediately—simply ignored the pointed remark. Philip had been fussing over her from the moment she had announced her intention to be included in the sudden teatime visit.

"It would be improper for Mariposa to call accompanied by only two gentleman not related to her," Sorrel had pointed out.

Mariposa had very nearly objected but recognized the look in Sorrel's eyes—determination and near desperation. She thought of how she would feel if she were confined to the same rooms for weeks on end. Sorrel, it seemed, was ready to venture out and was not averse to using Mariposa's unexpected arrival as a means to achieve that end.

Mrs. Douglas ushered them all farther inside. Mariposa tried to keep herself from growing too hopeful. She could not prevent herself from glancing all around her, praying she would catch a glimpse of her lost family. Every room they passed in the corridor sat empty. She could hear no footsteps nearby, no voices echoing around corners.

The sitting room was devoid of houseguests. Mariposa told herself that did not eliminate the possibility. She pictured her brother out running in the fields around the Douglas's home. Perhaps there was even a stream nearby where he sat fishing.

She studied Mrs. Douglas, the undertaking requiring a mere moment. A sudden lump formed in her throat. This woman she knew not at all looked remarkably like Papá.

"I must say, my lord, I was quite intrigued by your perplexing note," Mrs. Douglas said. "The identity of your guests puzzled me. But now, seeing this young gentleman, I have no difficulty ascertaining that he is one of your brothers."

"Indeed, ma'am," Philip smiled good-humoredly. "This is Mr. Jason Jonquil, barrister, come from London to pay his respects to his poor, ailing sister-in-law."

The appropriate expressions of pleasure were exchanged before Philip moved to the next inevitable introduction. "And quite happily met is another family friend up from Town. Her acquaintance with another brother, Captain Stanley Jonquil, is of quite long standing."

Bless him, Philip had legitimized her presence by implying an intimacy between their families.

"And though I had not made the correlation earlier, I was quite intrigued to determine if she is connected to *you* as well, Mrs. Douglas."

"To me?" The kind lady's confusion was obvious, as was her rampant curiosity.

"Yes." Philip obviously enjoyed the role of mysterious storyteller. "Mrs. Douglas, may I present Miss Mariposa Thornton, late of Spain."

Mrs. Douglas's sharp intake of breath was likely heard all the way back to London. The instant presence of tears further indicated the impact of that simple introduction. "Oh, dear heavens." Mrs. Douglas pulled a handkerchief from her cuff and dabbed at her eyes. "You are Richard's daughter!"

"Yes, I am," Mariposa answered, sitting farther forward on her chair. Richard was her father's name. Mrs. Douglas knew her, knew to whom she belonged. Mariposa's heart pounded in anticipation.

"Why, it is obvious now," Mrs. Douglas said. "You are the very picture of your mother, at least as I remember her. This infernal war has put years between meetings."

Mariposa felt as though her heart stopped. *Years.* Mrs. Douglas had not seen Mamá in years. That could mean but one thing—Mamá was not here. Santiago was not here. She still had not found them.

This could not be another fruitless search; it simply could not be.

"How are you related to my father?" Mariposa asked.

"I am your aunt," was the answer. "Richard was my baby brother."

Her aunt. "I did not remember that he had a sister."

"Come," was the gentle instruction. Mrs. Douglas matched word to gesture, indicating Mariposa should join her on the settee.

She reluctantly did so. Although Mrs. Douglas was family, she was also very much a stranger, which made Mariposa wary.

"Where is the rest of your family?" Mrs. Douglas asked gently.

"*Mi abuela*, my mother's mother, she is visiting the Dowager Countess." Mariposa indicated Philip in hopes of conveying the identity of the person to whom she referred. "My mother and brother are not here."

Out of the corner of her eye, she could see that Jason's focus did not waver from her. He alone understood the significance of that statement. Her mother and brother were not here. They, the last remnants of her family, were still missing.

"Did you know that your father's brother, Robert, his only other sibling, passed away a little more than a year ago?" Mrs. Douglas asked.

"I did not know that." Mariposa fought to keep her voice steady. She had been so certain her family would be with their English relations, but her father had no other living siblings. There were no other possibilities besides here, no place else she might look.

"He never married, I am afraid," Mrs. Douglas said. "Thornton Manor in Norfolk and the income attached to it have passed to your brother Marcos. You and your younger brother have inherited sizable portions as well. Our solicitor did not know how to find you. There was no response to the letters sent to your home in Spain."

"The war drove us out." Mariposa could not bring herself to say anything else. They should have remained. Should have stayed behind. The letters Mrs. Douglas referred to would have reached them had they remained at home. They might have found safe haven in England after all.

"Give me the direction of your solicitor, and I shall have the Thornton solicitor contact him to relay the details of Marcos's inheritance."

A sharp pain radiated through Mariposa's heart. Marcos was dead. How many years would have to pass before hearing his name did not cause her immediate pain?

She could not think on her brother any longer and, so, forced her thoughts back to Mrs. Douglas's question. "I do not have a solicitor."

"I am acting as her legal council," Jason interjected.

"Ah yes. I believe Lord Lampton indicated you were a man of the law." Mrs. Douglas nodded her head. "Then I shall be sure to give you our man's direction."

Mariposa glanced at Jason. She was forced, however, to look away almost immediately. The fact that he no longer despised her to the point of refusing to help her, combined with the look of compassion in his eyes, very nearly undid her.

"Come. Come," Mrs. Douglas said decisively. "Let us leave talk of inheritance and legal matters to another time. We have a sumptuous tea awaiting us."

And they were swept willy-nilly into myriad topics of discourse over multiple cups of tea.

Mariposa only vaguely listened to the conversations swirling around her. Santiago's voice filled her every thought.

"Everyone will forget me."

"I will not ever forget," she had vowed.

Did he think she had? Did he believe himself forgotten?

She knew not where else to look for him. She knew not how to find him. He was not forgotten; he never would be.

But he was so utterly lost.

Chapter Twenty-Two

MARIPOSA ONLY JUST MAINTAINED HER composure. After returning to the Lampton hunting box, Philip carried Sorrel upstairs to rest, she having begun to look excessively pulled and pale.

"I am so sorry, Mariposa," Jason said when they were left momentarily alone, except for the distant vigilance of a maid tucked in a corner for propriety's sake.

"I was so certain," Mariposa managed to say without the tears she fought spilling over. "I have no other family here, nowhere else they might have gone."

She shook her head almost compulsively, straining against a growing feeling of helplessness. If Mamá and Santiago had not come to the only remaining members of Papá's family, Mariposa had no idea where they could be. Unbidden into her mind came the fear she had pushed down for months, that Bélanger had made good on his threats and they were truly gone. She would not allow herself to dwell on the horrifying possibility.

"Perhaps you should consider hiring a Runner to investigate," Jason suggested.

A flash of panic seized her. "No." Hiring a professional investigator would only draw attention, the last thing she wished to do if, indeed, the French spy was involved in their disappearance.

"I fear Sorrel cannot endure the splendor of this ensemble a moment longer," Philip declared, entering the room and tugging at his foppish jacket. "The enjoyment would be too much for one person to experience all in one day."

Mariposa would, under normal circumstances, have smiled at his overdone dandy façade. She simply continued to wring her hands and endure the twisting in her stomach. What was she to do now? Where could she even begin to search?

"Mariposa, are you quite well?" Philip apparently sensed her distress.

She took several deep breaths. No words formed, no convenient half-truths or dismissive phrases.

"Mar—"

"*No están aquí.*" She paced, fighting down panic. She had lost her family. "*Mi familia no está aquí. No sé dónde están.*"

"*Señora Douglas es su familia,*" Philip answered. "*Ella está aquí.*"

Mariposa spun on the spot and stared, wide-eyed. "*¿Habla español?*"

Philip just smiled back as if to remind her that the answer was obvious.

"How is it you speak Spanish?" Mariposa asked. In the months she'd spent in England, she'd not come across a single person conversant in her native tongue, yet she'd met two in as many days.

"I found it a valuable thing to know," Philip replied rather evasively.

Mariposa glanced at Jason only to find a look of surprised confusion on his face. He hadn't known that aspect of his brother's education, obviously.

"How do you find my accent, Señorita Thornton?" Philip asked with a grin.

"Atrocious." Mariposa actually smiled a little herself.

"Ah, but my accent on paper is far better."

She laughed at that. "Just as I can understand Portuguese quite well, written or spoken, but when I attempt to speak, it is only too obvious that I am not a native speaker. Unlike my abuela, who speaks with hardly a hint of an accent. Her French is also far superior to mine, but she cannot begin to compete with my English."

She had thought her remark innocuous enough, but Philip's face grew stern. "Your grandmother speaks Portuguese and French?" he asked rather pointedly.

Mariposa nodded, sudden butterflies in her stomach. She ought not to have said that. Their linguistic capabilities had been a boon to Wellington's aides but were unique enough to make it possible to identify them as members of that network. How lax she had grown in the company of these Jonquil men.

"And I understand from Mater that you lived outside Orthez," Philip pressed.

She pulled in a tense breath. There was no point in denying it, though knowing where she'd lived was another rather crucial piece of the puzzle.

Philip dismissed the maid. The moment the door closed behind her, his attention turned back to Mariposa.

"Your name means 'butterfly,' does it not?"

Mariposa backed up a step, her heart suddenly racing. The Butterfly was what Wellington's aides-de-camp had called her in order to disguise her identity. She had been referred to as The Butterfly in all written correspondence involved with her work for the British. Instinctively she knew Philip had realized it. But how did he know about her role in the war?

"You need not fear me, Mariposa."

Despite his reassurances, she glanced at the door before returning her wary gaze to him. "How do you know all of this?"

"Know all of *what*?" Jason asked, jumping into a conversation he, no doubt, did not even remotely understand.

"You were invaluable, you realize," Philip said. "I know personally that your efforts saved lives."

She shook her head, unnerved. "No one is supposed to know any of this."

"Further, you more than once provided information to an individual known only as The Daffodil."

Mariposa nodded, wide-eyed. The Daffodil had been involved in discovering and uncovering traitors among the British, most especially among the upper class. The Daffodil's reports had always been considered of utmost importance by those in the field. She'd translated and passed along scores of communications from the unknown source.

"Well met." Philip offered an ironic smile and a minuscule bow.

"You?" she mouthed silently.

"I fear inventiveness is not a characteristic of those involved in providing pseudonyms for those of us in need of cover," Philip said with a light chuckle. "A jonquil is a flower, you understand, more commonly known as a daffodil."

Mariposa stood dumbstruck. Could it be true? Had she truly been unknowingly sending information to one of her beloved Jonquil brothers? Stanley could not possibly have known.

"Philip, what are the two of you speaking of?" Jason demanded.

Mariposa looked between the brothers, wondering what came next. She did not feel it her place to divulge information that so closely involved Philip.

"This is as much your secret as mine," Philip said, leaving the decision in her hands. "Do you trust him?"

Mariposa knew her answer in an instant. She had come to trust Jason more than any person she had ever known.

"I trust him," she said. "And he deserves to know the truth."

☸

I trust him. Jason stood in shocked confusion. That one sentence, that sincere declaration of trust wiped away weeks of difficulty between him and this whirlwind who'd entered his life. She trusted him, and he knew how hard that was for her.

He waited for Philip to undertake some kind of explanation for the odd conversation he'd had with Mariposa.

"For years, I have worked for the foreign office," Philip said quite as if he were relating some little bit of inconsequential Society gossip. "They needed someone in the *ton* to keep an ear out for carelessly mentioned information. You would be amazed the sort of sensitive secrets Society matrons are unknowingly in possession of. Being young and relatively unknown, not to mention anxious to do my part in bringing to an end the war that threatened the life of one of my brothers, I seemed the perfect candidate. All that was needed was a persona that invited confidences and indicated a lack of intelligence significant enough to appease any unease about dropping information."

"And *that* is the reason for—" Jason indicated Philip's ridiculous attire.

Philip offered a nod. "Enduring ridicule seemed a small price to pay for King and country, not to mention a much-loved brother. Ending the war meant Stanley's safe return. The guise worked well. I learned a great deal. I even apprehended more than a few dangerous spies, both foreign and domestic. I'd like to think I've made a difference."

"Do you still spy?" Jason asked.

Philip tsked, the consummate dandy once more. "*Spy* is such a horrid word, my man. I gather information. Far different."

"Does Sorrel know?" Jason asked, still unable to reconcile what he was hearing. The mindless dandy was an informant for England? It seemed all but impossible.

"She helped with my last mission," Philip informed him with an appreciative grin. "And it was my *last*. The foreign office relieved me of all duties after that very successful endeavor."

"But you continue the masquerade." Jason felt an overwhelming need to sit down, which he did.

"If I suddenly dropped the act, brother, people would grow suspicious. And anyone with nefarious ideas would begin to think too much on the change and those things they had let slip over the years. In time, Society will look back on my transformation and be convinced that Sorrel simply had a very good influence on me."

"All these years." Jason shook his head. A few of his own less-than-kind comments came back to him in that moment. "I accused you of being irresponsible, of neglecting your duties."

"A mistake I doubt you will repeat," Philip said rather more seriously than before.

"And what, Mariposa, is your story?" Jason turned to her, feeling almost too shocked for comprehension. "Are you an informant as well?"

With a nervous sigh, she began. "Shortly before the British troops arrived at Orthez, I overheard a conversation between French soldiers during my weekly trip into the city, information giving their future plans and the fortifications they were reinforcing. I passed this tidbit on to the British regimental leadership in the area. It proved invaluable. After that, I acted as a relay point between aides-de-camp, passing on information in whichever language I was instructed to. Abuela helped when necessary."

She was a spy. A spy! How absurdly convoluted could this become? He'd thought for the past few hours that he'd finally learned all there was to know about her past. What else was she not telling him?

"After Napoleon abdicated, we thought the danger had passed." Mariposa wrapped her determination around herself like a protective blanket. Philip listened intently as well. "I received a letter in December from a man I knew to have been one of Napoleon's informers. He was infamous, known for his cruelty. He is responsible for the death of more than one person involved in the exact activities I undertook. He knew what I had been doing and wrote in no uncertain terms of the retribution he intended to enact upon me and my family."

"And that is why you came to England?" Jason guessed.

Mariposa shook her head. "Not exactly. My mother and brother disappeared only three weeks after that letter arrived, too close for me to be at all certain that it was merely a coincidence."

Jason took a sharp breath. This was the part she hadn't told him, the reason for her anxiety. Her mother and brother weren't merely missing. They were quite possibly in danger, perhaps even dead.

"The threat had mentioned my family members specifically," she said. "Part of me fears he has taken them. I know Bélanger well enough to be certain that if he is the reason for their disappearance, they likely are . . . They are not—"

She shook off the words, but Jason understood. *Not alive.*

"*Bélanger* threatened you?" Philip asked.

"You know of him?"

Philip raised an eyebrow and gave her a pointed look. She nodded her acceptance of the gesture. Apparently his knowing of Bélanger should have been assumed.

"When did you receive this threat?" Philip asked.

"December the twenty-fifth."

"Christmas Day?" Jason blurted. "Of all the—"

"And when did your family disappear?" Philip asked.

"January the thirteenth."

"Miss Thornton." Philip crossed the room and took Mariposa's hands in his. "I can assure you that Bélanger did not abduct your family members."

She watched him, her gaze unwavering and anxious.

"Bélanger was apprehended on British soil the twenty-ninth of December of last year. If you require proof, I have a scar from the ball he put in my shoulder that night." He tapped his shoulder significantly.

"You said that was poachers," Jason jumped in. He vividly remembered the nasty wound, having been at the estate where the incident had occurred, though he was not present for the actual accident. *Except, apparently, it wasn't an accident.* Good heavens, what else had occurred at the holiday house party that he'd not been aware of?

"Poachers seemed the safest explanation," Philip said. "The lie was necessary."

The lie was necessary. He didn't often think of untruths in that light. Philip's façade. Mariposa's deception. They were . . . necessary lies.

"Bélanger couldn't have escaped?" Mariposa asked, not straying from the topic. "You are certain of this?"

"Bélanger is dead." Philips spoke bluntly. "He was hung for his various crimes. I assure you he could not have harmed your family."

Mariposa sat silently, her pale face looking particularly drawn, her eyes glossed over and unfocused.

"Ought I to fetch the smelling salts?" Jason offered.

"I never faint," she insisted, though her tone wasn't reassuring.

"You look as though you might."

She shook her head. "I am simply overwhelmed. I have lived in utter terror of this man these past months. And now . . . now he is suddenly no longer a threat." She rubbed at her mouth and chin, her eyes focused firmly on the floor. Her brows pulled down at a sharp angle. "I do not know what to think or feel or—I cannot comprehend it."

"You are certain you won't faint?" Jason truly worried she might.

Philip chuckled. "I suspect she is far too similar in temperament to my Sorrel, who is more likely to take me to task than have a fit of the vapors."

Mariposa's smile of acknowledgment was fleeting and obligatory. She was quickly lost in her thoughts once more.

Philip was as well, though his thoughts seemed less heavy than Mariposa's.

"How is Sorrel faring?" Jason asked.

"She looked quite done in when I escorted her up to rest just now," Philips said. "But I'm not overly worried. She had fortitude enough to tell me in firm tones that I was to stop being a 'cosseting old nursemaid' and make arrangements to take her to Lampton Park." Assuming an unnaturally high voice, he added, obviously giving an imitation of his wife's directions, "'When one is ailing, Philip, one wishes to be home.'" Philip shook his head. "A characteristically astute observation. Home *can* be a comfort when nothing else is."

Jason's gaze returned to Mariposa. Her coloring was still a touch alarming, and her focus was decidedly elsewhere. He meant to give her a moment to collect herself, to reach some level of calm.

"I spent a few days at Lampton House last week," he told Philip. "I suppose I needed a little of the comfort of home myself."

They both continually glanced in Mariposa's direction, though they had, by unspoken agreement, decided not to press her.

"Do you remember when we would play hide-and-seek at the Park and, inevitably, one of us would become ridiculously lost on that absurdly vast estate?" Philip asked. "There was nothing so comforting as the sight of that house after being upended."

Jason nodded. "I do remember, though I confess I'd not thought in those terms for many years now."

Philip laid a hand on his shoulder. "I think it is time you came home again. You have not spent more than a few days at a time at the Park since Father died. Ten years is too long to mourn that deeply."

Jason looked at his brother. How long had Philip known the reason for Jason's avoidance of his childhood home? Jason himself had only recently come to understand. "I think I will," Jason answered, nodding decisively.

Philip embraced him, honestly, sincerely embraced him. "It will be good to have you truly home again."

For perhaps the first time in a decade, Jason saw the brother he had once so idolized.

Philip stepped back a bit. "I believe I will go sit awhile with Sorrel." At the doorway, he turned back. "Oh, and I believe Cook has prepared her creamy potato soup to have with dinner. It's excellent." He slipped from the room.

"Those poor potatoes," a faint voice said, pulling Jason's eyes away from his brother and to Mariposa's face.

Relief nearly pulled a sigh from him. She looked a little better. Her expression was the tiniest bit less burdened.

Following her lead, Jason adopted a lighter tone. "It could be worse. It could be turnips."

"True." She offered a shaky smile. Pain remained in the depths of her eyes.

He sat beside her, touching her cheek with his hand. "I am so sorry you didn't find your family, Mariposa."

She did not immediately respond but seemed to be fighting against her own reaction to that disappointment. After a moment's struggle, a forced calm spread over her. How often had she been required to push aside her emotions, to clamp them down so she could move forward?

"To know they are safe from Bélanger, that is a relief."

And yet it wasn't the same as having them near or even know-ing what had become of them. "What will you do now?" he asked.

She hesitated, her face creased in thought. She sat up a little straighter. "I will tell Abuela that Bélanger is no longer a threat. And"—she squared her shoulders and stiffened her posture—"I will keep looking. So long as my family is lost, I must continue to search for them."

Chapter Twenty-Three

EVEN IN THE SUMMER, THE air in Scotland held a bite. Mariposa pulled her borrowed cloak more tightly around her shoulders. She likely felt the chill more than others, being accustomed to the warmer weather of the Continent.

After a nearly sleepless night, she needed a brisk walk to clear her mind. Her tears had dried in the dark hours of night but now threatened to spill over at any moment. Too much had happened and in far too quick a succession. She had found an aunt but not the rest of her family. The man she'd watched over her shoulder for these past months was dead. She knew not where to look nor how to explain her mother and brother's disappearance. She felt so very lost.

She stopped at the edge of a small sparkling brook not far from Philip's cottage. With a sigh, she leaned against the sturdy trunk of a tree and watched the water as it flowed over rocks and around bends in its journey farther downstream.

With her eyes closed, she could perfectly picture her younger brother. She had raised Santiago from the time he was six, being the only member of her family emotionally capable of doing so. She remembered him as he'd been then, so young, so trusting, and yet his beloved eyes so often filled with worry. How precious he was to her, a constant reminder of why she could not stop struggling to survive. He deserved a better life than one spent foraging for scraps and cowering in near-constant fear. She wanted so much more for him.

"Where could they be?" Mariposa whispered. She had concentrated so hard on locating her Thornton relatives that she had never stopped to truly ponder the possibility that Mamá and Santiago might not be with their relations. Mariposa slid to the ground, sitting with her back against the tree trunk, her knees bent, and her folded arms resting across them. She laid her head against her arms.

She had failed them. She had allowed her family to be separated with no means of reuniting them. A shaky breath preceded a sudden return of tears. She could not remember the last time she had cried as much as she had the past twenty-four hours.

Rather than fight the emotion, Mariposa simply let the tears fall. Her lungs heaved as she sobbed. Years of frustration and struggle and heartache surfaced. She was sinking, drowning in agony and loneliness. Since her father's death, she'd pushed herself relentlessly, but the exhaustion that had always lingered under the surface suddenly caught up with her.

She heard a slight rustling beside her but didn't look up. A hand rested lightly on her arm. She knew without even looking that it was Jason. With a gentleness that would have surprised her only weeks before, he eased her away from the tree enough to put an arm around her.

"I promised him, Jason." Sobs broke the words. "I promised Santiago I would always be with him, that he would not ever be forgotten. But I cannot find him. What if he is alone and afraid? He is only a little boy."

Jason did not offer empty words of reassurance but simply held her. Somehow he must have realized that was precisely what she needed most, to know she was not alone, that someone knew her agony and cared that she was suffering. "Tell me about him," he said.

The quiet invitation proved a lifeline. "Santiago is tall for his age," she said through sniffles and dripping tears. "Mamá says he has more of the Spaniard in him than I do. She says I take after my father and that is why I am so short."

Jason leaned his head against hers. "Shortness is an English trait, is it?"

"According to my mother. My father was shorter than she is. I take after him in more ways than being ridiculously tiny." Speaking of something other than her loss and sorrow helped calm her heart.

"In England, we have a term for ladies who are graceful, beautiful, and alluring, who also happen to be 'ridiculously tiny.'" He adjusted his position a little, settling her more comfortably in his arms.

Mariposa pressed her palms together and rested them against his chest, laying her head atop them. She could not recall ever feeling as safe as she did with him. She closed her eyes and lost herself in the rare moment of peace. "Is this term the English have coined a flattering one?"

"Indeed. The term is 'Pocket Venus,' and I assure you it is a high compliment."

She allowed her head to grow heavy against him as exhaustion took over. For more than six months, nay, for four years, she had struggled to rest, let alone sleep. Fear-fueled insomnia had been her constant companion. Why was it, then, that she could relax so entirely in Jason's embrace despite the crushing blows life had dealt her these past hours?

"How tall do you think Santiago is now?" she wondered aloud. "I think he may be nearly as tall as I am."

"That is not such a feat, my dear." A smile rang in his tone and added a tenderness to the endearment that warmed her heart. "But, yes, he is likely approaching your height and is a bit gangly and awkward, as growing boys often are."

"Were you gangly and awkward?" She smiled at the thought.

"Painfully so."

She felt him chuckle. Jason Jonquil presented such a pristine and perfect image to the world, a gentleman whose life was planned and executed down to the last detail. She'd seen such a different side of him these past days.

"I wish I could have met your father," she said. "Stanley spoke so fondly of him. He sounded wonderful."

"He was." Jason stroked her hair, the steady rhythm of it lulling her further into quiet relaxation. How she needed the restful moment. "I have never known a better gentleman or a better father. Every good thing I have done in my life I owe to his influence."

"Do you ever wonder, Jason, if your father would be proud of you?" she asked. "I think often of my papá and what he would think of the person I have become. I worry that he would be ashamed of me." The last few words shuddered out of her, even as tears sprang to her eyes once more.

"I know only a small portion of who you are and what you have accomplished, Mariposa," Jason said, his words slow and quiet. "But I can say with complete confidence that your father would be inordinately proud of all that you are."

"I want to believe that," she whispered. "If only he were here to tell me."

Jason's arm settled low around her, holding her comfortably close. "I have thought that of my own father many times and asked myself that same question."

Jason wondered if his father would be proud of him? How could he possibly doubt that? "Stanley spoke often of the good you have done," she said. "The many things I learned of your generosity are the reason I sought you out. You are a talented barrister, yes, but it was the goodness he spoke of that gave me confidence. Your papá would be so very proud of that."

"Where have you been these past years, Mari, when I have needed someone to tell me I was good enough?"

Mari. He'd spoken the shortened name like a Spaniard, with a soft *a* and a gentle *r*.

She smiled for the first time all day. "I very much like the way you called me Mari. I like having a pet name."

He adjusted a little, shifting his back against the tree. "Wait until you meet Caroline, Layton's daughter. She has a pet name for everyone. And I do mean *everyone*."

He held her in his arms, not rushing her or pressing her for conversation. Mariposa did not know how much time passed as they sat thus. The tension in her body dissipated. Her tears dried at last.

"I am falling asleep," she whispered. He likely had no idea how significant that was.

"Perhaps we should walk back to the house so you can sleep on a warm bed instead of the damp ground," Jason said.

"It would not be the first time."

He helped her to her feet. "Those days and that life are behind you now." He guided her, his arm securely tucked around her waist. She let her head fall against him as they walked.

"I still do not have my family," she said. "They are still lost to me."

"We have neither of us given up. We will keep searching."

Jason kept his arm about her all the way back to the house. Pain still resonated in the hollowest parts of her broken heart, but his support eased some of that ache. She could still believe her family would be found so long as he would help her look for them. He would stay with her, just as he'd promised so many times. And at last, at long last, she wouldn't be so alone.

At the doorway to her bedchamber, Jason laid a chaste kiss on her forehead. "Sleep well," he instructed gently.

Mariposa managed a nod before proceeding wearily to her bed, where she dropped fully clothed onto her mattress and fell deeply asleep.

Jason walked away from Mariposa's door, his mind and heart heavy. He had certainly seen women upset, crying, distraught. That happened in matters of the law. Never before, however, had a woman's suffering shaken him to his very core.

"He is just a little boy," Mariposa had cried, desperation breaking her voice. "I promised him."

Her brother's fate would eat away at her the rest of her life if she did not discover what had become of him. Jason wished he knew how to take that burden from her, but he was helpless. He had no better idea of where to look than she did. Yet how could he possibly stand idly by and watch her drown in such agony?

Surely there was some clue, some possibility they'd overlooked. Jason had ample experience unraveling complicated and seemingly impossible situations. Somehow he would make things right for her. He *would*.

"You realize," Philip said almost the moment Jason entered the drawing room, "you may very well have compromised Miss Thornton's reputation beyond repair by traveling all this way with her unchaperoned."

"We traveled as a lower-class married couple," Jason said. He had taken pains to protect Mariposa's good name. He did not mean to cause her greater difficulties than she already faced. "We gave false names and only disembarked at two stops. I took stock of the assembled crowd both times and saw not a single familiar face."

"Suppose by some twist of fate your flight becomes known?" Philip pressed. "What then?"

"Are you asking my intentions toward Miss Thornton?"

Philip laughed and shrugged. "Quite presumptuous, aren't I?"

"I would, of course, marry her if her good name were compromised," Jason said.

"And if it is not?"

"I think I would marry her anyway," Jason heard himself confess. His surprise at his own words must have shown. "Good heavens."

Philip chuckled. "Sneaks up on you, doesn't it?"

Jason nodded. Marry Mariposa? He'd thought to help her, to ease her suffering. But marry her? When had he come to that conclusion?

"I was top-over-tail in love with Sorrel before I even realized I *liked* her," Philip said, shaking his head amusedly. "She was probably far more perceptive."

Jason smiled at his brother. "I like Sorrel."

"And I like Mariposa," Philip said. "More than that, I like Mariposa's influence on you."

"She makes me want to be a better person, to look beyond myself," Jason answered, echoing Philip's words of the previous day.

"I have a feeling, brother"—Philip gave Jason a thump on the back as they made their way to chairs near a low-burning fire—"our wives are going to be good friends and terrifyingly efficient coconspirators."

"Do not be too precipitous," Jason warned. "I haven't so much as asked the lady. Lud, I didn't even know I was going to ask her until a moment ago."

"Then take some advice from your older, wiser sibling," Philip said with an air of feigned, overblown self-importance that Jason was finally able to find humorous. "Give her a chance to recover from her current despondency before posing the all-important question. Nothing destroys a well-versed offer of one's hand like a fit of hysterics."

Jason nodded. There was a great deal of wisdom in that. "I suppose I ought to ask someone's permission, though I don't know who. Mariposa is, for all intents and purposes, the head of her family." A thought occurred to him that made him chuckle. "Perhaps I should ask Stanley. He's the one who started all of this."

Philip didn't laugh along as Jason had expected. In an extremely somber tone, Philip asked, "Has Stanley written to you lately?"

"He hasn't," Jason answered, caught by the strain in Philip's voice.

"He has not sent word to me either. More worrisome still, Mater has not heard from him."

"Stanley hasn't written to Mater?" Jason was shocked. He couldn't imagine any of his brothers, least of all Stanley, who had always been very attentive to their mother's needs, neglecting to write to her when so far from home.

"He has not sent so much as a single word since being recalled to his regiment," Philip said.

"That is very unlike him," Jason said. Things Mariposa had said flashed through his mind. *He hates being a soldier. He has spent half a decade surrounded by death, and it is destroying his soul.* "Mariposa is concerned about him."

Philip looked Jason in the eye, his gaze unwavering and heavy. "I am more than concerned," Philip said. "I am deeply worried."

Chapter Twenty-Four

MARIPOSA FELT TERRIBLY CONSPICUOUS IN red. Unmarried ladies simply never wore such a deep, exotic color. Sorrel, however, had insisted that she borrow a gown to wear to dinner that evening. After three days of donning her most weatherworn and plain dress in the name of blending in, Mariposa had been rather easy to convince.

Though the dress was decidedly too long, it fit nicely otherwise. The wine color proved flattering. Perhaps if she ever married and were granted the privilege of wearing such colors in public, Mariposa would acquire a dress very much like this one.

Her cheeks likely darkened to match her gown when she stepped into the drawing room. Philip nodded in what appeared to be approval. Jason's expression, however, proved the most disconcerting. Something akin to disbelief mingled with shock on his face. Did she look so horrible? Or had she simply been so unappealing up until that moment that a flattering gown and the ministrations of Sorrel's maid had rendered a shockingly enormous difference? Neither possibility was pleasant.

Sorrel entered behind her. "Quit gawking, Jason, and walk the poor lady in to dinner."

Jason made his way directly to Mariposa's side. She hadn't felt so uncomfortable in his presence since the day she'd stepped into his office to confess her many lies.

"The dress is Sorrel's," she quickly admitted. "I didn't have anything appropriate to wear to dinner."

Jason didn't say anything.

Mariposa shifted uncertainly. Where she had once been indifferent toward Jason, she had come to long for his approval. If only he would say she looked pretty or that he was pleased to be in her company again. Anything would be better than the awkward silence between them.

"Sorrel was kind to let me borrow the dress." Mariposa could think of nothing else to say.

Jason's brows drew together, his expression not striking her as particularly pleased. "She ought to have chosen something else."

A lump formed in her throat, though she pushed it down. "You do not like it?"

He shook his head empathically. "I do not like it at all."

A gentleman who had caringly held a woman in his arms while speaking kind reassurances to her ought not to insinuate mere hours later that she looked hideous. No matter how true he might feel the sentiment was, it was cruel to actually speak it.

He had been so wonderful these past days. Why must he return to being cross and difficult?

She had kept her emotions under control for the better part of the afternoon. One less than complimentary comment from him and the stinging had returned to her eyes. "Blast you, Jason," she muttered. She refused to cry again. "*Con vuestro permiso,*" she offered her host and hostess. Head held high, she spun on her heel and made a quick retreat. She took the stairs swiftly, determined to reach her bedchamber, where the isolation would allow her a moment to reel in her agitation and growing despondency. She would have herself under control again before facing the world.

She'd only just reached the upstairs corridor when someone suddenly appeared in front of her. How in heaven's name had Jason arrived there before her? "How did you—?"

"Back stairs," he answered and swiftly spoke again, leaving her no opportunity for further comment. "Before you rage at me or cry or"—he looked at her with a wariness that bordered on panic—"or anything like that, let me explain."

His obvious conviction that she hovered on the edge of an emotional breakdown was nearly humorous enough to make her smile.

"I am a man," Jason said.

"Yes, I've noticed."

"Noticed, perhaps, but I do not think you completely comprehend the significance of that in this particular situation."

She took an unsteady breath, still too near to tears for any degree of stability.

Jason pressed on, his demeanor obviously the one he assumed when arguing in court, his hands clasped behind his back. He appeared properly somber and authoritative. "As a man, I am prone to say things that are universally misunderstood by women, *particularly* by women. Men say something, and at some point between our mouths and your ears, it twists around itself and transforms into something inexplicably insulting. We can't help ourselves. I am absolutely certain it is an inborn flaw."

"That is rather tragic." Mariposa retained enough of her sense of humor to manage an appropriately exaggerated response. Unfortunately, she also remained too overset by all that had happened to prevent her next breath from shaking with long held-back emotion.

Jason inched closer, eyeing her with palpable uncertainty. "The mere hint of tears, you understand, only makes the problem worse. We sense their approach and invariably panic. Not knowing what else to do, we generally begin talking again and are deeply in trouble in no time."

Mariposa felt like a pendulum swinging between amusement and despair. "You said you didn't like my dress."

Jason shook his head. "I never said I didn't like it."

"You most certainly did. You said, 'I do not like it at all.'"

Jason leaned against the wall near her. "But I didn't mean I didn't like it."

That made no sense. "I do not understand."

"My point exactly."

She stepped closer to him. "Then you do like it?"

He folded his arms across his chest. "That is not a simple yes or no question, Mariposa."

Now he was just being difficult. She propped her fists on her hips.

Jason shook his head. "Do not slaughter me. As I said, men can't help digging themselves into holes too deep for escape." He smiled at her, and she lost the last remaining bit of her heart to him. How could she possibly help herself? The high-in-the-instep Jason had all but disappeared. Though she did not always understand him, and he still at times ruffled her feathers, the Jason who had emerged from that staid exterior was inarguably lovable.

"Have I thanked you, Jason, for coming with me to Scotland?"

He kept smiling, leaning casually against the wall. The man was ridiculously handsome standing there as he was. "You have. Many times."

"I meant, have I thanked you *enough*? You have been a godsend. I cannot begin to imagine what I would have done without you, not only in the mail coach but here as well. After not finding my . . . my . . ."

He abruptly moved away from the wall and to within easy arms' reach of her. "I meant what I said about tears. You'll send me into a panic."

She meant to say something, a witty reply of some kind, but Jason lightly touched her face, and she found words entirely impossible. He held her face tenderly in his hand. Each breath caught in her throat. She was certain he was inching closer to her.

"Mariposa?"

Somehow she managed to push out a "Yes?"

"I . . ." The word trailed off even as he moved closer. Only a scant inch or two separated them.

His hand slid from her cheek to cup her chin at precisely the moment his other arm wrapped around her. Mariposa's pulse pounded hard in her neck, ears, and chest. Jason leaned toward her excruciatingly slowly. The moment seemed to stretch and pull as though each second became an hour. She stood as still as she could manage, all her thoughts focused on that instant in time, afraid if she so much as breathed, it would vanish.

Jason suddenly stopped with his lips a mere breath from hers. His posture grew instantly rigid. He dropped his arms to his sides. "What am I doing?" he muttered, his voice as quiet as a whisper.

Mariposa wanted to grab hold of him to keep him there. Even before he pulled away, she knew he would. He had meant to kiss her, but something had changed his mind.

"I'm sorry," was all he said before turning on his heels and walking away. He didn't entirely abandon her but stopped at the far end of the corridor, his back to her.

For a moment, Mariposa stood frozen in place, unsure of what had happened. She hesitantly moved closer to where he stood. "Jason?"

No answer came.

"Jason?" She spoke a little louder.

"I lost my head for a moment. I'm sorry."

He was sorry for nearly kissing her? Or sorry he hadn't? She could hear the strain in his voice but couldn't say what exactly had put it there. Maybe she'd been too forward or . . . or something. "Did I do something wrong?"

"No." The word sounded curt, his voice rigid. Though he would not admit it, he was obviously perturbed.

"If I did something to upset you, I am sorry."

He spun around and faced her, tension clearly written in every line of his face. "Blast it, Mariposa. Why must you constantly apologize? That's all you've done since leaving London. It makes a fellow feel so deucedly guilty all the time."

She hadn't seen that outburst coming. "You would rather I didn't apologize?"

"Not when you have nothing to apologize for."

"But you are angry with me," she said. "Does that not warrant an apology?"

"No, it does not." His taut jaw gave the words an edge.

"I do not understand you, Jason Jonquil." Her own frustration was beginning to bubble.

"My anger . . . anyone's anger with you is not your fault, Mariposa. You need never apologize for what is not your fault, just as you need never blame yourself when things happen for which you do not bear responsibility."

His admonition had merit, yet her experiences had taught her a different lesson. "Anger makes dangerous people more dangerous. Apologizing nullifies them."

"I am not dangerous."

"I know. I do." Now she felt "deucedly guilty." "Old habits do not die easily. I know no other way to respond when a person is angry with me."

"I am *not* angry with you." His voice had taken on something of a growl.

"Well, you certainly sound angry," she snapped.

"It's not you." He ran a hand through his hair, a gesture clearly indicative of his growing irritation but one she had never seen him employ before. Worse yet, he didn't look at her—his eyes shifted about as though he were determined to not so much as glance in her direction. "It's that ridiculous dress and that perfume and this blasted empty corridor."

"Do you wish me to leave?" She asked the question, though she feared the answer.

He nodded slowly and with emphasis. "Yes. I need you to leave."

His words sliced through her like a knife. Still, she knew how to retain her dignity even in the most harrowing of moments. She straightened her shoulders and assumed her most impassive expression. "Very well," she said. "You will be pleased to know I had planned to depart in the morning anyway. I will simply stay out of your path for the remainder of the evening."

He stood between her and the stairway. She did not know the house well enough to make her way to the back stairs he'd used. Leaving required she pass him. Mariposa kept her chin up and her posture confident. She refused to fall apart, no matter how many pieces her heart had broken into.

She forced herself to move with a fluidity that belied her growing desire to flee with all possible speed. As she passed the place where he stood, she kept her gaze forward, not looking at him, just as he had worked so hard not to look at her. A hand on her arm, however, prevented her from passing. She pointedly ignored the frisson of awareness that accompanied his gentle but firm touch.

"You are leaving?" His voice held equal parts surprise and concern.

How utterly confusing could one man be? He could not insist that she go in one breath and then sound perplexed at her departure with the next. "In the morning." She kept it at that. Long, drawn-out speeches tended to break down her defenses when she felt as painfully vulnerable as she did in that moment.

"When did you decide this?"

He did not release her arm, nor did she turn back to look at him. She simply couldn't. Her heart was breaking, her mind spinning with his constant contradictions.

"Earlier today," she said. "Too much has happened, too much disappointment and upheaval." She took a breath to calm herself. "When a person has been through so much, home beckons with increasing urgency."

"Home?"

"Well, London. That is the closest I have to a home now."

His hand slipped away from her arm. She hazarded a glance in his direction and found him with brows creased in apparent thought. His distant expression told her she'd been all but forgotten already.

"As I said, I will be leaving tomorrow, so you need not worry about being further assaulted by my ridiculous dress or putrid perfume or—"

He took a single step, placing himself directly in front her. "I want you to try very hard not to misunderstand this. It is rather important, in fact, that you don't." He brushed his fingers gently along her cheek.

How many ways could he possibly torture her in a single conversation? Her heart picked up pace even as she told it quite firmly not to get its hopes up. As usual, her heart paid little attention to her.

"I have discovered this evening that an empty corridor is not the wisest place for two people to be when you are one of those people and I happen to be the other. The dress you have chosen is, in a word, stunning. And your perfume is intoxicating. And the temptation to kiss you in this isolated and wholly private location is, as I have demonstrated once already, too great to resist. Yet doing so flies in the face of everything I have been taught about decorum and propriety and gentlemanly behavior. I have my failings, but being an honorless cad is not one of them."

How his admission lightened her heart! "One would almost think you don't find me entirely repulsive, Jason."

He smiled a touch crookedly as he stepped back. "Fishing for compliments?"

With a smile of her own, she said, "Perhaps a little."

"Then I will tell you that I do not, in fact, find you entirely repulsive."

Her smile grew at the welcome show of levity. "That was not precisely what I had in mind."

"There is a time and a place for flowery words," Jason said.

Mariposa sighed. "And an empty corridor is not that time nor place."

He took hold of the doorknob leading to the bedchamber directly behind him, his bedchamber, in fact. "I'll ask you to please give my excuses to my brother and sister-in-law. I will not be joining them for dinner."

"But—"

"I need to pack."

"Pack?" He hadn't said anything about leaving. Did he intend to go with her in the morning? Perhaps he felt the need to see her home.

"And"—his determined look cut off anything further she might have said—"I need you to promise me you will not take the mail coach back home but will wait a couple of days and return with Philip and Sorrel. They can take you to the Park to collect Abuela and see to it that you have a proper carriage and footmen to return you to London."

For a moment, she could not seem to sort his words out. She was to wait a few days. But he was still leaving in the morning? "You are not waiting?"

He shook his head. "I have some business awaiting me that cannot be further delayed."

Of course. He likely had clients he'd neglected in order to protect her from her own madcap scheme. That explanation felt far safer than assigning his precipitous departure to a lack of desire to spend several days in a carriage with her. It also rang far more true. He had said he did not dislike her. In fact, she felt rather certain he liked her quite a lot.

He half sighed, half chuckled. "You wear a very particular expression on your face every time you are debating over which dire explanation lies behind something I have said to you."

She wouldn't have to argue with herself so often if he weren't so very confusing.

Jason reached out and took hold of her hand, raising it to his lips without moving so much as an inch closer to her. "Yesterday you said you trusted me. I hope you meant that."

"I do not trust easily."

"I know." He let her hand slip from his. "All I ask is that you try."

She nodded.

"Farewell, then," he said. "For now."

"*Ve con dios,*" she answered quietly.

He closed his door. She brushed her cheek with the back of her hand, remembering all too vividly the light kiss he'd placed there. She did not know with complete certainty why he was leaving so suddenly, but she would do her utmost to trust him.

Chapter Twenty-Five

JASON AROSE EARLY THE NEXT morning, intent on beginning his journey as quickly as possible. Stepping inside the small dining parlor where every meal was served in this small house, he found he was not the first to seek out his morning meal. He gave his brother a quick nod before taking up a plate and beginning to fill it from the sideboard.

"For a dandy, you keep very early hours."

Philip's eyes opened wide, and he took in a sharp breath. "If word of this reaches Town, my reputation will be in tatters."

Jason would have rankled at the reaction only a few days earlier. Mater had encouraged him to discover the person his brother was beneath the mask of frivolity he wore. "You might both be surprised by what you discover," she had said. Jason looked forward to telling her how very right she had been.

Philip pushed his empty plate aside but did not move to leave. "Mariposa told us last evening that you are leaving us this morning."

"Yes." Jason took a seat at the table. "I have clients in need of my presence."

Philip leaned back in his chair. "I have been a spy for years, Jason. I know when someone is lying to me."

"Father once said something similar to me when I attempted to tell him a fib." Jason smiled to himself at the memory. "'I've spent years with your older brothers,' he said. 'I can sort out when one of you is lying.'"

"Lud, he certainly could. Nothing slipped past him."

Jason pointed at Philip with his fork. "The Jonquil Freers of Prisoners managed that a few times."

Philip chuckled quietly. "We had some larks, didn't we? Those were good years."

Snippets of his childhood swam through his thoughts. Memories of his father, which he'd worked so hard to keep tucked away, joined the others. This time, however, they brought comfort instead of strictly pain.

"Where are you actually going when you leave here today?" Philip pressed.

"I have a theory about Mari's family." Jason pushed the food around his plate, his mind spinning once more. "I don't know if I am right or even leaning in the right direction, but I need to follow it through."

"You know where they might be?"

He shook his head. "It is only a theory, and a thin one at that, but I have to pursue it."

"Does she know?"

Jason had debated that aspect of the situation for long hours the night before. "I have seen her hopes dashed and her heart broken. If this proves to be yet another dead end, it will only bring her more pain."

"Her ability to detect a lie is likely as keen as mine, having spent years as a spy as well. How do you mean to explain your absence to her?"

That had been tricky. "I told her I had some important business to attend to, and I asked her to trust me."

"Children of war do not trust easily."

Children of war. How heartbreakingly apt. "I know she struggles to have faith in people. She is trying, though, and she is doing better."

"You have been good for her and her for you." Philip looked genuinely pleased. "I wish you all the best, Jason, both in your courtship and your search for her family."

"Thank you."

"If there is anything I can do to help, please ask."

Jason set down his fork. "As a matter of fact, there is."

✹

"This is Westerthon, Mr. Jonquil." Philip's coachman did not look overly impressed with the tiny hamlet.

Jason, however, was grateful to find the place so minuscule. His search would be far simpler that way.

"Thank you, John."

The coachman tipped his hat.

"And, John, be careful during your drive to Nottinghamshire. You will be carrying three people who are very important to me."

John nodded. "You 'ave my solemn vow, sir."

"And have a safe journey back to Haddington."

John climbed back onto the carriage and set the horses in motion once more. Jason turned his attention to the small collection of tightly packed houses. Which was the one he was looking for?

He stopped a man passing nearby. "I am looking for the Old Mill House."

He was forthwith provided with odd but detailed directions. Jason followed them with his characteristic precision and soon found himself at the door of a small building with a stationary waterwheel attached to one side. He pulled a folded piece of paper from his pocket, checking once more that the Old Mill House was indeed his destination.

He knocked, and a moment later, the door opened.

His presence received a look of shock followed by a gasped, "Monsieur."

"Good afternoon, Jean," Jason said.

"You look very different." Jean eyed him with curiosity. "You sound very different as well."

"Yes, well, there is a lot I suspect Mariposa did not tell you during our journey, things I did not tell you either."

Jean held the door and motioned him inside. "I know what it is to have secrets," he said. "I do not begrudge that necessity in others who have survived horrors."

"I am very pleased to hear that"—Jason did not continue past the small entry but turned to face the Frenchman—"because Mariposa needs our help."

Chapter Twenty-Six

"So help me, Philip, if you do not stop coddling me, I will subject you to a closer acquaintance with my walking stick."

If Mariposa had learned anything about Sorrel over their first day of southward travel, it was that Lady Lampton bristled at nothing so much as people making a fuss over her, however justified their concerns might be. Yet there was so much vulnerability behind her protests that the only possible response was to feel ever more pained for her.

Philip, however, was more than adept at navigating that particular quagmire. "I am actually quite fond of your walking stick, my dear," he said, sitting beside his wife in the private parlor he had hired at the public inn where they would be breaking their journey for the night. "After all, we did first meet when you accused me of stealing it."

"You know perfectly well you did the accusing, and it was your walking stick you suspected me of pilfering."

Philip's brows pulled downward. He tapped a single finger against his chin. "I do not remember it that way at all."

Sorrel's expression lightened a bit, and some of the pain in her posture seemed to diminish. The journey had been a difficult one for her, recovering as she was from such a difficult surgery. "You likely also don't remember that you were insufferable," she said.

"It's pronounced 'irresistible.'"

Sorrel slowly smiled, even as she shook her head. "Actually, I suspect it is pronounced 'impossible.'"

Philip slipped his hand around hers. "I have heard a rumor that you are very fond of 'impossible.'"

"I am inordinately fond of 'impossible.'" Sorrel tipped her head to one side, the look one of subtle but unmistakable flirtation.

"Would the two of you prefer that I leave?" Mariposa acted as though she meant to stand.

Philip simply laughed. "Sit, sit. We'll behave. *I* will, at the very least."

"Do not believe him, Mariposa. He has never behaved a day in his life."

These two were blessedly diverting. Despite her heavy heart and the weight of uncertainty, Mariposa had felt lighter during their journey than she would have believed possible.

Their meal was humble but filling. The parlor contained a fainting couch, one faded with age but well cared for. Sorrel was able to lie down, something for which she appeared incredibly grateful. Philip occupied an armchair near her. Mariposa opted for a spindle-backed chair near the fire, her blood still having not adjusted to the cold air of England.

"I do not know what your plans are, Mariposa," Sorrel said, "but I hope you realize you and your grandmother are most welcome to remain at the Park for as long as you wish."

What are my plans? Tension knotted her stomach. She had no plans. She, who had devised strategies and made preparations for every imaginable situation, hadn't the slightest idea what to do next.

"I haven't given up the search for my family." Searching for her family had consumed every thought these past months. Keeping her family safe had occupied every moment of her life for years. "My disappointment at not finding my mother and brother at Mrs. Douglas's home clouded my judgment for a time. Not until last evening did I realize that she had given me a bit of valuable information. The estate my brother has inherited from our uncle would be the family seat. It is the home my father would have grown up in. My mother likely would have thought of Norfolk when thinking of my father's home and family. That is likely where she would have gone." Her tone of conviction died quickly, however. "I will send a letter and inquire as to whether or not they are there."

"Send a letter?" Philip sat with his hands casually steepled in front of him, watching her with an unmistakable intelligence. His foppish persona must have been incredibly thorough for anyone to ever have believed he was a dolt. "You do not mean to make the journey yourself?"

"Mrs. Douglas indicated that the Thornton solicitor has been attempting to locate my family for a year now. Had my mother and brother arrived unannounced, the estate manager or the butler or any number of neighbors would have sent word." Her spirits drooped at having to make the admission out loud. "Though I hope I am wrong, I do not believe they are actually there."

"Receiving that information by way of a messenger would be far less painful than seeing the truth of it in person." Philip spoke as one who understood the pain of repeated loss. "And if they are not there, what do you mean to do then?"

"I will find new information . . . somehow." She rose and began pacing a small circuit in front of the fireplace. "I have been gathering information for years, information no one else was able to find. I am good at it. I will simply do that again."

She met Philip's gaze. His was an expression of deepest empathy. "Life is not a war. You cannot navigate it the same way. For a soldier, often the most difficult battle is the one that cannot be fought."

Mariposa eyed him again, unsure what he meant. "I am not a soldier."

"Well, no, not in the truest sense of the word," he said. "But you have spent years of your life shouldering the burden of the battles around you. You have learned that the only way to survive is to fight, and you've learned to be good at it. Fighting has saved you and your family. But the battle stretching out before you now is vastly different from any other you've known."

His words rang painfully true. Her style of "fighting"—assuming personas, telling half-truths, slipping in and out of locations, facing down the dangers of enemy soldiers and violent spies—had kept them all alive throughout the years of warfare and had kept her going during this fruitless search for her family. She had focused so exclusively on preparing to face Bélanger, and it all had ended with no confrontation, no battle, no fight for survival. There was no immediate threat and no clear direction for moving forward.

She shook her head, pacing ever faster. She hadn't allowed herself to think about this overly much. Still not knowing where her family was had dealt her a blow, but not having the least idea of how to proceed entirely upended her.

"My father died when I was nineteen years old and ill-prepared to shoulder the burden of my family's well-being." Philip spoke to her, she assumed. "I did everything I could for my mother and brothers, protected them in any way I could, though I often fell short. When Stanley joined the army in the middle of a war, I was terrified. I couldn't bear the thought of losing my brother, but I didn't know what I could possibly do to prevent that. I took on the role of spy in order to help end the conflict early and bring him home safely. I changed my entire life to make that possible. I assumed a façade that embarrassed my family and undermined my own standing in Society, alienating myself from most of my one-time friends. But I was fighting a battle, you understand. I was confronting the enemy."

She understood that perfectly.

"But in time, that endless fight began changing me. The mask I wore grew comfortable until the line between the person I was and the person I pretended to be became all too blurred. It was my battle weapon, and I didn't know how to stop fighting."

Mariposa pressed her hand over the ache in her heart. If she had stopped fighting, she would have died. All her family would have died. What choice did she have but to fight in her own way?

"At the end of last year, I decided it was time for me to drop my weapons. Napoleon was in exile. Stanley was home. The battle, it seemed, was over." Philip sat forward on his chair, his elbows resting on his legs, his air entirely devoid of dandyism. "I ought to have felt relief or some sense of accomplishment. Instead, I felt lost. But putting my mask back on and playing the dandy for the world was no longer helpful. I couldn't simply take up my weapons and charge the enemy because there wasn't one."

Just as Bélanger was no longer her enemy and she was no longer living in close proximity to the battlegrounds of the Continental war. How did she defeat an enemy she could not identify?

"My mother and brothers weren't facing a despot and his armies," Philip continued. "They were struggling with life and all of its cruelty and complications. They didn't need Philip the spy; they needed Philip, their son and brother. They didn't need me to fight their battles; they needed me to walk beside them."

Abuela needs me to do that as well. She had, after all, endured the death of her husband, son-in-law, and grandson, and she too was mourning the loss of her daughter and only remaining grandson. Mariposa's grief was shared, but they had never truly mourned. There had never been time or the freedom to do so.

"You spent the remnants of your childhood struggling to survive," Philip said. "I suspect you never learned how to live."

"Did you?" she asked.

His smile was tender as his gaze fell on his sleeping wife. "I am beginning to."

"How did you begin?" She was too overwhelmed and too lost to know even that.

"Before you can learn to live the life you were meant to live, you need to discover the person you were meant to be."

She let out a long, tension-relieving breath. "I need to figure out who I am and what I want in life."

Philip nodded. "You have more to offer than your ability to fight and survive, but you need to see that. You need to know that. It won't always be easy, but in the end, it is the only way."

That, then, would be her next campaign—making the acquaintance of the person she was meant to be.

Chapter Twenty-Seven

JASON STOOD IN A VAST field, awed by the seemingly endless countryside. He had long since shed his coat—a lifetime in England had ill-prepared him for the humid heat of Spain in the early summer.

He pulled his gaze away from the landscape long enough to glance at his traveling companion. Jean had proven invaluable. The man knew the area and the language. Jason knew neither.

"Looking around," Jean said, "one struggles to believe that a mere four years ago, not far distant, thousands lay dead and dying."

Jason tried to shut out the image Jean had painted. Mariposa had lived here, then, or very nearby. She would have seen those thousands, would likely have heard their cries.

"Badajoz," Jean continued, "sits a little farther still." He shook his head, his eyes heavy with sadness. "The suffering there, I understand, was unspeakable on all sides of this war. An entire trail of loss and heartbreak winds its way through these countries." He sighed, and Jason heard years of sorrow in the sound. "War exacts such a heavy toll."

Jason had come to understand that over the past weeks. The realization made him worry ever more for Stanley. What price was he paying?

Jean thumped him on the back, a gesture he had utilized many times since their departure from England a week earlier whenever he noticed Jason's spirits flagging. "We are but a mile or so from Albuera," he said. "Prado Verde we know to be nearby."

Jason nodded. Prado Verde was Mariposa's childhood home. The odds were highly stacked against the possibility of discovering clues there about Mariposa's mother and brother, but Jason could think of nowhere else to look. As Philip had said of Sorrel, Jason could not bear to see the pain in Mariposa's eyes any longer. He'd sworn to himself that he would do everything in his power to find her family.

"Our wisest course of action would be to find someone local of whom we might ask directions." Jean's reasoning was sound, though Jason did not feel entirely confident in the outcome of his approach.

"After all that has happened," Jason said, "do you think the locals will be very forthcoming with two strangers, one of whom does not even speak their language?"

Jean wiped at a trickle of sweat on his forehead. "To that list of shortcomings, you must add my 'unbearable accent,' as your Mariposa described it."

Jason chuckled at the memory. "So we may be doomed from the start?"

"No endeavor motivated by love is ever entirely doomed."

They'd had far too many hours together onboard Philip's yacht and in rickety hired carriages for personal conversational topics to have been entirely avoided. Jason had learned of Jean's late wife and the stillborn child she'd died delivering. In turn, Jason had confessed his inability to entirely overcome the loss of his father. He hadn't needed to admit to his feelings for Mariposa. Jean had ascertained as much during their ride on the mail coach.

They walked in companionable silence. Jean whacked at the tall grass with a stick he'd found along the way. Jason took in the vast expanse of open country and tried to picture Mariposa there as a child.

"She was like a butterfly, light and soaring," Abuela had said.

Jason had seen hints of that in Mariposa. He wanted her to feel that way always. She ought to live a life in which she felt safe enough to no longer hide behind masks and half-truths. He wanted her to be free again.

A full quarter hour passed without a house or barn in sight. Just when Jason began to wonder how far from civilization they truly were, a bend in the road revealed a farmhouse not too far distant.

"I will make our inquiries," Jean said.

Jason accompanied him to the front step, but when a tired and suspicious-looking woman opened the door, he left the entirety of the conversation to Jean. His French-influenced Spanish did little to lessen her wariness.

Convince her, Jean. We need to find Prado Verde.

A few more exchanges conducted entirely in Spanish led to a reluctant gesture up the road. Jean copied it and asked her something. She answered, then quickly closed the door.

"I understood not a word of that," Jason said.

"Your Mariposa will wish to hear Spanish from time to time. I will be happy to teach you a word or two."

"I will accept that offer. First, though, did our guarded señora offer any useful information?"

Jean nodded as he stepped away from the humble dwelling. "She says that we must continue on this road until we reach a very large tree. At that tree will be a wide path leading through a meadow. At the end of that path will be a tall stone wall. Behind the wall is Prado Verde."

Jason was impressed. "That is a great deal of useful information."

"It seems my suggestion to ask of the locals was a good one." Jean gave him a look of feigned haughtiness—one with which Jason had become incredibly familiar. The older Frenchman had shown himself to be an enjoyable companion. He had a bouyant and optimistic view of life and the world despite his tragic history, and his was a sense of humor that never failed to lighten any situation.

"We were going in the right direction after all." Jason felt some relief at that. Despite having planned the journey as much as possible, this last stage of it was both the most crucial and most complicated. The Spanish countryside had not recovered from the war. Accommodations were nearly unheard of, and many once-proud houses no longer stood, their resident families long since fled.

But Jean had known how to reach Albuera, and they knew Prado Verde sat near enough to that city to have headquartered a portion of the British army.

They passed a barn a few minutes later, and the directions they had received were confirmed.

"We are close, Jason," Jean said as they continued onward. "I am certain of it."

"Close, yes. But will we find anything beyond that wall other than an abandoned estate?"

Jean slapped a hand on his back. "You must have faith, *mon ami.*"

Somewhere in the distance, birdsong echoed. A breeze picked up. How idyllic the scene was. Mariposa might find some peace there once the war was finally over. Of course, that meant she would leave England, an eventuality he was not yet ready to consider.

"How long have you been in love with Mariposa?" Jean asked without preamble. They had become such swift friends that the question did not at all feel prying or presumptuous.

"I honestly have no idea." Jason picked a long stem of grass. He vaguely remembered using grass as a whistle in his childhood. The time he'd spent with Philip and his conversation with Mater weeks earlier had kept those almost-forgotten moments fresh in his memory of late. "I did not feel it coming on by degrees. Rather, in a sudden moment of clarity, I simply realized I couldn't live without her, that her happiness had become paramount."

"Not the most comfortable of notions, is it?" A marked degree of empathy accompanied those words.

"Not comfortable in the least." And yet it wasn't miserable either. "Ours was not the easiest of beginnings. This was not at all the outcome I had expected."

"My wife and I began much the same way." Whenever Jean spoke of his late wife, a poignant mixture of pleasure and pain entered his expression. "We were employed in the same home, I as tutor for the sons of the house and she as governess for the daughters. She found me quite lacking in my post. I thought her overly proud and possessing too high an opinion of herself."

Jason chuckled. "That is not the most promising of beginnings." He tied his stem of grass into interlocking circles, just as Mater had always done when the two of them had sat on the banks of the Trent eating pilfered ginger biscuits and talking at length on any number of subjects. Whether the contentment he felt beneath the uncertainty of this search stemmed from the pleasant companionship of his new friend or the inherent beauty of his surroundings or the inevitable influence of love, he couldn't say. But something had changed in him.

"It is not the beginnings that matter, Jason, neither the endings, but all the many moments in between." Jean, Jason had discovered, was something of an amateur philosopher.

Though Jean could not have yet reached his fiftieth birthday, Jason could not help thinking of him, to some degree, in a fatherly role. He offered advice and insight and support that Father would have had he been there to do so.

"The degree to which my wife and I disliked each other on the day we met did not come close to matching the love we felt on the day we were parted," Jean said. "The two were not even comparable."

"If you could go back to that first day and live it again, give yourself the chance to not misjudge her," Jason asked, "would you?"

Jean did not immediately answer. His lips pressed together, and he swallowed with some difficulty. The usually unflappable man struggled a moment against a visible surge of emotion. When he spoke, his words were quieter, heavier, and the slightest bit broken. "If I could relive any day with her, any at all, I would without hesitation. I think that is why I was so frustrated with you in that mail coach. Watching the two of you was like seeing my Elizabeth and I all over again. You had everything within your reach, and you didn't even know it."

Jason tossed his grass chain out into the field beside them. "I didn't know it," he acknowledged. "I had no idea I was in love with her."

"And," Jean added, "no idea she was in love with you."

Jason wanted to believe that. He held out some hope, but Mariposa had never said the words. Until she did, he couldn't be certain.

"Would you relive that first day you met Mariposa?" Jean asked.

"The first several," Jason said. "I thoroughly misjudged her. The opportunity to rectify that mistake is more than tempting. If I could undo that, I would."

"Her lies no longer bother you?"

Jason shook his head. "I will always value honesty, but she taught me to not be so quick to condemn."

"The very best of relationships encourage us to be better than we are, to become more."

Mariposa had most certainly done that for him.

Jean motioned ahead. "I believe that is the very large tree we are searching for."

There was, in fact, a tree far taller and wider than any of the others growing directly at the side of the road they walked on. And as predicted, a path, smaller than the road they were on but wide enough to accommodate a carriage, turned off the road directly beside the tree.

"Shall we see if we find a meadow down this path a bit?" Jason suggested.

"*Oui.*"

Just as they were told by their cautious guide, the path led to a wide, open meadow. A tiny voice carried on the breeze—not spoken words but a lilting song.

"Do you hear that?" Jason looked around in all directions, attempting to locate the source.

"A child, I would guess."

Jason agreed. The voice definitely belonged to someone young, though where that person might be remained a mystery. "How is it that we are surrounded by a meadow and can see for some distance yet can hear someone we cannot see?"

"The vagaries of fate, my friend." Jean stopped on the path and narrowed his eyes as he scanned the surrounding countryside. "If I am not mistaken, we are searching for someone small, perhaps easily hidden."

Jason's ears perked as the song continued. The tune was unexpectedly familiar. After a few bars, he recognized it. He caught the flow of lyrics and began stumblingly and quietly singing along. "We sing, and we roar, and we drink and call for more and make more noise than twenty can." Jason shook his head in amazement. "Though the lyrics are hard to understand with such a heavy accent, I know that song. I've heard former soldiers sing it. Stanley himself did on occasion."

"I would guess, then, whoever our songbird is, the child was likely here at the time of Albuera and heard the British soldiers singing their ditties." Jean's search became ever more determined. "The child would be that much more likely to know the location of Prado Verde, even if it has been abandoned for years."

Jason could see nothing around them except grass and the occasional tree. "But how do we locate the slippery fellow?"

"Sing," Jean said.

"*Sing?*"

Jean nodded, still searching for their serenader. "Perhaps if he hears you singing, his curiosity will bring him out of hiding."

"It isn't the most appropriate of songs."

The look he received clearly communicated Jean's annoyance at the pitiful objection.

Jason groaned in defeat and, in a voice far louder than it was refined, sang out. "I am the king and prince of drinkers . . ."

Jean laughed out loud.

Jason continued with gusto, hoping the embarrassing interlude would prove beneficial. "Ranting, roaring, rattling boys . . ." He searched as he sang. Before he'd even completed the brief chorus, a head popped up from around the back side of a thick-trunked tree.

"Keep singing," Jean instructed in a low voice.

"We despise your sullen thinkers." His voice broke as he reached for the high note. He was certain he saw the little imp laugh. "'And fill the tavern with our noise.'"

A high but confident voice joined in with the nonsensical refrain that followed. "We sing, and we roar, and we drink and call for more and make more noise than twenty—"

The boy must have been struck in that moment with the realization that the men with whom he sang, albeit at a distance, were strangers. He stopped abruptly, then turned and ran.

Jean shouted something after him in Spanish. Whatever he said worked. The boy stopped and turned back, eyeing them cautiously.

Jason kept his mouth shut and let Jean do the negotiating. He recognized only a few words, among them *Prado Verde* and *sí.*

Jean leaned closer to Jason and said, "The boy says we are very near Prado Verde."

"The locals have been very helpful," Jason acknowledged.

"He also warned us it has been empty forever."

Jason's confidence flagged significantly. "Forever?"

Jean shrugged. "It likely seems that way to him."

They followed the lad at a distance of several paces, something the boy seemed to insist upon. The child could not have been much older than ten, perhaps eleven years old. He wore clothing little better than rags. Dirt covered every visible inch of him. His midnight-black hair stuck out in every direction. Jason had seen the boy's English counterparts on every corner in London. The world had far too many children with no one to look out for them.

As they trailed the boy across a field, he began whistling. Jason listened a moment, then smiled. His smile quickly gave way to a laugh.

"I take it you recognize this tune as well?" Jean asked.

"Whoever is responsible for that boy's musical education ought to be whipped."

"Another inappropriate song, then?"

Jason chuckled. "To listen to his repertoire, one would think the boy was a drunkard."

"And we are following him around the Spanish countryside." Jean looked exaggeratedly horrified. "We ought to have limited our guides to wary farm women and men working in their barns."

"If you had told me six weeks ago that I would be following anyone around the Spanish countryside, I'd have thought you mad."

Jean sighed and grinned. "But that, my friend, is what love does to a man."

"Undermines his sanity?"

"Absolutely, monsieur. 'Tis a sweet madness indeed."

Chapter Twenty-Eight

"This 'ere's Conway, late of the infantry. He spent his childhood in the country and is keen to go back."

Mariposa wrote down the information Black shared with her. He had been invaluable in the work she was doing. Philip's admonition had remained with her long after she had returned with Abuela to London. She needed to discover who she was and what she meant to do with her life.

Stepping inside her rented London house and seeing Black there, as well as Will, she'd had a sudden burst of insight. She knew firsthand the toll of war, and she had seen far too many of England's soldiers forgotten and neglected on the streets of London. Papá had willed her an income sufficient for her and Abuela's comfort. The unexpected boon from her late Uncle Robert gave her the ability to do something more.

"Conway," she said, attempting to set the nervous man at ease with a reassuring smile. "I know of an estate in Shropshire in need of an assistant gamekeeper. Do you have any experience with animals?"

Conway nodded eagerly. "Me grandfather was a gamekeeper. Took me along on his walks over the fine estate where he worked."

Mariposa loved that these arrangements fell so nicely into place. "We will provide you with the funds to reach your destination. The rest will depend upon you."

"I ain't afraid to work," he told her. "And I'll do anything not to sleep on the street anymore."

Over the past two weeks, she had heard the same thing again and again from men who had placed their very lives on the line only to return home to poverty and hopelessness. Mariposa had not entirely overcome her struggles. The war still haunted her, and she yet grappled with feelings of failure, but she was finding some peace in offering hope to others who had lived through similar horrors.

She sent them each off to their new lives with her best wishes, with encouragement, and with the request that should they meet a dark-haired woman or brown-eyed boy with the name of Thornton, they should send word back to her. She could help and change lives. She could give meaning to her survival of the conflict. Perhaps in time her efforts would also help her find her family. As she had feared, her mother and brother were not at Thornton Manor in Norfolk. They never had been. She had no idea where else to look for them.

Mr. Jones, a man of business recommended to her by Philip, made note of the arrangements she wished put in place for Conway. The one-time soldier was summoned by Hansen, Jason's kindhearted and invaluable secretary, who, upon hearing of Mariposa's endeavors, had volunteered his own time to help. He would explain to those who would be traveling how they would make their journey, whom to ask for when they arrived at their new place of employment, and the many other things they needed to know.

"Conway was the last for today," Black said. "Heaven knows there'll be plenty enough more by next week."

There would, she feared, always be more.

Abuela shuffled over to Conway, whom she'd not met, and lovingly patted his cheek. She had embraced Mariposa's endeavor with a tender compassion. None of their soldiers ever left feeling anything less than cared about and valued.

During these weekly arrangements, Mariposa often thought about Stanley Jonquil and the despair she had seen in his eyes. How she hoped someone was showing him compassion and reminding him that he was loved.

It was, however, Jason who most occupied her thoughts. She had not seen nor heard from him in the three weeks since he had abruptly left Scotland. Not a single word had come from him, no note saying he regretted not being able to call on her, no explanation of his continued absence. Hansen had indicated that Jason had not, in fact, returned to London, that he had not been in his office in more than a month. He had made arrangements for his colleagues to see to his clients, but no one seemed to know when he would be back.

Just as she'd sworn to Jason, Mariposa was doing her utmost to trust him. She told herself his absence had a reasonable explanation, that he hadn't forgotten her or decided she wasn't worth his time or attention. She tried very hard to have faith in the strength of his word and, much to her surprise, was not struggling as much as she once had.

Perhaps she was beginning to heal.

"Thank you for your help, Mr. Jones. As always."

He neatly stacked his papers. "It is my pleasure to honor my brother's memory by helping those who fought as well."

Mr. Jones had lost a brother in the war. Mariposa had learned of loss in Hansen's family as well. The decades of strife had left few families unaffected.

Abuela sat beside Mariposa at the parlor table. She held out a folded missive. "This—it is for you."

Mariposa hesitated. "Do you suppose this letter contains bad news? The previous one certainly did." It had brought word that her last remaining hint as to her family's whereabouts had proven fruitless.

Abuela shrugged in the customary way.

Mariposa took the letter, curious. When she had first come to England, the arrival of an unexpected note or letter had struck fear deep in her heart. That she now felt intrigued rather than scared stood as a firm testament that life had indeed changed.

"It is a dinner invitation," she told Abuela after reading the missive's contents. "A dinner to be held tonight." She allowed her excitement to bubble over into a grin. "At Lampton House."

"Jasón is returned?"

She looked over the brief invitation once more. "There are few details. A small family dinner at Lampton House. That is all it says."

"Do you wish to go?" Abuela asked her.

"I do." She did not even have to ponder. If there was any chance Jason was there, she very much wished to go.

Abuela smiled at her. "Then we will go. And we will wish very much for your *amor* to be there."

Mariposa had seldom been so nervous. Black grinned as she descended the stairs, and she returned his smile with a tremulous one of her own. Abuela had produced, seemingly from nowhere, a gorgeous gown, white with a sheer red overdress, the color beneath rendering the color above less scandalous. Mariposa felt beautiful.

She stepped into the entryway only to find Jason himself standing there waiting for her. Mariposa's heart simply halted, stunned into silence.

And then he smiled. "Good heavens, Mari. I have missed you."

It was quite the most wonderful thing he could have said. She intended to return the favor and say something tender and sentimental. Instead, she blurted, "You look tired."

He silently chuckled. "I imagine I look tired because I *am* tired."

"Are you ill?" The possibility immediately struck fear into her heart. Was something wrong? Did he need a doctor? A tisane?

Jason took her hand and raised it to his lips. "I am not ill. I have simply had a great deal of work to do lately."

"Oh." Mariposa knew her discouragement surfaced in her voice. All those weeks, his work had kept him away? That couldn't be correct. Hansen's report belied that explanation. Business away from London, perhaps?

"Now you think you have discovered my priorities, don't you?" His thumb caressed the back of her hand, sending shivers up her arm. "Two months ago, you would have been correct. My career occupied my every moment and nearly every thought. Then a lovely young lady came into my life and nothing has been the same since."

"I don't believe *lovely* was the word you used at the time."

Jason's hand brushed along her jaw. "It ought to have been."

She leaned into his caress. "I have missed you as well."

His hand still holding her chin, Jason kissed her cheek. He stayed there, his face nearly touching hers.

Mariposa took in the spicy scent of him. How had she lived so long without this man?

He sighed her name, and she melted. Jason shifted, and his lips hovered over hers, his warmth washing over her. Mariposa slid her arms around his neck. He wrapped his arms around her, his embrace both firm and gentle.

"My Mari," he whispered against her lips. "My dearest Mari."

Abuela stepped into the entryway in that precise moment. "You say Mari almost like a Spaniard, Jasón, but it is not enough for me to allow such closeness."

Jason pulled away but with a look of amusement. "What is it about you and empty corridors, Mariposa?"

"This is an entryway."

He shook his head and smiled as he put her at arms' length. "Apparently there is very little difference."

Mariposa willed her heart to slow down and hoped the heat in her face was not too obviously a blush.

"Lest we forget," Jason said, "there is a dinner party awaiting our arrival."

"We should probably be on our way." She felt rather proud of herself for managing such a sensible response.

"Remind me sometime," Jason added under his breath as he slipped her arm through his, "to greet you in an entryway while your abuela is not at home."

"I heard that," Abuela said.

Mariposa could not hold back a broad and joyful smile.

Jason raised her hand to his lips once more. "It is good to see you smile."

"It is good to have a reason." Indeed, she had a number of reasons. Jason's kindness. The impact she was having on the lives of the unfortunate former soldiers in London. Her correspondence with her aunt Douglas. The feeling at last that she was finding herself beneath the thick layers of protective armor she had worn for so long.

Jason handed her up into the carriage, followed by Abuela. He took his place across the carriage from them. Mariposa simply could not stop smiling.

"What have you undertaken these past weeks?" he asked.

"Philip found me a reliable man of business who has helped me use a portion of my inheritance from my uncle to find employment for returned and impoverished soldiers. We have found positions for nearly a dozen already."

"That is wonderful." His words rang with sincerity. "You know all too well the miseries they've endured. What better person than you to aid them in recovering?"

"Our butler and footman have helped. They are former soldiers themselves. And your secretary has offered his assistance."

Jason settled more comfortably on his bench. "Tell me more about it."

For the entirety of their ride to Lampton House, she spoke of her newfound passion, and he listened with every appearance of being enthralled. He asked questions, praised her efforts, and asked what he could do to be of assistance.

Philip had been correct. Finding who she was and what she was meant to do with her future had given her a reason and a means of moving beyond mere survival.

They arrived at Lampton House and were quite properly ushered inside and taken to the formal drawing room to await the announcement of the meal.

"Where are the other guests?" Mariposa asked, her curiosity piqued by the fact that no other Jonquils were present.

"What has convinced you that there are other guests?" His eyes danced about.

"Why do I suspect you are up to some mischief, Jason?"

"Mischief?" His feigned innocence could not have been less believable.

"You are hiding something."

Jason's smile grew ever wider. "If you put your mind to it, you might think of a way to convince me to spill my secrets."

Her cheeks flamed at his playful tone and crooked smile.

"Mater would scold me viciously for putting you to the blush," he said.

"Is Mater here?" Mariposa would love to spend an evening with Jason's mother.

He shook his head no.

"Your brothers?"

"No." His enjoyment of her growing curiosity could not have been more apparent.

"Do stop tormenting me, Jason."

"As you wish," he said. Jason left her where she stood in the midst of the room and walked to a door, different from the one through which they'd entered. Mariposa glanced at Abuela, where she sat on a chair. Abuela offered a shrug, obviously not knowing any more than Mariposa did.

"They've arrived," Jason said to someone apparently just out of sight around the door.

Footsteps sounded. Jason motioned for the mysterious person to enter.

"Jean," Mariposa blurted out, too surprised by their erstwhile traveling companion's sudden arrival to remember her manners.

Jean smiled as he crossed to her. He bowed. "A pleasure to see you again, Mademoiselle Mariposa."

"Mademoiselle?" They'd told him she was a married woman, yet he'd referred to her with the French equivalent of miss. "You know, then?" She watched Jean for signs of disapproval at the ruse they'd enacted.

"He knew almost from the beginning," Jason said, still standing across the room.

"You never said anything," Mariposa said to Jean.

"I assumed there was a reason."

"There was."

Jean nodded. "Yes, Jason explained enough."

"And you do not hate us?" How she hoped he didn't.

Jason spoke from the doorway. "I held Jean hostage until he agreed to think the world of us." That sparkle of devilment remained in his eyes.

Jean chuckled. "I have discovered our Jason has quite a sense of humor when he sets his mind to acknowledging it."

"He is a man of many facets," Mariposa said.

"And you have missed him," Jean said under his breath.

"Horribly," she answered.

"Would it set your mind at ease to know he has talked of little but you these past three weeks?"

Three weeks? "You have been with him that long?"

Jean nodded. "And have found he improves upon acquaintance."

Jason had turned his attention back to the corridor down which Mariposa could not see. "Come along, you ragamuffin. Don't dawdle."

"What have you two been doing?" Mariposa asked.

But Jean refused to answer. Jason seemed to be looking at someone. Another guest? He motioned with his head toward the drawing room, then stepped back. A young boy, all gangly limbs and thick, unruly hair burst into the room, his large eyes taking in every inch of it.

Mariposa pressed her open palm to her heart, even as her legs buckled beneath her. Every ounce of breath seemed to rush from her lungs. "Santiago," she managed to whisper as she dropped to her knees.

"Mariposa!" her brother shouted, sprinting across the room and throwing himself into her open, waiting arms.

She gasped against the sobs that racked her body. She could form no words beyond his name, which she repeated again and again. Mariposa held him tight, half afraid that if she let go, he would disappear.

"*Mi niño,*" she whispered, rocking him back and forth. Her Santiago was in her arms again. Her little boy. He was safe. He was safe, and he was with her. "*Mi niño. Mi niño hermoso.*"

Endless prayers of gratitude filled her heart at the miracle unfolding before her. Somehow this child was alive and well despite being lost for half a year. She studied every inch of him, desperate to convince herself she was not imagining the reunion.

"*¿Eres real?*" She stroked his soft, sun-darkened cheek. "*¿Estás aquí?*"

Santiago grinned. "*¡Pues, claro que sí,* Mariposa!*"

"*Mi niño.*"

Her brother threw himself once more into her embrace. She knelt there in the middle of the room holding him to her, memorizing the feel of him.

"*Te quiero,*" she whispered. "*Te quiero.*"

"Let your sister at least stand up," Jason said from just outside Mariposa's very watery vision. "Don't you know it's unforgivable to wrinkle a lady's dress?"

"Oh, Mariposa is no worried of her dress," Santiago said.

Mariposa held him tighter. "Your English is a bit improved."

"Jasón has promised he will me teach to speak the English *correctamente.* El Señor Beauchene *y* Jasón *y yo practicamos* from *España.*"

Mariposa looked over Santiago's head to where Jason stood watching her. "*España?*" she whispered, emotion continuing to break her voice.

"Come now, Santiago, let your sister up."

Santiago climbed off her lap despite her efforts to keep him there.

"No. Do not leave," she said, grabbing for Santiago's hand.

He smiled as though he had not a care in all the world. His eyes widened. "*¡Abuelita!*" Santiago rushed across the room.

Mariposa remained kneeling on the floor, unable to move. She looked up at Jason, feeling herself fall to pieces. He held out his hand. She took it without hesitation. Jason helped her to her feet, but she could not find the strength to stand on her own. Before she could say a single word, he slipped his arm around her waist and supported her as they left the room. She walked beside him as one in a daze, hardly aware that she even moved.

"I do not understand," she said, blinking back further tears. "You were in *España*? *¿Encontraste a Santiago?*"

"That last night in Scotland, you told me that after all you'd been through, home had begun to beckon to you." Jason laid his hand on top of hers as it rested on his arm. "I immediately began to wonder if perhaps, after years of struggle and warfare, your mother felt that same pull."

"Prado Verde," Mariposa whispered, her throat constricting painfully. Home for Mother would always be Prado Verde. In Spain. "But how did you—? Spain is so very far away."

"I am fortunate to have a brother who has a 'boat very large,' as your brother described it," Jason said. "And our good friend Jean knows the area in and around Albuera. He also speaks the language, something I found invaluable. With such resources at my disposal and the assistance of several people living in the area, finding Prado Verde was easier than I had anticipated."

"You have been to my home?" She was unable to speak the word *home* without a crack in her voice. How she missed it. How she missed everything good it had once been in her life.

"It is beautiful, Mariposa," he said quietly, gently. "I can only imagine the agony you must have felt leaving it behind."

She could do nothing but nod, her next few breaths caught on the emotion continuing to build within her.

"We found a filthy imp of a boy running around the fields near Prado Verde," Jason continued. "His vast knowledge of English-language drinking songs was impressive, to say the least. He led us to your home—*his* home."

Santiago. They had found Santiago in a field in Spain? "Spain." Mariposa breathed out the shocking thought. "He was in Spain." Mariposa shook her head repeatedly, mechanically. "But we were supposed to come here," she said. "To England. It was the plan. It was what we agreed on. Mamá was supposed to come here. She was supposed to bring Santiago with her. We were all supposed to come here. England was our safe haven."

Had her mother tried to come but was unable? Had something happened to her?

"Sometimes, my dear Mariposa," Jason said, "in times of fear and uncertainty, we make decisions here"—he touched his heart—"instead of here." He touched his head. "I thought perhaps your mother had gone where she felt most safe, where her heart was."

Jason pushed open the door to a sitting room. A woman sat at the tall windows overlooking a back garden. Her hair, once a deep black, was now liberally sprinkled with silver. Her figure was a little too thin, a testament to some degree of deprivation, but she still carried herself regally.

Mariposa knew her in an instant. "Mamá." She could hardly get the word out.

Her voice must have carried, for her mother turned from the window. Mariposa held her breath.

"Mariposa." A quiet smile pulled at her lips. "*Estás aquí.*"

"*Sí, Mamá.*" The sight of her mother, the sound of her beloved voice, brought its own measure of peace despite the loss of the vibrant woman she'd once been. Footsteps sounded behind Mariposa. She glanced over her shoulder. Abuela stood in the doorway, Santiago tucked into the crook of her arm.

"Jason found them both," Mariposa said to her grandmother. "In Spain."

"*Sí.* A miracle."

Abuela, Santiago with her, crossed to where her daughter watched the evening downpour through the tall windows. The three of them stood silently, focused on the scene outside. Abuela's arm slipped around her daughter's waist. She glanced back at Mariposa and gave a firm and calm nod. Abuela had not crumbled, had not retreated into quiet isolation as she had done for so long after her husband's death. She had begun to heal as well.

Mariposa leaned against Jason. "*Gracias*, Jasón," she whispered, feeling his arms encircle her once more. "*Muchas gracias.*"

He held her as she watched her beloved family, still broken in so many ways but together again at last. She spotted Jean standing at a respectful distance across the room. She owed him and Jason more than she could possibly repay. Her whispered "*Merci*" to the beloved Frenchman felt horribly inadequate.

Jean pressed his open hand to his heart and bowed. He raised his eyes to Jason's and nodded. The gesture meant something between them, though Mariposa did not know what. In the next instant, Jean stepped silently from the room.

"I believe he was sent to us by heaven, Jason," she whispered, fresh tears falling.

His arms tightened around her. "I know he was. I know it without a doubt."

Chapter Twenty-Nine

HAVING SECURED PHILIP'S PERMISSION TO do so, Jason offered Mariposa and her family the use of Lampton House for as long as needed. Mrs. Thornton, they all feared, remained too mentally fragile to endure more upheaval than their trek to England had already created.

With the family settling in, Jason made the lonely journey to his rented rooms near Lincoln's Inn. He'd insisted only months earlier when Philip had suggested otherwise that his small flat was more than adequate. It no longer felt that way.

Jean was staying with him for the foreseeable future, he being in the process of finding another position as a tutor. Jason welcomed his company. The man was easy to talk with. He had a knack for getting to the heart of any problem and offering precisely the advice or encouragement Jason needed.

"You did a beautiful thing today, Jason," Jean said as they sat in armchairs on either side of his small fireplace. "One cannot help but be touched by the abundance of love that family has for one another."

Jason nodded. He too had been moved by their reunion. What he'd wanted most to see, however, he had not. He'd hoped having her family together once more would wipe the pain from Mariposa's eyes. Jason prayed that in time her grief would lessen.

Jean appeared deeply contemplative. "What do you think the chances are of Mariposa wanting to hire a tutor for her brother?"

The unspoken question could not have been clearer. "I think her only objection would be that hiring you would feel rather like paying a family member to be a family member."

"Do you truly think she views me that way?"

Jason had seldom heard someone sound so cautiously hopeful. He knew that underneath the strong, resilient exterior, Jean was lonely and had been for a long time.

"*I* think of you that way," he said. "You've become far more than a friend, Jean. And I can tell you without hesitation that little Santiago took to you from nearly the moment we met him."

Jean smiled. "The imp won my loyalty the first time he sang '*Dodo, l'Enfant, Do.*'"

"His French is better than his English," Jason acknowledged. "Not to mention his song selection is far superior in your native tongue."

Despite the quip, Jean's smile faded. His eyes grew unfocused and distant. "My little one would have been almost exactly Santiago's age had he lived."

Jason had thoroughly pitied himself in the years since his father's death. But Mariposa and Jean and little Santiago had shown him the meaning of true, overwhelming loss and the strength of deep and abiding love.

Moisture gathered in his friend's eyes, and a look of such stark need crossed his face. "Do you think she would allow me stay, Jason? I would not even require a salary, only a roof over my head." He shook his head, his brow furrowed with heavy concern. "That child is entering a world so foreign to him. I cannot bear the thought of him facing it without guidance and support. Not that I doubt Mariposa will do all she can, but . . ." He let the words dangle, the sentence unfinished.

Jason rose and crossed to where Jean sat. He laid a firm, reassuring hand on his shoulder. "I know she will."

"Thank you, my friend." Jean looked less burdened. "But let us not bother her with this yet. She has quite enough weight on her shoulders just now. Allow her time."

"Allow her time" became Jason's motto over the next two days. He sent around a note each of the mornings, reassuring Mariposa that the staff and home were entirely at her disposal and that he would call on them after they'd had an opportunity to settle in.

The wait was excruciating. He dove with enthusiasm back into his work, grateful that his colleagues had taken on some of the burden he'd left behind. Concentration came only with effort, but he managed. Jean proved invaluable as a distraction the two nights he spent away from Mariposa. He felt very nearly sure of her feelings, but he meant to find out for certain.

Almost forty-eight hours to the minute after he'd collected Mariposa for her reunion with her family, Jason pulled on his outer coat, preparing to call on her at Lampton House. Anticipation mingled with nervousness, leaving him more than a touch rattled.

"Might I make a suggestion?" Jean grinned at him in a way that spoke of bottled-up laughter.

Jason silently motioned for him to proceed. He could use all the sound advice he could get.

"Pay a visit to the young flower seller you've told me of and purchase the loveliest bouquet he has," Jean said. "Then offer them to the young lady as gallantly as possible."

"Flowers? Are you playing matchmaker, Jean?"

"Unabashedly."

"For that," Jason said, "you have my undying gratitude. I have been attempting all day to convince myself that I am not about to make a blasted mess of the whole thing."

Jean looked more confident in him than Jason felt. "She loves you," he said. "Having been in your position, I know that is hard to feel confident about. But I have watched her and know it to be true."

Jason fought down a smug look. He dared not grow overly sure of himself before things were more certain.

"You need not plead your case," Jean said. "Nor ought you to worry so very much. She does not need to be convinced of your worth."

"Then what does she need?"

"She needs to know you love her."

Jason smiled. "I think I can manage that."

He stopped on his way to Lampton House to purchase not one but two bouquets from Benny. Armed with such potent ammunition, his efforts couldn't help but succeed. A few examples of inarguable failure from his past resurfaced, but he pushed them down.

Upon entering his childhood home, Jason happened first upon the youngest Thornton. Santiago eyed Jason's floral tributes with disdain. "*Flores?*"

"Yes," Jason said. "But the *flores* are not for you."

"*¿Para quién?*"

"Who are the flowers for?" Jason guessed at the translation. Santiago nodded impatiently.

"These"—Jason held up the pink bouquet—"are for your mother."

Understanding lit Santiago's eyes. He took hold of the front of Jason's jacket and pulled him farther into the house.

"Mamá!" Santiago called out as they made their way up the stairs.

Being dragged about by his shirtfront was not precisely the dignified entrance Jason had intended to make. Still, the child was in such earnest Jason couldn't possibly hold it against him.

"Mamá *es* here," Santiago said, pointing to the drawing room doors a few paces ahead of them. "She *es* stuck."

"Stuck?" Good heavens! Had no one helped the poor woman? Jason stepped around Santiago, careful not to knock him over.

"*Sí.*" The child kept pace with Jason, reaching the doors just as he did. "She does not want to go anywhere."

Relief and exasperation immediately flooded over Jason. The boy's word choice had been unfortunate. Jason had pictured Mariposa's mother in rather dire straits, wedged behind a heavy piece of furniture or something equally as troubling. As they stepped inside the drawing room, his eyes immediately sought her out and found her quite comfortably situated near the tall windows, watching the gardens just beyond.

Santiago pulled Jason to where she sat. Mrs. Thornton looked at them, the somewhat blank, somber expression she always wore unchanged. The boy said something to her in Spanish, something that drew her eyes to Jason. He had quickly learned upon finding her in Spain that Mrs. Thornton did not speak English. Whether she did not know the language or simply refused to speak it, he could not say.

Jason held out the bouquet. "*Flores para—*" He could not remember what should come next.

Santiago took pity on him and whispered, "*Usted.*"

"*Flores para usted,*" Jason said, praying he'd come close enough to at least be understood.

Her gaze shifted between him and his offering. For the first time in the two weeks since she'd been found in Spain, Mrs. Thornton smiled. Hers was not the bright, full-of-life smile her daughter had but a simple show of contentment. She took the flowers he held out for her and motioned him closer.

Jason leaned down, expecting to be told something and hoping Santiago would translate. Mrs. Thornton did not speak. She touched his face ever so gently before lightly kissing his cheek. Though Mariposa had once done the same, Mrs. Thornton's kiss felt like the countless good-byes and hellos he'd received from his own mother.

"*Dios te bendiga,*" Mrs. Thornton whispered before turning her eyes back to the scene outside her window.

Jason looked to Santiago. The boy shrugged, perfectly matching his sister's signature gesture. Apparently translating his mother's sentiment was beyond Santiago's grasp of English.

"*Aquí estás,* Santiago."

Jason turned back to face the door at the sound of Mariposa's voice. She smiled at him, and his heart jumped in his chest.

She gave her brother a look that was 100 percent scolding older sister. "Did you wash behind your ears, young man?" she asked, miming the question.

Santiago's expression grew instantly mutinous. "Jasón no make me wash *las orejas.* On his boat, he says wash *las manos*"—he held up his hands—"*la cara*"—he motioned toward his face—"but no says wash *las orejas.*"

Mariposa propped her fists on her hips. "You think Jasón will agree with you?"

Santiago's grasp of the English language apparently extended that far. He gave Jason a look filled with hopeful expectation.

Jason ruffled the boy's deep black hair. "Having once been your age, I empathize with you, but as a grown gentleman, I have to support your sister in this."

"And what have you to say to that, Santiago?" Mariposa asked.

He waved his hand dismissively, a gesture that precisely mimicked one Jason had seen dozens of times from Mariposa. "Jasón, he uses the big words. I no understand."

Mariposa gave her response entirely in Spanish, and it was immediately effective. Santiago sulked from the room, no doubt on his way to see to his behind-the-ear ablutions.

"I am afraid I am not the most popular sister in London just now." Mariposa sighed. "Mamá, as Santiago has told me many times, never made him wash behind his ears."

"Considering how he looked when we first found him in that field, I doubt she made him wash anything."

Mariposa turned back toward him, and the frustration in her eyes dissolved.

"I brought you *flores,*" Jason said. He'd nearly forgotten the bouquet he still held.

"*Flores.* You are learning Spanish?"

"A word here and there," he said.

She took the flowers and immediately raised them to her nose. The gesture was endearingly feminine. "You are very sweet."

"Sweet enough to warrant a dinner invitation?"

She brushed the tips of her flowers along her cheek. "Did you wash behind your ears?"

"Would you like to check?"

Color spread across her face, but she continued to smile. "I think you can be trusted." Her eyes focused somewhere behind him. "Are Mamá's flowers from you as well?"

"They are." Jason looked back at Mrs. Thornton. Though her gaze remained on the view, her fingers lightly stroked the flowers she still held. He thought she seemed more peaceful. That, in turn, would bring Mariposa a measure of peace. "Can anything be done for her?" he asked.

Mariposa laid her head against him as they both stood watching her mother. "I do not know. We never had the luxury of a doctor to consult."

Jason put an arm about her shoulders, holding her to him. Somehow, having her there made Lampton House feel more like home than it had since Father's death. "Perhaps a doctor might be found now that she is here in London."

"I refuse to send her to an asylum," Mariposa said vehemently.

Reminding himself that trust did not come easily for Mariposa, Jason did not allow himself to be ruffled by the insinuation that he would advocate institutionalization. He simply bent enough to press a kiss to Mariposa's temple. The small show of support earned him a quick glance.

"You are giving me your 'Mariposa needs to have more faith in me' look," she said.

"Am I?" He tried to imagine that look. "Is it working?"

She only smiled and stepped away from him, crossing to her mother. "Mamá. *Las flores necesitan agua.*"

Jason watched her tend to her mother, her love evident in every word and gesture. She no longer hid behind the mask she'd worn when first they'd met. Her wit and humor and zest for life had not disappeared. Rather, his understanding of her character had deepened.

"She does not wish to release her flowers long enough to have them placed in a vase." Mariposa spoke as she crossed the room, obviously intent on summoning a servant to bring the necessary vase and water for the bouquets, both of which Mrs. Thornton now held.

Jason took hold of Mariposa's hand as she passed, preventing her from leaving. He had come to confess a few things and, despite having been with her for several minutes, had not managed a single item on his list.

"Might the flowers wait? I was hoping for a moment of your time."

She reached up and touched his cheek. "You may have far more than a moment, *mi cariño*."

"I will, for my own sake, assume *mi cariño* is not a vicious insult."

Santiago's voice answered before Mariposa could. "It means 'my dear.'" The boy stood in the doorway, his repulsed tone surpassed only by his disgusted expression.

My dear? Jason's nerves actually settled a bit at that revelation. He felt less and less unsure of Mariposa's feelings.

"Are you"—Santiago eyed them both warily—"wanting *los besos* now?"

Jason had no idea what "*los besos*" meant, but Mariposa's eyes flew open wide.

"*Vete*, Santiago." She shooed him off. "Go . . . clean some part of yourself."

"No more cleaning." With a determination that in any other situation might have been admirable, Santiago stepped fully inside the room and crossed to an empty chair not far from his mother's. He sat and gave them a mulish look.

"To his credit," Jason said, "no happily dirty boy ever wishes to clean any part of himself."

Mariposa sighed with all the drama she usually did. "This, I have discovered, is quite true."

"Perhaps you would be so good, Mariposa, as to tell me just what '*los besos*' means."

Jason didn't think he had ever seen Mariposa blush as deeply as she did in that moment. "It is . . ." She grew rather flustered. "It means 'kisses.'"

He laughed on the spot. "That mischievous little imp."

"It is not so very funny," Mariposa protested. "Why must you laugh that he thinks you want to be giving me kisses? This is not so *ilógico*."

Jason kissed the hand he held. "I laughed at his audacity in posing the question. I assure you, the idea is not at all *ilógico*, my— How did you say that? *Mi clarín*."

Her lips twitched. "You just called me your bugle."

"What word was I trying to say?" He thought he'd remembered correctly.

"*Mi cariño*," she answered. "Although if you are saying it to me"—she grew even more flushed—"you would say *mi cariña*."

"And that means 'dear,' does it not?"

She nodded. "'Dear.' 'Darling.' 'Love.' It is an endearment."

Jason took hold of her other hand. "But is it an endearment you truly meant?"

Mariposa took in a rather sharp breath. "Are you asking if I am in love with you?"

That was rather more abrupt than he'd planned the conversation to be. Still, he was not one to pass up an unlooked for opportunity. "That is exactly what I am asking."

Abuela chose that precise moment to join the rest of the Thornton family in the increasingly crowded drawing room. The woman had the world's best—or, in reality, *worst*—sense of timing. "*Buenas noches*, Jason."

How was a man supposed to have the all-important conversation with his lady love when every relation she had insisted on gathering around?

"How are you, Mrs. Aritza?" He could hear the irritation in his voice. Abuela merely nodded and continued on, joining her daughter near the window.

Mariposa's eyes were firmly fixed on him when he looked back at her. Her complexion had grown more than a touch pale, an unmistakable nervousness in her eyes.

She spoke before he could. "I do not think I can answer that question with so many people about."

"My sentiments exactly."

She very nearly duplicated her brother's earlier actions, pulling him from the room but by his hand and not his jacket. As they stepped just out of sight of the drawing room, she stopped and turned to face him. "Will this do?"

He glanced around. The family was not breathing down their necks, but it was not quite the setting he would have chosen. "A corridor?"

"An *empty* corridor," she corrected.

His smile was immediate. "Perfect," he said and meant it wholeheartedly. "Now, where were we?"

"You wished to know if I love you." Beneath her still-apparent nerves, a bubbling excitement seemed to be growing. "You would not ask that if you did not love me. I am certain you would not."

"But we were not discussing *my* feelings." She was getting a vast deal too far ahead of him.

She looked him directly in the eye, determination obvious in her expression. "I love you, Jason Jonquil," she said quite seriously. "The how or the when"—she waved a hand—"I cannot say. But it is true."

"I—" Jason managed nothing more than that single syllable before she kissed him.

She kissed *him*. He quickly joined in the effort, reveling in the joy of having her in his arms once more, of stealing a moment together without interruption, without worry and heaviness. He closed the small gap between them. Her fingers brushed his face. He kissed her more tenderly, more deeply.

Though he regretted it, he recognized the necessity of ending the exceptionally pleasant interlude. He had not actually declared himself. Another moment of her intoxicating *besos* and he'd forget everything he intended to say.

Though he didn't actually kiss her again, he kept her close, enjoying the familiar scent of her. She melted into his embrace, her cheek resting against his chest. "How does one say 'I love you' in Spanish?"

She took a somewhat ragged breath. "That depends on who is saying it," she answered, "and to whom the words are being spoken."

He stroked her hair, refusing to let her go. "Let us assume, then, that the words are being spoken by a hopelessly besotted young gentleman to the lady he knows he could never live without."

She raised her eyes to his. A single tear trickled from the corner of her eye. "*Te amo,*" she whispered.

"*Te amo,*" he said. "I love you with all my heart."

"In spite of everything I did?"

Jason shook his head. "There is no 'in spite of' or 'except for.' All my heart, Mari. I mean that. If there were limits to my affection, I would not have run after you nor journeyed to the Continent in the midst of a war. A man does not do that for a woman unless he is entirely devoted to her."

She raised up on her toes and whispered, "*Mi cariño*" in the brief moment before pressing a tender kiss to his lips. "And you will not leave me," she said still but a breath away.

"Not ever," he said. "If I have to chase you across every ocean, every continent, I will."

"Are you asking me to marry you?"

"I am *begging* you to marry me."

Mariposa's expression sobered.

That look worried him. "What is it?"

"I do not think my mother will ever be well again, and I cannot leave her. And I am responsible for Abuela and for raising Santiago. That is a large burden to ask you to share."

"One I will gladly carry with you. I happen to know Jean is hoping to convince you to hire him on as tutor for your scamp of a brother. Abuela can help with your mother. Who's to say your mamá won't improve with time?"

"She might not."

He kissed her forehead and pulled her fully into his embrace again. "We will cross that bridge when we must."

"Where will we live?" Mariposa asked. "There are too many of us for a flat."

"Your brother inherited a very sizable estate from your uncle," Jason reminded her.

Mariposa nodded her understanding. "Thornton Manor. But that was Marcos's inheritance."

"It is now Santiago's," Jason said. "Your family will have a place to live for years to come. And when the war is over, which I hope it will be soon, we might consider spending time in Spain."

"I would like that, Jason. I should dearly love to see Spain again."

Jason stood with her in his arms, quite content with life. "What else shall we do, my dear?"

"Raise turnips," Mariposa said. "And then refuse to eat them."

"And I can repeat myself dreadfully, and you can threaten to fire me."

"No, my love. Never that. I intend to keep you forever."

"*Qué es esto?*" Abuela asked without warning from the doorway.

Jason kept Mariposa pinned to his side as he grinned at the knowing look in Abuela's eyes. "*Te amo.*" He felt certain he'd remembered the phrase correctly.

Abuela raised her eyebrows in surprise. "You are in love with me?"

"Oh, dear," he muttered.

Mariposa giggled. "No, *Abuelita*. Jasón *me ama*."

Abuela clucked her tongue and shook her head in obvious exasperation. "You speak the Spanish *horriblemente*, Mr. Jonquil. You will have to work on that. Our butler, he will help you." With a crisp nod, she returned once more to the drawing room.

Once she'd given up the pretense of speaking no English, Abuela had quickly become one of Jason's favorite people. Mariposa's entire family, in fact, had become decidedly important to him. "Did I really tell her I was in love with *her?*" he asked.

Mariposa laughed, a sound far lighter than he'd heard from her in the first difficult months of their acquaintance. "You did. I, for one, was quite shocked."

He loved this lighter side of Mariposa, to see her happy enough to smile so freely.

"I suppose Black will have to help me with my Spanish, after all," he said.

"We will all help you, dearest," Mariposa said.

"I cannot tell you how grateful I am to see you so happy," he said.

She looked up into his eyes. "I have my family and yours. And I have you, the finest gentleman in all the world. How could I be anything but happy?"

He wrapped his arms more fully around her. Nothing short of providence could have brought about such a blessed ending to their many misadventures. Theirs would never be a sedate nor boring existence, but they would, indeed, be excessively happy.

Chapter Thirty

THE JOURNEY FROM LONDON TO Norfolk was not a quick one, but the trip passed quickly for Jason, knowing that Mariposa would be waiting for him at the end of it. He had been away from her for more than a week, despite having been married only three. There had been no avoiding it.

Her mother needed the stability of a permanent home. Seeing them settled at Thornton Manor was a priority. Thus they had obtained a special license allowing their wedding to occur sooner rather than later. They'd had a few precious days for an abbreviated wedding trip, then had returned to Nottinghamshire for Corbin's wedding. Jason had accompanied Mariposa and her family to Thornton Manor before hying himself to London. In time, he would learn how to best divide his time between Town and the country, but for the moment, they were still sorting it all out.

He moved swiftly through the front entryway, pausing only long enough to give his hat and gloves to the butler. Black had remained in London. He and the footman, Will, had continued Mariposa's efforts to assist their fellow former soldiers. Jason called upon his own connections throughout Society to find the needed employment opportunities. The work meant a great deal to Mariposa. Absolute joy filled her expression every time she offered hope and a future to these men whom far too many chose to forget. He loved her all the more for her kind and generous heart.

The Thornton estate, while not as expansive as Lampton Park, was vast enough to cause Jason a little difficulty in locating his love. He found her after a time sitting on a wickerwork chair on the back terrace. She wore her hair in a loose chignon and sat with a relaxed and peaceful posture. The rigidity that had filled her when first they'd met, a tension that even her pretense of vacuousness had not kept entirely hidden, had dissipated over the past weeks.

She still had moments, a great many of them, truth be told, when the fear and anxiety and strain of her past settled heavily on her once more. But there were also times when the loneliness and upheaval he'd kept tucked away since his father's passing resurfaced as rigidity and surliness. They saw each other through their difficult times and came through their struggles stronger and better.

They were not perfect, but they were perfect for each other.

Mariposa called out in Spanish in the very moment her brother ran across the back lawn. He waved back to her, answering in the same language. Tucked in the midst of all the words Jason didn't know, he recognized his name. In the next instant, Mariposa spun in her chair.

"Jasón!" She leapt up and ran directly to him, throwing herself into his embrace. "You were gone too long, my love."

"I wholeheartedly agree." He trailed light kisses along her cheek and jaw. "In time, you will be able to go to London with me, then we will not need to be apart."

"I know my family has burdened you—"

"Mari," he gently cut off the all-too-familiar expression of regret. "They are no burden."

She brushed her fingers along his cheek. "I do love you. I hope that you know that."

"I know that." He turned his head enough to kiss her fingers. "Though I have no objection to you reminding me."

Another shout, this time in a mixture of English and Spanish, echoed up from the grass. Jason felt Mariposa laugh from within the circle of his arms.

"Jean, bless him, is doing all he can to improve Santiago's English, but the poor boy cannot seem to manage sentences entirely in the less-familiar language."

Jason turned a little to face the lawn but kept his beloved firmly in his embrace. "I cannot manage more than two words in *my* less-familiar language, so I certainly cannot fault the boy."

"And when you do attempt Spanish, you end by confessing your undying love for my abuela."

He shook his head. "You will never allow me to forget that moment, will you?"

His eyes lighted on a grouping of chairs beneath the expansive branches of one of the estate's many grand trees. Mrs. Thornton sat there watching her son run to and fro. Jean sat nearby, doing the same.

"How fares your mother? She seemed less burdened when last I saw her."

"A little, yes. Jean has been an invaluable friend to her, able to speak of Spain as she remembers it and in Spanish, as she is most comfortable." Mariposa leaned back against him, resting her arms atop his where they wrapped around her middle. "His kindness has brought life back to her eyes."

"I have said it before, and I will do so again: Jean's presence on that mail coach was nothing short of a miracle."

"Oh! You will be so happy to hear this." Mariposa spun around, enthusiasm filling her expression and tone. "Benny arrived a few days ago."

While he missed having Mariposa in his arms, Jason took tremendous delight in seeing her eyes dance with happiness.

"Is the gardener upset with me for sending Benny here?" Jason asked.

Mariposa shook her head. "The sweet boy works hard, and he is surprisingly fond of plants and flowers."

That was precisely the reason Jason had thought Benny would do well as an under-gardener.

"Jean, however, insists that Benny learn to read and write." Mariposa looked back out to where her brother was climbing a tree. "The two boys have become fast friends. Benny has helped Santiago with his English."

A London street vendor was offering English lessons? "What precisely has he taught him?"

Mariposa's brows pulled down. "I do not recognize most of the words."

Jason held back a laugh. "That is likely for the best." He spent enough time interacting with the urchins of London, searching for those he could help, to know their language was not always genteel.

Mariposa looked out at her brother once more. "He will make a very. . . unique English gentleman one day. A vast estate, an enviable income, an accent that is somehow both French and Spanish, a sprinkling of impolite words and phrases."

The laugh he had forced down could not be prevented any longer. "Society may never recover."

Mariposa smiled up at him. "I am not worried for him. He has you, and you will teach him how to be a fine gentleman."

Jason took her hand in his and raised it to his lips. He pressed a light, gentle kiss to the back of her hand. "Have I told you that I love you, my Mariposa?"

"You have."

He stepped closer to her and slipped his free arm around her once more. "I do have a disconcerting tendency to repeat myself."

"Yes, you do."

"*Je t'aime.*" He kissed her forehead, lingering over the gesture. "*Te amo.*" He kissed her lips. "I love you."

About the Author

SARAH M. EDEN IS A *USA Today* best-selling author of witty and charming award-winning historical romances. Combining her obsession with history and her affinity for tender love stories, Sarah loves crafting witty characters and heartfelt romances set against rich historical backdrops. She holds a bachelor's degree in research and happily spends hours perusing the reference shelves of her local library. She lives with her husband, kids, and mischievous dog in the shadow of a snow-capped mountain she has never attempted to ski.